"A story woven with the prejudices and desires that fill the Cajun land-scape." —*New York Daily News*

"Martin Pousson's debut novel is like a long, sad Cajun ballad. . . . Pousson writes about his angry, embittered souls with an insight that illuminates their fragility." —*The Atlanta Journal-Constitution*

"A remarkably sure-footed and rich first novel, admirable not only for the clarity of its voice and the fluidity of its style but for the coherence of its vision." —**Lis Harris, author of** *Holy Days*

"I haven't felt myself in the grip of a voice this powerful since I first read Dorothy Allison and Frank McCourt. Martin Pousson is that kind of major new talent." —**Christine Wiltz, author of** *The Last Madam*

"A moving, compelling story, and above all else, it's a good read. . . . *No Place, Louisiana* should whet any voracious reader's appetite with its strong, realistic characters and high drama." —*Genre*

"A tightly wound novel about a claustrophobic . . . marriage . . . confi-dently eschews the style of a Faulkner or the charm of a McCullers to evoke the prejudices and limitations of Cajun culture. . . . Fans of Richard Ford and Larry Brown will respond to Pousson's dark perspective and adept prose." —*Publishers Weekly*

"Sure-footed, richly textured and deeply tragic." —*The Cleveland Plain Dealer*

"Pousson evokes the doomed passion of Tennessee Williams." —*The Advocate*

continued . . .

NO PLACE, LOUISIANA

Martin Pousson

RIVERHEAD BOOKS

New York

Riverhead Books
Published by The Berkley Publishing Group
A division of Penguin Putnam Inc.
375 Hudson Street
New York, New York 10014

Epigraph on page ix from *Wise Blood* © 1952 by Flannery O'Connor, renewed 1980. Permission to reprint granted by Harold Matson Co., Inc.

Copyright © 2002 by Martin Pousson
Book design by Amanda Dewey
Cover design and imaging by Honi Werner
Cover photographs © Elizabeth DeRamus

First Riverhead hardcover edition: March 2002
First Riverhead trade paperback edition: April 2003
Riverhead trade paperback ISBN: 1-57322-976-8

Visit our website at www.penguinputnam.com

The Library of Congress has catalogued the Riverhead hardcover edition as follows:

Pousson, Martin.
   No Place, Louisiana / Martin Pousson.
      p.   cm.
   ISBN 1-57322-200-3
      1. Married people—Fiction.   2. Louisiana—Fiction.   I. Title.
PS3616.O87 N6   2002   2001031883
813'.6—dc21

Printed in the United States of America

10   9   8   7   6   5   4   3   2   1

Dedicated to
my parents and
grandparents and
in memory of
my sister

What follows is a work of
fiction. All characters, events,
and dialogue are imagined
and not intended to represent
real people, living or dead.

Where you came from is gone,
where you thought you were
going to never was there,
and where you are is no good
unless you can get away from it.

FLANNERY O'CONNOR

Part One

1

LOUIS AND NITA ON A BLIND DOUBLE DATE. A THICK, rainy night in February. No crickets are out since it's too cold. As Nita tells it, the motor in Louis' brand-new '65 Falcon turns over twice before starting. From her side of the car, she sneaks a glance at her date. He's mean-looking, she thinks. With that long face and furrowed brow, he's not at all the dreamy high school graduate she pictured. He has hard dark eyes, red splotchy skin, and stiff hair that, like him, seems obstinate and pumped up with pride.

Nita turns her head to cast a look at her brother, Claude, in the backseat. Claude and his steady girlfriend, Kayla, set her up on this date. Kayla and Louis both live in Iota, which is only about twenty miles away. Nita's never been there, but she figures anything has to be nicer than the dumpy little town of Jennings where

she and her brother live. She was disappointed when Claude told
her they weren't going out in Iota, but she brightened when he
said that Louis worked in a rice mill and that he was a quarterback
at St. Francis, a *Catholic* school. Immediately, Nita pictured a
broad-shouldered boy with bright eyes, a wide grin, and an easy
way about him—a boy who might take her to a *real* restaurant,
not just a dingy old diner like the one where they're headed.

Though she's not at all happy about going to Aggie's, which is
only a hair, a short and skinny little hair, better than the diner
where she works, her picture of Louis doesn't change until she
sits next to him in the car. Right away, she's surprised by how awkward he looks. His head seems much too big for the rest of his
body. And, though his hands look like the thick strong hands she
expects of a guy who was a quarterback, his constant tapping
makes her nervous. Even as he drives, he taps his finger against the
steering wheel. It's that tapping and something about the look on
his face that leads her to turn around in her seat.

Nita is sixteen and a sophomore and she knows that any other
girl in her school would kill to go out with a guy who has a car *and*
a high school diploma—even if they were just going to Aggie's
Diner. In fact, all week long she looked forward to bragging about
her date to the girls in class who call her No Shoes Nita and who
are always telling her that she should paint her bare feet and tie
her toes up with lace if she ever hopes to have a date. When she
was set up with Louis, she borrowed a pair of brown and white
oxfords from her married older sister, Vina Lee, and she planned
to tell those girls that her date had drunk cherry cola out of
her shoe.

But Nita can't imagine this guy anywhere near her foot and
she starts to worry how long the date will last. Do I have to go
through with this?, she thinks as she stares at her brother. Claude

can't read her eyes or he plays dumb, so she turns her head back to face Louis. When he catches her staring at his slicked-up crew cut, his chest fills with air and he punches the accelerator with his foot.

Not one hour rolls by before Nita knows she hates Louis. He's rude, so rude that he barely says a word to her in the car. She hasn't been out on many dates, but other boys have always said *something* about how pretty she looks. Even her brother told her she was *bien jolie* when the horn honked outside their front door. But Louis says not one word about her hair, which she ironed herself that morning, or about the dress she rehemmed especially for tonight. It's only a hand-me-down from Vina Lee, but it's her best one. She sewed a patch of blue roses on the left sleeve to cover a small tear. But Louis notices nothing, and she can hardly budge without him glaring at her. He won't even let her fiddle with the radio dial, and she doesn't dare roll down her window for the hope of cool air.

When they get to Aggie's, Louis forgets to hold open the door, to pull out the chair for Nita. And when the bouffant-haired waitress drops the laminated menus on the table, he refuses to let Nita take one. Instead, he calls the waitress back over to the table with a sharp whistle and doesn't wait for Claude and Kayla before he orders. "We'll have two cheeseburgers with grilled onions and some of those crinkly fries, just water to drink," he says in a rush as if he rehearsed it.

What if she didn't like onions or cheese, what if she wanted a *pop rouge,* a bottle of strawberry soda to drink? He's cheap, she decides. And all he talks about is his car. Three times he tells her how it's brand-new and souped up with a V-8 engine and a glass-pack muffler set. He washes and waxes it every other day, and every night when he parks it under the light of the front porch, he picks the gravel out of the tires with a butter knife. Nita nods her head as he talks and talks, but she doesn't say a word.

When the food arrives, she eats a few bites, then pushes the blue-lined plate away from her. "Gonna finish that?" Louis asks. After she shakes her head no, he snatches the burger and gobbles it in a few quick chomps. Nita stares at him. Greedy, she thinks, cheap and greedy he is. When the plates are cleared and the check is dropped onto the table, he eyes the total with a frown, counts out the exact change twice, and gets up to leave. Claude throws in his share, plus an extra dollar. Right then Nita sees it: Louis left no tip, not even a quarter. That does it, she thinks, doesn't he know I wait tables too? How could he be so stingy?

At the end of the night, they part—Nita swears—with no kiss. Louis doesn't even pull the car all the way up to the house before he stops to let her and her brother out, and when he drives off, his tires leave a black line in the road. "Some date," Nita says, then rolls her eyes.

When she and Claude walk in the house, all the lights are off and their mother's bedroom door is shut. Nita is glad since she won't have to face Buford Cormier, her mother's third husband. At least tonight, Buford won't poke her in the rib with his sharp fingernails and call her *maudite* or *canaille*. Every day her stepfather tells her mother, Gilda, that Nita is an evil girl, a conniving moocher who wastes too much toilet paper. When she goes to the bathroom, he presses his ear to the door to count the number of sheets she pulls from the roll. He tells her that he can figure by the sound of the cardboard hitting the plastic spindle just how much paper she's taking. If she takes too much, he kicks at the door until she opens it. Then he marches her to the kitchen where he makes her face Gilda. *"Elle est canaille."* He points at Nita, then pokes her in the rib. "If this little witch wasn't your daughter," he yells, "I'd throw her out with the shrimp heads and crab shells! She's taking food from my plate every time she steps in that bathroom!"

Nita never can figure out the big deal, but it's always the same. Buford lifts her dress and places his hand on her bottom (she thought it might stop when she turned sixteen, but it hasn't). He's liable to hit her with anything: a spatula, a wet dishrag, even the wrong end of a mop. But when he's really mad, he cups his hand, blows hot air into his palm, and smacks at her backside until she screams. Gilda stays silent, with her mouth drawn in a thin line and her hands clasped behind her jet-black hair. She doesn't move until Nita starts to cry, then she says, "*C'est l'heure du lit.* Time for bed."

But tonight Gilda's bedroom door is already closed and Nita can take all the toilet paper she wants. She lingers in the bathroom and, when she goes to bed, she forgets about Louis and the awful date.

The next day, just after Nita gets home from school, Louis calls. He says nothing about her or how pretty she is or even how much he liked meeting her. He only asks about his car, wasn't it something and didn't she like riding in it? She almost laughs. He's so full of himself, she thinks. Did she want to go out again? They could go riding in the Falcon, maybe go to a drive-in. "No," Nita says, "I can't."

Again and again and call after call, Nita refuses Louis' offers for another date. But then Gilda has one of her spells: after she has another fight with Buford about money, he storms out and she locks her bedroom door for three days. She makes Nita stay home from school to wait for the dented cans of *petits pois* and huge blocks of gray cheese that people from the welfare agency send over once a month. Then, after her stepfather comes back, Nita misses another two days of school. Buford tells her to stay home and scrub all the hardwood floors by hand, and he even makes her wash his dirty old Pontiac when he finds a whole roll of toilet paper missing and blames it on her.

"She's got her *tetons,* she should be on her own," he says to Gilda. "Instead she's gonna eat this paper like it was lettuce and you know who's paying? *Pas moi!* She can buy her own roll with the tips she makes from that weekend luncheteria. *Mais moi?* I've had enough!"

When Nita shoots back that it doesn't matter, that her *real* dad is coming back soon, Buford runs his fingernails through his long hair and sneers, "*Mais oui,* soon as he gets out of jail."

That night, Louis calls for the seventh or eighth time and Nita doesn't rush to say no. She lets Louis talk for a minute while she stares out at the bald yard with no driveway, only dust and bits of shell. She thinks how a date with Louis would get her out of this ratty house at least, and she wouldn't mind having someone buy her a burger—even if he is cheap with the tip. She twists the phone cord around her hand and turns toward the living room. There are throw rugs everywhere and plastic bubble wrap covers the couch. Huge patches of tin foil in the windows block out the sun and the one good fan in the house shakes from side to side. Nita looks at the phone and is surprised to hear herself say, "Okay, next Saturday then."

On their second double date, her brother announces his engagement to Kayla. Without thinking, Nita elbows Louis. "Hey, maybe we should get married, too," she jokes.

He doesn't get the joke.

The next weekend, Louis appears at Nita's front door with a ring. He stands there with the open box in his hand, but doesn't speak. My God, she thinks, he thought I was serious. Nita doesn't know what to do, especially since Louis just keeps staring at her, not saying a word. She looks past him at the yard and remembers that Louis works at a rice mill in Crowley. Maybe he'd want to live there, she thinks. She heard that her father's new wife lives in Crowley and figures he'll move in with her when he gets out of jail next month. And Nita would like nothing more than to see her dad again.

The last time Nita saw Hilton, she was thirteen and in the hospital. She'd been in an accident and lay in bed with a steel rod in her leg. A few nights before, she'd gone for a ride with Claude and Vina Lee, who were both drunk. Her brother took a curve fast and way too hard, and the car flew into the post of a barbed-wire fence. Both Nita and Vina Lee were thrown over the fence and into a cow pasture, while Claude sat pinned but unharmed behind the wheel of the car. Her sister had back surgery and was released after a few months, but Nita was stuck in a hospital room for close to a year. Hilton came to see her only once, but he brought more candy and presents with him than she got the rest of her time in that room.

Before that, it was six years since Nita had seen her father. She was seven, her mother had just thrown Hilton out of the house for the last time and he snuck back in to talk to his baby daughter. Gilda was pregnant with her younger sister, Monetta Lou, but her father didn't seem to take much interest in the new baby. Nita was his favorite and she was sure that would never change. She was the only one he'd let near him when he took his medicine. She'd hold her finger against the steel needle in her father's arm while he slowly pushed the plunger and a brown juice flowed into his vein. When he pulled the needle out, Nita sometimes joked that it looked like a giant mosquito couldn't get enough of him, that it had gone crazy and bit his arm again and again. "Does it itch, Daddy?" she'd ask and Hilton would laugh his big-chested laugh.

Other times, her father just stroked her hair for a while in silence or he'd hum until his voice became softer and he'd tell her about all the things he'd done before he met Gilda: he'd been a casino croupier, a champion boxer, and a top-rated chef in New York. Nita didn't know anyone else who'd been to New York; most people she knew hadn't even been to New Orleans.

Her father was also a *traiteur,* he could heal just about anything. He made roach tea for people with lockjaw and fried up chicken gizzards with bayou gum and old grease to cure the croup. He sewed a string of chinaberries for Nita's fever once and constantly ground up water moccasins and valerian root.

When the medicine in Hilton's needle started to work, he always sent Nita out of the bedroom. If Gilda was away, one of his nurses would come over and they'd stay locked up in the bedroom together. One time, when Nita was five or six, her brother busted open the door and she saw a nurse in a bra and panties sitting on her father's chest. He'd taken his shirt off and Nita could see the long stitched-up scar he'd gotten from a fight. His skin looked dark against the white of the sheets and his black hair lay back against the pillow like fur. She could see why the other kids on the street called him Chief, but she couldn't figure out what the nurse was doing on top of him.

If Hilton and the nurse needed medicine, they'd find the money Gilda stashed in a canister for groceries, or they'd search Claude's room for the change he made from mowing lawns and washing cars. There were days when Nita, Claude, and Vina Lee ate nothing but two-day-old hunks of bread dipped in cane syrup, and when they complained, Gilda said, "Your father is a monster. He's a *loup-garou.*"

But Nita didn't think her father was a werewolf, even if he did smash up all the furniture in the living room and even if it took six cops to hold him down each time they came to arrest him. Her mother shouted that he was a junkie and a voodoo doctor, but she never feared her father until he circled their house in a pick-up truck and threw a bloodied black chicken on the front porch. He threw *gris-gris,* too, tiny burlap sacks filled with ground-up valerian root and stinkweed. "That's the Black Voodoo," her mother said. "That's pure evil." But Nita still didn't believe it. If anyone was evil, it was Buford and his toilet paper rations.

It's her stepfather that Nita thinks of when she looks at Louis, then at the yard and the old Chevy jacked up on cinder blocks across the street. Louis still hasn't said a word. He stands silent on the steps with the open box in his hand until Nita looks past him and says, "Yes." Once she says it, the unasked question seems answered. She takes the ring and the box from his hand and shuts the hurricane door. The screen of the door has a large hole near the handle and she stoops toward it to say, "Good night." Nita watches as Louis puts his hands in his pockets and turns back toward the car. She's almost glad he didn't try to kiss her.

2

LOUIS AND NITA ON A BLIND DOUBLE DATE. A THICK, rainy night in February. No crickets are out since it's too cold. As Louis tells it, the motor in his brand-new '65 Falcon cranks up with a quick turn of the key. He lets the car idle for a minute and the steam from the dual exhaust covers the side and back windows like a low-lying cloud. With the car still in park, he presses the heel of his Dingo boot down on the rubber accelerator pad. The engine races a little, then Louis throws the gear shift out of park and the Falcon roars into reverse. The wheels of the car hit asphalt and he grips the hard leather pad of the steering wheel before guiding the Falcon from a dead-zero first gear to a full-throttle third. All eight valves pop open and the back left tire screeches as the Falcon carves up the road.

This is his favorite part of every date—watching alarm creep into a girl's eyes as the car races forward and she reaches back for the metal clasp of a seat belt. Her hands flap around the edge of the sideboard, then plunge into the crack of the seat—all in vain. Louis had the seat belts stripped out when he bought the Falcon—they messed up the hard line of the car's interior, and without them, the car's speed is always fully heeded. When the accelerator pad reaches the floor and the speedometer's needle starts to twitch, he looks in the rearview mirror at his friend Kayla and her date in the backseat. But they're so wrapped up in each other that they haven't noticed his fast moves behind the wheel.

Louis turns his head from the mirror to look at his date for the night, Nita. She's gotta be squirming by now, he thinks. Yet when his eye catches hers, he sees not a fidgety panic, but a steely resolve. Her head is cocked back and her mouth is drawn into a thin hyphen. No fear flashes in her eyes; she seems barely aware of the Falcon's speed. In fact, Louis realizes, she's been looking not at the road, but at him. He can't tell what she's thinking; her expression is too hard and glassy for him to penetrate. Yet her hands are soft against the leather seat and she looks small in her *cotonnade* dress. Her mouth is hard, yes, but there's something fragile about her, too. Like a china doll, Louis thinks. She has the same dark, flowing hair and permanent fragility. She'd stay this way forever, if he didn't touch her. Her eyes would show nothing and the neat line of her mouth would never break or bend into a smile. Her skin would stay this way, too. A porcelain tinted with olive and chicory. She'd sit there forever in a dark, unknowable glow. She'd never take her eyes off him, but would never so much as say hello.

Louis is so mesmerized by Nita that he doesn't see the yellow light flashing overhead. The Falcon flies through the intersection and narrowly misses a head-on collision with a one-eyed Comet coming from the left. Louis swerves the car a little and, right then, he sees it: he's lost her. Nita has turned away from him to face the passing storefronts. She presses her face against the side window, then turns to the backseat where her brother and Kayla sit. Nita hangs her head on the cool leather of the seat back. She runs her hand through her hair and clicks her tongue against the roof of her mouth. But Claude and Kayla lock lips and pay her no attention, so she turns around to face the road. Then she does it: she puts her hand out to the radio dial.

Louis tries to hold back, but no one, *no one,* touches his radio, *not* when Jan and Dean are on, and *especially* not when Jan and Dean are singing "Dead Man's Curve." Louis can't help it, he snaps, "Don't touch that," as his hands turn white against the steering wheel. "Don't touch a thing in this car!" Nita draws her hand back to lay it on the seat. Her mouth stays set, but her eyes narrow and she sinks into her dress. Louis' voice rings in his head as he realizes that this is the first time he's spoken to Nita since she stepped into the car. *Couillon,* he thinks, stupid, stupid, stupid. Now the song is over and she won't even look at him. But Louis can think of nothing to say, so he hunkers down before the wheel, with a furrowed brow and no thought in his head except how to get this girl to like him.

When the Falcon pulls up at Aggie's, Nita opens her door before Louis turns off the ignition. She walks into the diner and straight toward the rest room. Louis, Claude, and Kayla take a table and wait for Nita to find them. Louis starts tapping his foot against the linoleum tile, then stops. He shifts in his seat. This is crazy, he thinks. He's been out with practically every girl from St. Francis, even Anna Forêt, the most popular girl in his graduating class. (Anna told him he was the best-looking guy in their class—even if there were only eight other guys, Louis took it as high praise.) *They* always want *him*. After all, he was the captain of the football team, the Fighting Wolves, and the son of one of the best-known farmers in town. His mother is head of the P.T.A. (his little brother is still in school), and he's the only guy in his class who left the family farm for a job outside of Iota. Louis works at one of the biggest rice mills in Crowley and he drives a new, a brand-spanking-new, shiny black Falcon, a little deuce coupe—just like the one in the song. He's never been the nervous one on a date. He's never had to *try* to get a girl to like him. And he's never even been out with the same girl twice. He's got a reputation as the boy least available, one-date Louis, *he'll never settle down*.

When Nita finds the booth and slides in, Louis decides to seize control. He whistles for Beulah, the bouffant-haired waitress, and, in his best John Wayne voice, barks out his order, "We'll have two cheeseburgers with grilled onions, some of those crinkly fries, and just water to drink."

No one at the table laughs at his imitation; Claude and Kayla haven't parted lips since they stepped into the car and Nita just stares straight ahead. Louis tries to get her attention by asking, this time in a Marlon Brando warble, "So, uh, what d'ya think of my ride, the Falcon over there?"

He points his thumb toward the window. She doesn't respond, so he goes on to tell her how he had it customized *special* over at Bubba Oustalet's. How it has a souped-up engine with a V-8 and a glass-pack muffler set. How he washes and waxes it once a week and how he picks the gravel out of the tires with a butter knife. Louis is still talking about the Falcon when the burgers arrive. He chomps his in a few quick bites and finishes the fries in a hurry, but Nita barely touches the food on her plate. He asks, "Aren't you hungry?" and she shakes her head no. So he calls for the check and they slide out of the booth.

The next day Louis can't get Nita off his mind. All day long he pictures her dark, flowing hair, that neat little mouth in a line. He sees her green, speckled eyes and the olive of her skin. She's darker than any girl he's been out with; his mother would have a burning fit if she saw her. She looks Indian almost, a Cajun squaw painted with honey. As he brushes his teeth, Nita's face fills the bathroom mirror. As he turns on the water hose outside, her dress dances in the stream. As he polishes his car, her long, dark hair falls over his face in cascades and finally her mouth opens to kiss him.

That night, he picks up the phone in the kitchen and calls her. Before he knows what he's doing, he's asking her out, "So, uh, what d'ya say to us getting together tonight?"

"I can't," she says.

"What about tomorrow?"

"Busy."

"Didn't ya like my ride, didn't ya like tooling around in the Falcon?"

"Look. I . . . I gotta go." Click.

Every night for the next week, it's the same. She can't go out; she's busy. Someone's coming, she's gotta go, click. The second week the calls last a little longer. "Claude really likes Kayla," she says once. Then another time she says, "I wish I had a car. I wish I could get out of here anytime I wanted."

Finally, toward the end of the second week, he coaxes out of her the first hopeful word, "Maybe. Maybe this weekend. If Buford goes away."

Buford, her stepdad, leaves for a hunting trip on Friday. Nita and Louis go out for another double date with Claude and Kayla on Saturday. On that date, Claude and Kayla announce their engagement. Louis can't believe it when Nita elbows him and says, "Hey, let's get married, too."

But—as Louis puts it—he knew from that first date, from that first moment he lost her, that there was no other girl for him. So he shows up at her house a week later with an engagement ring that he spent the whole week scrounging up money for. He asked for an advance at work and even put off buying new mag wheels for the car. When she opens the blue velvet box, the line of her mouth twitches a little. She looks not at him, but past him at the yard outside and says, simply, "Yes."

Louis doesn't bother to ask the question, "Will you marry me?" for it seems that without his asking everything is set. Anyway, he doesn't want to take a chance that she'll change her mind. So he says "Good night" and steps back toward the Falcon. Nita turns toward the hurricane door and Louis realizes that he hasn't kissed her. They're going to be married and he hasn't kissed her. Well, there'll be time enough for that, he thinks, soon we'll be doing nothing but kissing.

3

WHEN NITA TELLS HER MOTHER AND STEPFATHER about the engagement, Gilda starts to cry and runs to the bedroom where she locks the door. Buford looks puzzled, and just keeps staring at his fingernails. Then he mutters, "*Mais,* it's about time," as he walks out the door toward the Pontiac. Nita figures she's getting off easy, but wishes someone would make a fuss over her.

The fuss, when it happens, is not at Nita's house, but at Louis'. When Louis goes to his mother, Anna, with his announcement, she pulls one glove off her hand and unpins the powder blue pillbox hat from her head. Anna is a thin-waisted, tight-lipped Cajun blond. Only she isn't really blond—she wears a frosted wig to cover her prematurely balding head—and she comes from French-speaking German stock, not Cajun. Still, her eyes *are* blue and her skin as pale as a camellia and she tells Louis that she'll be damned if she's going to help any son of hers marry outside Iota.

"Where does this . . . *jeunesse* come from?" she asks.

Merde! Louis thinks. Shit! That's the one question he fears most and it's the first one she asks. Why couldn't she ask something easier like, "How old is she?" or "Are you sure?," anything but "Where's she from?" Place means everything in Louisiana, Louis knows that. Tell someone where you're from and they can guess your father's occupation and, if he's a farmer, what he plants. ("Rice? . . . Sweet potatoes, then!") The mark between parishes can go beyond differences of crop and even class to reveal a family's character. ("The Ville Platte Comeauxs, that's good people, *hein?* But down in the bayous I know a couple of Comeauxs, *méchantes?* That's not people you wanna fool with, no?") Louis stands there with the name of the place his fiancée is from ringing in his head, then the word *fiancée—fi-an-cée!*—rings out, too, until Anna asks again, this time in a sharper tone, "Where's she *from?*"

Then Louis coughs into his hand and says, "Jennings." Anna's upper lip twitches and she yanks off the remaining glove. Jennings lies west of Iota, on the border between Acadia and Jefferson Davis Parish and, as far as Louis' mother is concerned, that town belongs more to Texas than Louisiana. It's only twenty minutes away by car, but you could hunt and hunt, Anna tells him, and not find more than a half-dozen true-blue Cajuns there. Jennings is known in the Crowley–Iota sewing circles as a lawless town, full of ranchers and ex-cowhands left over from when the Wild West crossed the state line for the wide-open Texas plains. The land in Jefferson Davis Parish is less fertile than the land in Acadia, so Jennings replaced the cattle ranches not with amber waves of grain, but with black, slimy oil wells. Louis has heard Anna's lady-friends tsk-tsk at what they see in Jennings: "Those oilhands are worse than cowboys," the ladies always tell each other and nod in agreement. "They'd mix with anything: Redneck, Yankee, Indian, even a *negresse* or her little pickaninny girls."

"Jennings?" Anna cries, "Jennings! *Le bon Dieu!* Of all the places? What's wrong, *tête dure?* Couldn't find you a nice Cajun girl here in Iota? What about that Anna Forêt—she's popular, isn't she? Her family farms rice just like your *pére* and she's got those pretty blue eyes . . ."

"But Mama, I know all the girls in Iota."

"Exactly—we *know* them. In Iota, *nous nous connaissons, tous,* tous! What do we know about this girl? What do you know about her?"

"I like her . . ."

"*Like* her? *Écoute-toi,* in my book *like* and *know* are two different things. Me, I never *like* before I *know.* You say you like her—okay, *cher,* let's see just what we can find out about this girl and her people. How do they call themselves, then?"

If Nita's hometown makes Louis' mother nervous, that's nothing compared to the discovery of Nita's family name. Anna calls Louis into the kitchen the next afternoon when he gets home from work. All her lady-friends gather around the table before she asks him again how "that girl" calls herself. When he says, *"Moreau,"* she turns to her friends, who quickly reveal the real spelling and pronunciation: "Morrow."

"And what kind of French is that?" Anna asks Louis.

"Not French at all," the ladies jump in before Louis can say anything, "English."

"English!" Louis' mother nearly shouts.

Louis sits stiff in his chair as he watches his mother fume, while the ladies collect around her with their flapping hands and open mouths.

"She's not even French!" Anna shrieks. "She's worse than not French, she's English! And she's not even honest about it. She's gone and Frenchified her name to hide what she is!"

Then to top it off, the ladies announce that it's known, widely known in fact, that the Morrows aren't Catholic. They're not even regular Protestants. They're Pentecostal, the speaking-in-tongues kind.

Louis' mother slaps her hand down hard on the red and white tile of the counter and he watches as her knuckles go white.

"That does it," Anna whispers, out of breath, as she knocks twice on the tile, then presses her fingers to the side of her head.

But that isn't the worst of it. After Anna forbids Louis to tell his father, Louis Sr., about the engagement, she deploys every active member of the Crowley–Iota sewing circle on a fact-finding mission. Each day, she waits until her husband has left for the farm, then she calls her lady-friends over for the latest report from Jennings. Soon the dirt on Nita's family catches wind and shoots straight through the crack under the Toussaint family door. All day long Louis' mother sweeps, and still the dirt swirls at her feet. The voices of the sewing-circle ladies swirl, too, and as more and more dirt piles under their door, Anna tells Louis and the ladies as they all gather in the kitchen one morning that she regrets ever hearing the words Jennings or *Moreau*.

"To start with," Anna tells Louis, "*Moreau*—or Morrow—is not her mother's name. It's Lejeune. And even if that makes this girl you want to marry part French, it also makes her a bastard."

Anna shoots a look toward the ladies for confirmation. Louis wants to laugh at his mother, but instead he bites his lip.

"Even if Nita was born in wedlock," Anna says, "this Lejeune woman divorced Nita's father when the girl was seven—and isn't that just like being a bastard?"

The frosted heads of the ladies nod and their voices murmur in agreement. Louis watches as his mother circles herself around the kitchen.

"Maybe it's worse," she decides. "There's not even a name for what kind of child she is. Then this Lejeune woman—Gilda, and isn't there something a little off about that name?—this woman has married not just once, but twice more! And she never rests, not even between marriages. She walks the streets alone . . ."

Louis' mother hesitates and the ladies pick up the line, *"At night!"*

"She's never been picked up," Anna says. "She's never been charged, but then, it's Jennings, you know."

"Pauv' bête." The ladies rub Anna's hands and fan her face as she stumbles to the den and falls back in her padded cane rocker. *"Pauv' bête."* For there's more.

Even though he knows he'll be late for work, Louis follows his mother to the den. He's starting to relish her fury, and he can't wait to see what might happen next as Viola, the oldest of the sewing-circle ladies, speaks up.

"The *mère's mère,*" Viola says. "Well. Anna, I don't know if I should tell you this . . ."

She looks down at the white kid gloves on her hands. "I'm not even sure if there's any proof for it. But my daughter told me . . ."

Viola puts her hands to her eyes as if she was facing a brutally hot sun. Louis watches as—even before the old lady speaks—what she prepares to say collects a certain truth about it.

"Anna," Viola sounds as if she might cry, "the *grand-mère* is not even white, she's Indian, some kind of half-breed, Blackfoot, Chitimacha, something. Attakapa? *J'connais pas,* but she's Indian, I tell you!"

When Louis hears this, he can't help himself. He laughs out loud and the ladies stare at him until he walks out onto the front porch. He's still laughing when he reaches his car door. Nita isn't Attakapa, she can't be, Louis knows that. The Attakapa were cannibals, a blood-thirsty war-hungry tribe that ran a stretch of land from the Sabine River to the Mermentau Bayou. That area is now covered by the westernmost, and as his mother would put it, Texas-butting, parishes of Beauregard, Allen, Calcasieu, and Jefferson Davis. He remembers that from his Louisiana history class, junior year. Jennings is, sure enough, part of Attakapa country. But the cannibals were killed off more than a century and a half before in a battle with the Opelousas, Choctaw, and Chitimacha tribes. Louis figures the Chitimacha blood is what runs through Nita's veins.

But as he drives to the rice mill in Crowley, Louis' amusement turns sour. He can't believe his mother would check up on his fiancée like that. And then to call in half the town for the report! Doesn't he have the right to choose his own wife? Anna is always meddling in his life, always telling him what to do. She even tried to keep him from taking the job at the rice mill. She told him she didn't want him working so far away. (Louis laughed when she said this; Crowley is little more than fifteen minutes by car.) "Why can't you find something here in town?" she asked. "Why can't you work on the farm with your father?"

But Louis doesn't want to be like his father; that's why he decided to work in Crowley. It's not a big town, not like Lafayette. But it's a lot bigger than the half-mile strip he jokingly calls "downtown" Iota, where he can't get away from his father's shadow. Louis Sr., is not tall, but he's a big man in Iota. The other farmers often ask for his advice, and no one's ever been elected mayor without having been to his house first. He's even helped to stop property fights between neighbors. Everywhere he goes, people ask Louis, "How's your *père?* Where's your father been hiding?"

Sometimes he wants to tell them he has no idea *how* his father is. After all, they hardly talk anymore. Every night, Louis Sr. comes home late from the farm and cracks open a can of Dixie. But he never says much more to Anna than, "What's for supper?"

Ever since Louis can remember, Anna has harped on his father to add on to the house, to make the place bigger, to buy a new couch. They have one of the best homes in Iota, Louis knows that. His father even built a brick planter out front and put up a fence with a gate. But it's not enough for Anna. She wants him to build a gazebo and whitewash the trees in the backyard and she wants him to do it *now;* she says, she doesn't care how tired he is. Her work never quits, why should his?

His father used to turn purple and scream at Anna to shut up and leave him in peace. But then he had a nervous spell and was put into a clinic for several months where he never spoke one word to Louis or anyone else who visited. Louis worried that his father had lost his voice, but the doctor said he just needed some time alone.

Since he came home from the clinic, Louis Sr. has stopped fighting Anna, but he's also stopped saying much of anything to anyone else in the house. Even when they barbecue, his father stays quiet. He drinks his Dixie and shows Louis' younger brother, Rémy, how to flip an oyster on the grill without losing any juice. But when Anna asks his father what he wants, the gizzard or the neck, he just shrugs his shoulders and says, "Me? I'm like Patin's duck, I don't give a quack." Louis shakes his head and thinks, We used to wrestle for the neck.

As he parks the car in the shell-covered lot by the mill, Louis decides he doesn't want to turn into Patin's duck. He's going to marry Nita, no matter what his mother says.

That night after work, Louis is a little late getting home, but when he walks in, he finds a bowl of gumbo waiting for him on the table. *"Mange-toi,"* Anna says. "Eat." Then she unties the checkered apron from around her waist and bends over the chair where Louis sits. She's waited alone all afternoon for him to come home, waited all day to tell him her decision. She's hardly left the kitchen, in fact, she's scrubbed and rescrubbed nearly every inch of it. She seems strangely calm to Louis and her voice sounds almost soft when she tells him, "You can't marry that girl, you can't. I won't let you."

Louis looks around: the room is bright and buzzing with frilly curtains and glistening surfaces. Nothing is on the counter that doesn't belong there; even the hand-embroidered dish towel his mother uses to wipe her hands seems arranged, *draped,* where it hangs from the chrome handle on the bone-white stove. You'd never know anyone lived here, Louis thinks as he takes it all in. The green Depression-glass pitcher filled with water and dahlias, centered on the table. The glinting, steel knives hanging upside-down in descending order according to length.

"I'm gonna marry her, Mama," he says. "I said I was, and a Toussaint does what he says." Louis stares hard at his mother and silently dares her to buck up against his father's family code. Anna puts a hand out as if to rest it on Louis' shoulder, then draws it back. Her hand hangs in the air for just a moment, as if it had no place else to go, then it settles at her side.

"How can you still want to marry that girl, that dirty little Indian girl? How can you still like her when you *know?*"

But for Louis, knowing has nothing to do with liking. He likes Nita and, like it or not, he's already decided to marry her. Anna turns her back to him and jerks on the hot water in the sink.

"If you marry that girl, that little Indian *jeunesse,* that *negresse rouge* . . . I'll have nothing to do with it, do you hear? *Pas d' tout, comprends?*"

But that's perfect, Louis thinks. He can see how it all is perfect. He'll marry Nita and move away from here, from this house that holds its breath, from his mother who holds the house like a glass ornament in her hand. He'll marry Nita and rule his own house; *he'll* give it breath or take it away. Then he'll make a son. A little boy who will look just like him and who will carry his name. He'll marry Nita, he can see it. He'll marry her. He will.

4

THE WEDDING CEREMONY, WHAT LITTLE THERE IS OF it, is put together slap-dab and without any help from Louis' mother. Instead, the burden for both the wedding and the reception falls on Gilda, and Nita's mother is barely able to sustain the cost. She tells Nita that Hilton is out on parole. "But he's harder than a winter rabbit to track down," she says. And they both know that, when she finds Nita's father, they can't expect him to pay for a thing.

Then——when Nita insists on having Hilton walk her down the aisle——her stepfather also refuses to help.

"Either I'm her father or I ain't——*comprends?*" Buford shouts at Gilda. "How's it gonna look if you go sailing into that church with two husbands like some damn Mormon?"

"It's her wedding," Gilda says. "It's her choice."

"I am the man, here," he shoots back, "*personne n' plus,* no one else."

When Gilda finally finds Hilton and tells him she'd be happy to help him get his hands on a suit, Buford storms out of the house and drives off with the Pontiac and a loaded shotgun, leaving her to get around on foot. Three days later, he returns with a few head of duck, throws the shotgun on the table, then walks up to Nita, and says, "I won't pay for any of it, not a cent, *écoute-moi?*"

Nita waits until Buford turns his back, then she makes an exaggerated face that her mother calls the "*grimace.*" But even as she counts the days before she can leave her stepfather's house, she worries about how her mother will manage the wedding alone. All she has are the government checks that come once a month and a little extra cash she keeps stashed in a canister. Nita also worries that Gilda will have another spell, that she'll lock herself in her room and not come out for days.

But her mother pieces together the plans so quickly and so well that Nita almost can't believe it. Gilda tells her that she can wear her own mother's dress—the one her mother passed down from her *grand-mère*—all she'll have to do is pin it. She says she can do Nita's hair and makeup, too. And the flowers—she knows a place where she can get calendulas by the bunch and she can cut and arrange them with a little help from two of her sisters. Euna Mae and La-La are both good with flowers and they'll know their way around all that ribbon and wire. Gilda's four other sisters can help her sort out the groom's cake, the little deviled sandwiches with the cut-off crusts, and the punch bowls with their bobbing grapes and kumquats. And the *boudin* balls Gilda can make herself from a secret blood sausage recipe. "What else?" Gilda asks Nita, without waiting for a response. "It oughta be cool enough then, so a big tureen of gumbo and maybe a *sauce piquante.*"

The wedding is still three weeks away, but already Nita can see the shopping list swelling and the peppery steam rising in the kitchen. The dark syrup is boiling and pecans are toasting for one of Gilda's famous pies. Nita knows that her mother will make everything herself—*tous par main*—no true Cajun wedding would ever be catered. After all the groceries are bought, there will be just enough in the emergency fund left over for the frothy two-tiered bride's cake, which has to be store-bought and big enough to impress Mrs. Toussaint. *"Cettes madames catholiques,"* Gilda tells Nita, "these Catholic ladies, they love a big show."

Her mother seems to worry more about the wedding, though, than she does about Nita herself. Gilda has asked next to nothing about her fiancé. Although she's met Louis, all she said about him was that he looked serious and that she was impressed with his Falcon. She told Nita she ought to feel lucky getting married to a boy with a good job *and* a good car.

The night after Gilda pins Nita's dress, Louis calls to talk about their plans for the wedding and Nita asks her mother to say she isn't home. But Gilda tells her not to be *fou*. "He knows you're here," she says. "He's been calling all week. And, anyway, don't you have to go with him to St. Jude's?"

Nita has avoided seeing Louis and she's put off a visit to the church; she hasn't wanted to talk to the priest. She doesn't know if she wants to pledge Catholic. And she also doesn't know if she wants to drop out of school. But her mother tells her not to worry. "School is only to keep girls off the street and out of trouble," she says. "Marriage is the real diploma."

Nita hangs her head and goes to pick up the phone. She tells Louis that she doesn't feel well. "Is it all right," she asks, "if you go without me?"

When Louis agrees to see the priest alone and to make a separate appointment for her later in the week, Nita feels a volt of re-lief surge through her body. I can make it through this, she thinks, if I can just keep from seeing him.

She considers telling one of her sisters that she's not in love. But Monetta Lou is only nine and Vina Lee wouldn't understand. Ever since she got married, she's been telling Nita she needs to get hitched, too. "You'd better hurry," she teases. "You don't wanna be an old maid."

In fact, the only protest anyone in her family raises about the wedding is the date. Gilda tells Nita that March is not a good month to marry, and in order to convince Nita she takes her one morning to see her grandmother. Deola, Gilda's mother, is not a *traiteuse,* she can't heal what needs healing. But she can see things, sometimes, before they happen and she can often look back to see what has gone before.

As soon as Nita and Gilda join her at the kitchen table, Deola fills a white teacup with sassafras leaves and hot water. She turns the cup over a cast-iron pot, then shakes her head. The leaves have left a thick brown smudge of a line near the bottom of the cup, and the cards she dealt before they arrived haven't played out any better. "Not good," Nita's grandmother says in a rough whisper. Then she pokes a finger in the white coil of hair on top of her head and repeats herself, *"Pas bon, pas d' tout.* Not good, not good at all."

According to Deola, bad things always happen in March. That month is *trop vent,* too windy. Everything gets blown around and she tells Nita that she can never figure out if it's the last month of winter or the first month of spring. *"Attends à l'avril, ma chère,"* she begs. "Wait till April."

Nita thinks about telling her grandmother that she's not even sure if she wants to get married. But she decides against it, and she decides against changing the date, too. She doesn't want to talk to

Louis any more than she has to. He told her he wants to get married as soon as possible, and he chose the earliest date they could get at St. Jude's. And, anyway, what would she tell him? That they had to change the wedding because her grandmother's cup had a brown line in it?

No, she has to find another way around Deola's worries. Nita remembers that both her mother and grandmother were married before they turned seventeen. So she tells Gilda and Deola that she wants to be married before her next birthday, which falls on the last weekend in March, and they both relent. "I may be an old widow, *chère,*" Deola says, "but I remember how it is. I couldn't wait to get married either."

With Gilda and Deola's approval, then, Nita and Louis are set to be married on Friday, March 13.

5

TWO WEEKS LATER, THE WEDDING DAY ARRIVES AND
Louis' mother breaks out in hives, or at least that's what she tells
him when she remains too long in the bathroom. Louis knocks on
the door several times, and when his mother steps out she looks
just fine to him. But Anna tells Louis that her throat feels tight and
that her skin itches—always a bad sign. Louis wants to laugh; he
knows his mother reads her skin the way other people read an as-
trology chart. He also knows that she's still searching for some
way to convince him to call off the wedding.

As Anna looks at Louis, she presses her index finger to the
place below her right eye. Her fingernail leaves a mark in her
makeup, like a tiny purple comma, and she drops a powder box
and a vanity mirror in her purse before stepping out of the bath-

room. Before Louis closes the door, she spins on her heels. "You know," she says, picking up the only conversation they've had for the past few weeks, "this whole thing looks to me like the rice on the bottom of a pot—sticky and not worth the effort."

Louis ignores his mother and slides the door closed behind him. He hasn't told her this, but he's started to worry about the wedding. He's hardly seen Nita at all since they were engaged. The only real time they spent together was at the rehearsal with the priest. Louis was so nervous about getting everything right, he could barely look at Nita. And even when he calls, it seems that she doesn't want to talk long. Maybe she doesn't want to jinx us, he thinks. She's probably just nervous, that's all.

A few hours later, shortly before noon, Louis and his parents arrive at St. Jude's in Jennings. Someone is at the organ, pumping out the opening strains of "The Wedding March" in different keys, and Gilda pokes her head out to see who is in the church. Louis catches sight of Nita's mother and he points her out to Anna. Then he looks around the room while, in a loud whisper, Anna ticks off at least half a dozen things that are not just wrong, but hideously wrong. She tells Louis that there should be a ring boy, a flower girl, bridesmaids. When Louis tells her there wasn't enough time for all that, she says there should at least be petals on the carpet and candles on the altar. Then she tells him the flowers are all mixed up. There are too many calendulas; their perfume is *trop doux,* too sickly sweet. There should be white camellias for honesty and a simple trellis of wisteria for trust. "And geraniums," Anna says. "Geraniums would act like a good *nanaine,* and keep the whole thing looking proper."

"But more than the flowers," Anna turns to her husband, "there's Nita's mother, that Lejeune woman. She's wearing red!

That color is for roses and azaleas, for bricks and kitchen tile. No woman should ever be seen in red, much less a woman who happens to be the mother of the bride!"

Anna presses her lips together and looks at Louis. "And she's wearing glasses, cat-eye glasses at that! *I* would never wear specs in church—*never!* Let the *bon Dieu* look into my eyes direct, I would!"

She harrumphs, then turns back to her husband, who simply coughs into his hand. "Where was I?" she asks him, without waiting for an answer. "Oh yes, and that Lejeune woman's lipstick is too dark and smeared too wide around her lips. She looks as if she's pouting—what has *she* got to pout for?"

After Louis finds his place at the front of the altar, Louis Sr., the original to Louis' carbon copy, readies himself to walk down the aisle with Anna. He chuckles out loud, then looks down at his dark single-button suit to check that everything is in place. Louis knows his father is a man who believes in the power of clean lines. He watches as Louis Sr. tugs on the tail of his skinny black tie, then secretly tucks it into the waist of his pants. Louis' mother calls that trick of his *trop gauche,* but it works and he learned at least this from his father: no matter what anyone says, stick with the thing that works. Louis knows that his father is neater than he is, and he also knows that while they look alarmingly alike, his father's face is somehow sharper and he's a little taller, too. But Louis figures he's only nineteen. He's still growing, he might catch up with his father yet. Throughout this whole fracas, Louis Sr. has said next to nothing. Mostly he's just laughed to himself and cracked open another can of Dixie.

Once his parents are seated and Nita's mother takes her place, Louis' eye catches the first glimpse of his bride. Nita with that white frilly cloud about her head. That froufrou gown with poufed-up sleeves and a never-ending train. Even in that baggy sack of a dress that looks as if it was pinned and pulled to fit her, and against the tall, sharp figure of her father, Nita commands the room. She makes her way up the aisle inch by inch and seems to relish every turned head. Yet there is no gloss of vanity about her. Louis sees only a new bloom of a girl—opening her mouth for the first time in a nervous, but radiant smile. As she passes pew after pew and finally glances his way, he thinks that Nita looks more like a squaw than he remembered. Her hair rushes out from behind her veil in luminous jet-black waves. Her skin looks tinted, a dark burnished color like the hull of grain in the Iota fields. Just then, he recalls the Spanish meaning of her name, Bonita, "Beautiful."

Louis can see that the little church is maybe half full. He knows that his mother invited next to none of her lady-friends, only those in her immediate sewing circle, the ones who live down the street, whom she couldn't possibly exclude. Louis' mother was too embarrassed, too *honte,* to invite most of the Iota ladies to the wedding. He could see that some had come anyway, uninvited, and he figured others would show up at the reception, just to witness his mother's face as the band launched into *"Jolie Blon',"* Pretty Blonde, the unofficial Cajun anthem and the first song played at every *fais-do do.* For now, the uninvited ladies take up a few short rows behind his mother and father, and each presses a glass rosary to her chest as "The Wedding March" grinds to an abrupt halt and the priest in his purple cassock appears before the altar.

For Nita and Louis, the whole affair, from "Dearly Beloved" to "You may now kiss the bride . . . ," disappears at once like the Eucharist they take on their tongues. There is the awkward, impatient sound of someone shifting against a wooden pew. There is the loud drop of the kneelers against the church floor. There is a cough and the quickly muffled cry of a little girl. Then the double doors to the church fly open and the wedding couple is carried out with the clack and wheeze of the organ and a burst of camera flashes and rice. Nita can't remember the kiss and Louis can't remember slipping the ring on her finger. But it was done, and now they're out of the church and into the Falcon for the long drive to the reception hall.

THE DRIVE TO THE KNIGHTS OF COLUMBUS HALL IS A long, snaky affair if you follow the country roads—which is the only way Louis will go. Nita can't understand why he avoids the highway. She wants to get there quick and get this thing over with. The wedding was nerve-wracking enough; she can only imagine what the reception will be like. She keeps picturing that moment when she first walked into the church and all those eyes were on her. She knows her dress looked terrible and that was all she kept thinking about while the priest droned on. Nita was surprised when she heard her cue and the practiced words came tumbling out: I do. She felt as if she was called on in class and somehow got the answer right.

Then came the disappointment. Nita had pictured how free she would feel walking out of Buford's house forever, but she didn't feel free at all. As she walked down the aisle, she caught sight of Louis looking at her and she thought about what her mother had said, that this would be her graduation. But she didn't feel like she was graduating. All she felt was that she wanted to turn around and walk back out toward the marble steps. She wanted to walk down the street and keep walking until she got away from Jennings and away from Louis, too. Her mother told her she would like being married, but Nita isn't so sure. She'll be seventeen in a couple of weeks and she's never done anything except wait tables at Fiona's. What will she do when she's married?

Nita craves some time alone, but she knows that everyone in her family will be at the K.C. Hall. No one would turn down a chance at a good *fais-do-do* with free *boudin* and Styrofoam chests packed tight with icy cans and bottles of Dixie, Jax, and Bud. Though Bud is a Yankee beer, the rice they brew it with is Cajun and it's all her favorite cousin, Six-Pack, will drink. She knows Six-Pack will be there along with all the men who skipped the wedding because they couldn't find or afford a suit, or because they figured why bother with all that mess when you're just gonna jump right back in your overalls anyway? They'll all be there, cracking bottles of beer with their teeth, each man raising his cotton shirt to scratch at a mosquito bite on his belly. Hypolite, Jacques, and Ti-Boy, Gaston, Arcade, and Ti-Pep, they'll be there, crowded around the steaming pots while the raccoon-eyed *tantes* and *cousines* ladle out bowls of gumbo. The girls will hike up their skirt waist when no one is looking, to show a little more leg, and some of the crazier *tantes* will pull at their bobby pins until their hair falls to their shoulders in thin streams. Nita knows how these things go; the longer she takes to get there, the longer they'll stay. "Hurry," she tells Louis, "can't you hurry?"

It's the first she's spoken since they stepped inside the Falcon, and Louis thinks she can't wait to cross the threshold with him. "Look, I'm going as fast as I can. I don't want all this gravel to chink the new paint job," he tells her. "We'll get there soon enough."

Nita puts her hand up against the dash and under her breath says, "Yes, the car . . . the car . . ." Louis signals a left turn for the road out to Evangeline, then turns his head to face her.

"You like it?" Louis asks.

"What?" Nita says.

"Being married, silly."

"Yes," she says, then purses her lips, "I guess so."

Nita turns to the passenger's window to watch the road close up behind them. They're on pavement now and Louis gives the Falcon some juice with his patent-leather shoe pressed hard against the pedal. The tight streets of Jennings quickly disappear and the fallow fields of thistle and knee-high bluegrass give way to the dwarfed derricks and round oil bins of Evangeline. The rotten-egg smell of sulfur mixes with the almost sweet traces of petroleum in the air. This is the road Louis first drove to meet Nita; he doesn't tell her that, but he likes the thought of it anyway. He likes this mixed-up smell and the sight of the oil rigs drilling at the ground like a pelican pecking at its breast. He likes to think of the pelican on the state flag, how it pierces its breast with the pointy end of its beak, how blood falls from its breast to the young pelicans in the nest and how the oil is like that.

The little switchback road pulls away from the sulfurous air and the tarred fields and clips right and left several times before rounding a corseted S-curve for Iota. More than one car has spun out on the ramshackle bridge, and just last summer two juniors from St. Francis ran through the split-wood railing and into the muddy bayou waters below. Neither of them died, but Louis has called it "Dead Man's Curve" ever since. The Falcon takes the curve with ease and when the road evens out, Louis points out his parents' newly reshingled wood-frame house. Nita spots a brick planter up front, bursting with nasturtiums, white verbenas, geraniums, and her favorite—purple-laced pansies. In the back of the house, under more than a dozen massive live oaks, she spies a semicircle of azalea bushes in full bloom with a wisteria vine running along the fence. The tree trunks are painted white at the base and Nita wonders what the house looks like inside. While she presses her face to the window, Louis thinks how he can't wait to take her home, to watch his mother serve Nita at the dinner table. He looks at the back of Nita's head and thinks, She's mine now, mine.

The road turns back on itself again to bypass the two-lane one-block downtown of Iota where one small redbrick building functions as the city hall, the police department, and the office for the volunteer fire troop. There's a one-room library in a peaked wood frame and a Dollar General store under a sloped tin roof that looks something like an airplane hangar. One bar without a sign, a little glass-front drugstore, and an empty lot complete the strip. Nita sees none of this, though, as the Falcon sails past St. Francis and into the fertile prairie land between Iota and Crowley. The crops of rice sit squat under several feet of water, their stalks just beginning to push out of the ground. Mosquitos swarm over the stagnant water in search of a tall dandelion or a fat frond to spread their eggs under. Live oaks shoot up between the fields with tallow trees, water oaks, and clumps of cedar. The road turns in and out, cutting up the land of the farmers and keeping pace with the fast hum of telephone wires and the neat click of utility poles.

After more than twenty minutes, the Falcon jerks to a stop before the K.C. Hall. Louis and Nita push open their doors at the same time and a crowd of red faces surrounds them. Somebody throws a leftover purse of rice and the band starts up with *"Jolie Blon'*," the old Joe Falcon version. "That there's the real Cajun," Nita hears somebody say. "Joe recorded that song with Cleoma Breaux, his one true love, right here in Crowley."

"She looked just like Nita," Louis' father says as he takes his daughter-in-law by the hand. *"Exactement."*

The father-in-law gets the first dance at a wedding *fais-do-do,* but first he wants to show her a picture of Cleoma and her husband in the hall.

The black and white photograph is framed and dated 1928. It's cracked and, even with a frame pressing it down, it looks curled at the edges. But Nita can make out the ghostlike face of a French-Indian girl with a kinky bush of black hair tied behind her head. Sitting in a cane rocker, she stares straight at the camera and holds a guitar at a slight angle on her lap. Her feet just barely reach the ground, her head is cocked, and Nita thinks she looks just like a gypsy. Cleoma is small, but Joe, Cleoma's husband, seems dwarfed next to her. His hair is parted in a hard line down the middle of his head and he seems to have no eyebrows. His small hands cradle an accordion and there is the trace of a mustache above his lip. He has prominent ears and stares at Nita with a mournful face. There seems to be a greater charge between Cleoma and the guitar on her lap than between her and the man at her side. Nita looks at Joe and Cleoma staring at her in silence and wonders if that's it, if that's what a marriage comes to.

"You're married, now," Mr. Toussaint tells her. "You're a real Cajun bride, *la vraie chose.*"

Nita looks at him, but says nothing.

"That means you're my daughter, *ma fille,* a Toussaint girl," he says quietly. Then he shouts out loud, *"Allons danser!"*

Louis watches the two of them and is surprised to see his father take to Nita so quickly. He hasn't seen him this excited in a long while and he figures it's a good sign.

Nita sees Louis looking at her, and the thought of Joe and Cleoma fills her head as she steps onto the dance floor with Mr. Toussaint. "Call me Pop," he says, and she catches sight of a sour face under a powder blue hat as he twirls her around.

Anna, Louis' mother, folds her arms across her chest as Nita and her new Pop glide across the hardwood floor to the chank-a-chank of the seesaw music. Pop Toussaint cuts a mean two-step with one leg falling perfectly limp as the other slides in and out with the rhythm of the song, *"Quel espoir et quel avenir mais moi je va avoir? Jolie blon', tu m'as quitté moi tout seul . . . ,"* What hope and future will I have? Pretty blonde you have left me all alone . . .

How strange, Nita thinks, that they should dance so furiously to this sad song. All around her the *n'oncles* and *cousins* whoop and shout: "Louis' girl, *elle peut vraiment danser,* she sure can move, *hein?*"

As the song comes to a close and someone shouts, *"Ah yi yie!"* Nita closes her eyes and places her chin on Pop's shoulder. When the violin sounds the last high whine, a crowd of men from both sides of the family circle Nita to pin five- and ten-dollar bills to her bridal train and to claim the next dance. Pop Toussaint folds a fifty and clips it to the lacy trim of her veil.

Then Nita catches sight of her own Pop walking in the hall like a Texas cowboy with a ten-gallon hat on his head. Hilton sports a high shine on his boots as he crosses the floor to his daughter. The lights of the stage flash in the silver on his belt buckle and on the many rings on his fingers. In his right hand, he holds a hundred-dollar bill and Gilda gasps out loud. Nita's grandmother mumbles, *"De toutes les choses,* of all the things . . ."

But Hilton ignores his ex-wife and stares straight at his daughter as he asks the band to play "that Belle song." The accordion gathers air, then the bandleader sings, *"T'es' pour moi, malheureuse,"* You are mine, unhappy one . . .

And in all the fuss, Nita and Louis forget about their own dance until it seems too late to bother and the *fais-do-do* itself is done.

6

NITA LIES ON THE HARD BED, THEN STANDS UP. SHE walks over to the round Formica table near the window and sits down. She crosses her legs, then uncrosses them. Whatever she tries, nothing feels right. She tugs at the edge of the yellow chintz curtain and stares at the two stuffed blue marlins over the bed. *Two.* Nita can hardly breathe with the thought of those fish above her head. She would take a shower, hide under a warm stream of water, but she's already done that and he's sure to come back any minute.

Louis has gone for a bucket of ice from the machine outside. "No good drinking warm beer," he said. "Beer's just one thing that has to be cold."

She's glad to have him out of the room—even for a minute. That drive west from the K.C. Hall in Crowley all the way to Lake

Charles, more than an hour in that car with nothing but him and the radio and a few passing road signs, that drive wore on her nerves. Not that she wasn't nervous before. But the wedding was really just a walk, then a dance or two. This, this was the thing she dreaded for more than a month. The thing that stuck in her mind when she looked at that picture of Joe and Cleoma Falcon on the paneled wall of the K.C. Hall. Nita thinks how Cleoma looked worn and riddled with regret. With that bushy black hair and those dark gypsy eyes, she looked more like an Indian queen than a Cajun man's wife. But then who was *Jolie Blon'*, who was the blonde woman Joe was singing about as Nita danced with Louis' father? And why did Mr. Toussaint show her that picture? No, she won't become another Cleoma, playing guitar to her husband's lament. She isn't sure how she'll get out of it, but her mind is set.

When Louis returns with the bucket, Nita asks him to go down to the motel office for a *pop rouge*. "It's stuffy in here," she says. "I can barely breathe."

She pokes her head through a tear in the curtain to look down at Louis crossing the concrete lot. She thought at least they would have a view of the lake and the little strip of beach that runs alongside the highway. More than anything, she wanted to get outside Louisiana, to look at mountains or skyscrapers, to see all the things she had heard her father talk about. After all, she'll be seventeen soon and she's never seen anything west of Sulphur. She's never been to New Orleans or even Lafayette. But they couldn't afford a real honeymoon, Louis said, not without his parents' help. And there was no way Anna would pay for any more than a night in this Travelodge off I-10. Whatever money they plucked off Nita's bridal train, Louis told her, they needed for the apartment in Crowley. He picked that apartment without her. What would he have done if she hadn't walked down the aisle, if she hadn't even shown up at the church? He is so sure, too sure, of her. He barely even speaks to her. It's as if he knows beforehand what to expect. As if he knows what he's getting out of the deal.

As he crosses the car lot, Louis looks back at the room and catches a glimpse of Nita's face moving away from the window. She's crazy about me, he thinks, checking up on me like that. He almost can't believe that Nita is his. He hardly knows what to say to her when she's near. His tongue thickens when he looks at her and his jaw clamps shut. But soon, he knows, things will loosen up and they'll have plenty to talk about. And, anyway, a little quiet is all right. They're married, aren't they?

When Louis returns from the motel office, he hands Nita the strawberry soda and an opener. Then he cracks open a can of Dixie and pours it in a plastic cup, chock full with ice. A little foam spills onto the carpet and he lets rip with a laugh. "You talk about living," he says, "this is it!"

Louis twists on the knob to the TV and flops back on the bed. Good, Nita thinks, let him lie there. He kicks off the covers, kicks off his shoes. She stares at the twisting squares and circles on the bedspread, the shifting blues and reds in a bundle on the floor, while he watches Petula Clark on some variety show singing "Downtown" and complains that he's never seen the Beach Boys on TV, not even Ed Sullivan. "They're much better than her," he says. "Hell, they've even had those *negresse* girls on, singing 'Baby Love.' Why not the Beach Boys?"

Nita says nothing. She just pulls her nightgown over her knees, and draws her legs up close to her chest. Louis tries on an Ed Sullivan slur and warbles the opening to "Little Deuce Coupe." Then he watches the Nightly News, some bit about more changes with the Vatican II and the Voting Rights Act. "Damn niggers," he says, "they're everywhere. Anyway, that's enough of that. *C'est tout.*"

Louis walks over to twist down the volume on the TV and then he curls up in the middle of the bed. "Are you gonna sleep in that chair?" he asks Nita before patting the slim half of the pillow next to his head.

This is it, Nita thinks as she shifts in her chair, this is it. Soon as she stands, Louis throws off his shirt and pants, leaving on just a pair of crew socks, tight white underwear, and a stretched-out V-neck T-shirt. He tugs the V-neck over his head and lies back against the pillow. But when Nita reaches his side of the bed, she doesn't move. She just stands there staring at the blue marlins. He looks up at the wall, then back down at her. God, she's beautiful, he thinks as he grabs her hand and pulls her toward him. She stumbles and falls onto the mattress. Neither of them move for a minute, except that Nita chews on a fingernail and Louis' stomach moves up and down with the air he breathes. Then Louis gets up off the bed and drops his underwear to the floor. His socks are still on as he walks toward the bed. Nita looks up at the ceiling and thinks, I don't know him, I don't know a thing about him, and now he's standing over me. She draws her knees together and he crawls on top of her. "Nita," he says.

"What?" she asks. "What?" before Louis presses his lips against hers. He pushes up her white cotton nightgown and pushes apart her legs. He struggles with her knees, then jams himself into her. She bites her upper lip and wants to scream. She's sure he's ripping something inside her, doing something horribly wrong. But then he lets out a muffled sound and pulls back from her. Is that it, is he done? she almost asks as he stands up from the bed and stretches his arms toward the ceiling.

Louis stands by the bed for a moment and thinks maybe he's never felt this good. He's got everything he wanted. Nita is exactly as he imagined. She's tender and smooth, slim and warm, and totally his. The feel of her lips and skin burns in his mind even as he pulls away from her. But he tells her none of this; he's sure that it would come out wrong. Instead, he walks to the bathroom to brush his teeth.

Nita lies in her spot with the smell of Louis still on her. The sound of his breathing lingers in her ears and she can feel her eyes begin to tear up. But she doesn't want to cry in front of him, so she tells herself that at least it's over, the night she dreaded is over and she didn't give him a thing. All right, she thinks, it's all right. There's a warm trickle of blood between her legs, but she didn't give him a thing. Louis closes the door to the bathroom, then Nita stands up to change her nightgown and pull the bottom sheet off the bed. She looks toward the blue-green glow of the TV and nearly smiles. She didn't give him a thing, not a thing.

7

THE DAY AFTER THE HONEYMOON, A SATURDAY, LOUIS
and Nita arrive at their apartment in Crowley. Right away, Nita
sees that the place Louis chose for them is not really an apartment—it's the back end of someone else's house. The back upper
end, at that, and Nita has to climb a steep, rickety set of stairs
before she reaches the plywood-covered door. There she waits
for Louis. He wouldn't give her the key to the door, so she hangs
her head over the rail and shouts for him to hurry up. "I need to
pee!" she screams down at him. Then, remembering that there's
someone in the house below her, she says in a loud whisper, "I have
to *go.*"

Louis pulls a leaf from the lip of the Falcon's trunk, then steps
back toward the road to inspect the car. Satisfied that he can't find
any damage from the Lake Charles beach, he looks up at the little

white apartment and catches sight of Nita with her back to the paneled door. She has one hand on the rail and the other on her hip. Her hair spreads out behind her, a little black cloud of hair against the white of the house. He thinks he should say something, set down some rule. The keys are in *his* hand after all, he signed the lease to this place, why should he stand for her shouting at him? But he feels too good and all he can think to say is, "All right."

As he walks toward the stairs, he tosses the ring of keys up in the air and holds his hand out like a mitt. When the ring ricochets off the side of his hand and lands in the dust, Nita snickers out loud and points down at the place where he stands. "All right," he says again, "all right."

Once Louis opens the door, Nita bursts into the apartment to find her way to the bathroom. But she stops short when she bumps into a card table set up in the middle of the living room. What she sees makes her forget, for just a minute, why she was rushing. In the corner opposite from her, two winged-back chairs face each other, one made of woven cloth, the other a sunken Naugahyde. Besides the two chairs and the table, there's no other furniture in the room. Nita cranes her head toward the kitchen, which is separated from the living room by a narrow Formica-covered bar. There are three appliances in the kitchen: a fridge, a stove, and a range, each a dim, murky color somewhere between rust and orange. It's a color Nita's never seen before and some-thing about it makes her feel not only uneasy, but unwelcome. How is she supposed to cook in this gloomy kitchen? How is she supposed to feel at home here?

"What do you think?" Louis says, but he doesn't mean it as a question. "All this stuff I borrowed from Bootsy." Bootsy is Louis' racing, drinking, football-playing buddy, and there's a picture of him on the counter by an empty can of beer, which Nita thinks is weird. It's as if someone already celebrated here without her. And what's to celebrate? This place is no better than where her mother is. In fact, it's smaller and darker and it'll take weeks for Nita to get the floors anywhere near clean. The walls will have to be scrubbed, too, and the baseboards bleached. She feels a tremor inside, some emerging knowledge in her head as she puts the palm of her hand to the back of her neck and lets out a little sigh. She closes her eyes for just a moment, then looks back at the can of beer and remembers she has to pee.

Behind the closed door of the bathroom, Nita sits on the plastic seat of the toilet. She lets her head fall back in relief. Blood rushes to her ears and she cups her throat with her hand. The tremor grows stronger inside; she can't shake it off or blink it away. The tremor pops like a light behind her eyes. This is what she knows: she has made some kind of crazy mistake and there's no undoing it. She's married this man and moved into this house and neither is what she wanted, hoped for, expected, or thought she deserved. She doesn't think of divorce. It's not an option she considers. Even if she could get out of this, what would she do then? She couldn't go back to Buford's house and she dropped out of Jennings High without even taking a typing class. She can cook and clean and that's it. So that's what Louis will get, she tells herself, a maid. It's more than she wants to give him, but he'll expect something and this is the bargain she settles on.

While Nita is in the bathroom, Louis walks down to unlock the trunk of the car and haul up their bags. As he steps onto the sidewalk, he thinks he's found just what he's been looking for, a life on his own away from Anna and the farm. Maybe he has no TV or hi-fi yet, but he has an apartment, some more furniture on the way, a job as an accountant with one of the best rice mills in town, a wife. And the Falcon, Anna couldn't take that away from him. Louis walks toward the stairs, his shoulders hunched over with the weight of the bags. Yes ma'am, he thinks, all this. Right here. All this is mine.

Dinner is a bit of a mess. Neither Nita nor Louis can find a way to light the oven, so the frozen potpies stay partially congealed even after Nita throws them with a little oil in the only saucepan she can find. Louis promises to have the stove fixed "Pronto!" and assures her that she will have a cast-iron pot and a skillet and whatever little thing she thinks she might need. "Boo, you just tell me," he says, "you just tell me."

Nita nods, but says nothing. Boo? she thinks. Boo? What does he think she is, a spook? It's like he's talking to a baby. She's a woman, in case he hasn't noticed, his wife. Maybe she's not quite seventeen yet, but she's seen a whole lot already. Okay, maybe she hasn't been outside of Jennings, but he doesn't know the life she's had. And she can guarantee him this: it's not the life of a Boo.

All this fuss makes Nita's head throb, so she tells Louis good night and walks off to bed. The bedroom is tiny, but cleaner than the kitchen. There's no window, but there are also no duct-taped holes in the wall. Someone even tried a bit of decoration with a plywood valence running the length of the closet. The linoleum rose tiles on the floor are cracked in spots, but mostly they're hidden by the double bed. Which is soft, not the way Nita likes it. She sits on the edge of the bed and the mattress sinks almost to the floor. With her legs doubled up, she stares at her bag in the corner. I'll unpack tomorrow, she decides before closing the door to change.

Late that night Nita dreams she's suffocating: a sheet of cellophane settles over her and she can't breathe. Every time she moves, the cellophane moves with her. It pulls tight against the space between her legs and presses against her mouth until she screams and wakes to find that her arm has fallen asleep under the weight of Louis's chest. Her scream wakes him and he rolls over on his side. Nita stares at his back, watching it move with his deep breaths. She falls asleep again, but keeps drifting in and out of the dream, until finally the alarm goes off and it's Sunday morning.

Nita is not prepared for what happens next. Louis stretches his arms as he gets up from the table and says, "Well, we better get a move on if we wanna make the ten o'clock Mass."

Mass? Nita pledged Catholic to marry Louis, but she never pictured going to Mass with him. She has nothing to wear. The only dresses she has are cotton and they're sure to be crumpled after sitting in her bag all night. And besides, none of them fall much farther than her knees and all of them are short-sleeved. And aren't Catholic ladies supposed to wear those little lace things on their heads . . .

"Mantillas," Louis says. "They're called mantillas and all that's changing now anyway. And we're going to Sunday Mass, not a funeral, so calm down. It's gonna be all right."

Nita hates the way he talks down to her, like a kid, but she's too nervous to say anything. She falls into a studied silence until the Falcon pulls into a spot in front of St. Michael's. An altar boy pulls on the rope in the bell tower and the clanging fills Nita's head with a giddy sense of doom. Families slam car doors and file up the marble steps and into church as if someone, some invisible person, was commanding them. Single file, now, Nita hears the voice say, make a straight line. Everyone's hands automatically pull at their dress hems, their shirttails. Everything is tucked, tied, pulled back, or straightened out. Nothing ever looked this organized, this *controlled,* at the tent revivals her Aunt La-La brought her to. People there had hair that stood on end, in some kind of hallelujah stretch to heaven. Their skirts were always twisted from jumping up on chairs to shout Jesus' name or to testify about some healing going on at their house: "Lord, I just got to thank you, *Thank You!*, for givin' my baby back his constitution and dryin' up his tears. And thank you, Lord, for gettin' my Pierre that new job with the oil company and holdin' off them bill collectors . . ."

Their testimonies could go on for hours, full of moaning and crying and hair-pulling. Though Nita was married in a Catholic church, she's never been to a regular Catholic Mass. Still, she's sure there will be no jumping up on chairs and no hair-pulling. It's all so quiet and solemn, all she can do is laugh. Right there in the car with Louis staring at her, she breaks into a fit of giggles that doesn't die down until the church doors close and the bell stops its metallic ringing.

Louis feels nothing but excitement as he and Nita step out of the car toward the church. St. Michael's is his favorite church in all of Acadia Parish. He'd hoped to be married here, but he's glad at least that he and Nita live in Crowley and that they can come every Sunday. He loves the high dome of the ceiling and the century-old Gothic lamps that hang over the pews. And he always looks forward to the drama of the priest's entry: the gold cross raised high over the altar boy's head, the smoking candles, the bells, and the incense, all of it seems so much more powerful at St. Michael's than at the little church in Iota.

Louis can't wait for this chance to show off his new wife. He thinks about how jealous all the other men will be when he walks in with Nita. As he tells it, she looks excited, too, and he's only a little surprised when she grabs his arm as they cross the threshold to the church.

The first thing Nita notices when she and Louis walk inside the church is a sea of lace and satin, coupled with a velvet hush.

The silence seems not so much holy as decorative, some ornate design worked up and agreed upon by all the people sitting in the neat little rows. She feels like an intruder when her eyes catch sight of the square gold plaques tacked on the end of each pew. Each plaque announces a family name: The Delahoussayes, The Fuseliers, The D'Aquins; The Comeauxs, The Breauxs, The Doucets. Nita thinks it odd that these people should own a piece of the church, but she's also impressed by the display. How nice to know each Sunday just where you'll sit, she thinks. Then she wonders, do some pews cost more than others? Do some families pay for a better view or a longer row?

Nita turns her eyes to the front pews and feels her ears burn a deep red. Each lady's head is covered with a round web of spun lace. Louis said none of these Catholic ladies wear mantillas anymore, but there they are, a crest of ash-headed ladies in pulled, pinned lace like cloth halos. They're the Anna Toussaints of St. Michael's, Nita can tell, anointed ladies of the church nodding disapproval to one another. She tugs on Louis' sleeve. "Let's sit in the back," she whispers, "the very back."

Louis is disappointed; he was hoping to walk with Nita all the way to the front. But he looks at her and whispers, "All right," just as the priest bows before the altar and raises his hands up to the frescoed ceiling.

The ceremony itself is a bore. Nita finds herself wishing it was all still in Latin. At least then there might be a little something to wonder at. For all she can tell, the priest just mumbles a lot of words and the people in the pews nod forward and bob back. Every once in a while, the priest says something, and the people repeat after him. They rise and kneel and politely shake hands whenever he tells them to. Nita begins to think that the priest is kind of like a grade-school teacher smiling down at a well-behaved classroom. There's even what looks like grape juice and crackers and some sort of break near the end. Louis seems to enjoy the "Apostles' Creed" prayer the most. He shouts that one out in a loud voice while Nita searches for the words in a pamphlet left on the pew. She stares at the back page, which has a series of boxed advertisements and more family names. She feels small and unnoticed and she's glad for it.

When Mass is over and the priest and his altar boys bow before the giant statue of Jesus hanging on the cross, Nita thinks to sneak out a side door she spies on the right. But Louis shakes his head no and points toward the huge double doors behind them. "We've gotta stand outside," he says, "on the front steps. We've gotta make sure Father Préjean knows we were here."

Outside, the sun is high and bright and Nita's hands pull at the hem of her dress. It's too short, she can see that by looking around her. And she's the only woman on the steps without stockings. One of her ankles itches and she fights the urge to kneel down and scratch it. Then the priest suddenly appears on the top step and a crowd of people surround him to shake his hand and say a few words. She hears Louis' voice mumble something about being new to the parish, before he booms out, "And right here's my wife . . ."

Just then, the old ladies who surround the priest turn to inspect Nita and she can feel the heat of the moment rise like the vapor off a tar pit. Their eyes light upon her uncovered head, her ungloved hands, the hem hanging just below her knee. *"Pauv' bête,"* she hears one of them whisper, "poor idiot."

But the priest gestures for her to come closer and Nita hears herself say, "Hello, sir." Immediately she knows she fouled it up. Father, she thinks, call him Father. But it's too late. The priest and the circle of ladies turn from her to a couple approaching in front of Nita and she falls in step behind Louis to find their car in its spot on the street below.

That night after a dinner of fish sticks, which Nita cooks up in the saucepan like links of sausage, Louis lets loose a giant yawn, stretches his hands over his head, and announces that he is "fixin' to get ready" to go to bed. Nita stares at him and says, "So soon?"

She was hoping to beat him to sleep; now she lingers over the kitchen sink scrubbing a spot she knows will never come out. Louis hesitates, thinking she might want to join him or to talk for a while. But Nita says, "Go on, then, I've got some cleaning to do."

As he walks down the narrow hallway, she stares at his back and thinks he already has the heavy steps of a paw-paw, an old grandpa who likes nothing more than his La-Z-Boy and a can of cold beer. Except for that pimply skin and the goofy look on his face. That's what gives him away—he'll never be a man. He'll go straight from red-faced teenager to purple-veined paw-paw. He'll never be the man she pictured herself marrying. That man was tall and dark like her father. And there was something magical and grown-up about him. His breath filled the air like steam and his arms stole up behind her and circled her waist. He talked into her ear and told her how much he loved her, what a good wife she was. He didn't yawn or stretch his hands up over his head. He didn't say things like "fixin' to get ready" and he certainly didn't walk like a paw-paw.

Nita scrubs and scrubs the stain in the sink until her fingertips begin to pucker. Then she yanks the cord for the kitchen light and turns to face the dark stretch to the bedroom. When she opens the door to the room, she lets out a tiny sigh of relief. Louis has gone to sleep, so she won't have to talk to him or lie under his weight.

Fearing another suffocating dream, she stuffs a pillow between their two sides to prevent him from rolling on top of her again.

Nita quietly stoops over the bed. She can hear Louis' measured breaths as she turns to face the wall and slip into her nightgown. He's sleeping, she thinks, so it won't matter if I change right here. But without her knowing it, Louis rolls over and his eyes open to find the slope of Nita's back before him. There's that tiny freckle between her shoulder blades; the short but curvy line of her back. Her long, silky black hair, her round hips and dark brown legs. He looks at the shadowy brown of her skin, but can't decide on the color. Sometimes he thinks it's like caramel or creamy coffee, other times he decides it's more like cane syrup or dark green olives. In any case, he's glad she's awake. He can't wait to touch her again and thinks how he missed her touch last night. She was tired then, but now she would be ready. So as the cotton hem of Nita's gown falls down over her calves, Louis closes his eyes and pretends to sleep. He hears her peel back the sheet, then feels the bed sink a little as she settles into place. He waits until he's sure that she's closed her eyes, then he puts his hand across the pillow to touch her face. He lets his hand hesitate a moment by a swirl of her hair, then he puts the flat of his palm against her cheek. But instead of sighing softly, Nita screams and rolls out of bed onto the floor. Louis starts to laugh, but as he lies there looking at her figure in the dark, he hears a soft, muffled cry. "What's the matter?" he asks. "I was only playing."

"You scared me," Nita says. "I thought you were asleep."

"Boo, I'm sorry. How can I make it up to you? You just tell me."

Louis tries to muster up a face that says "Sorry" and "Please" at the same time. His brows meet in an inverted V, his lips press tight against each other, and his nostrils flare.

"Don't do it again," she says. "Just don't do it again."

The fuss dies down and Nita crawls back into bed. She's still sobbing a little, so Louis moves his leg over to her side. He wants to make Nita happy, but he doesn't know how. More than anything, he wants to touch her, to lie on top of her again. But as soon as his leg presses against hers, she says, "Don't."

So Louis rolls onto his stomach and buries his face in his pillow. Soon Nita can hear his breath slow down and she lets her eyes close to welcome a little rest. She's not asleep for long when she has another dream. This time, her father stands before her, wearing the Texas-sized hat and silver buckle he wore at the wedding. He puts his hands out to her, but when she goes to hug him, he disappears and she begins to cry. Her own crying wakes her and she finds herself staring at Louis' face on the pillow between them. His nostrils are flared and his face is frozen in a grimace and every two beats or so, he lets rip an enormous grunt like a pig's snort. She was dreaming, Nita realizes, dreaming of her father. And for the second time that night, hot tears fall down her cheek and she lets herself say out loud what she felt in the dream, "Home, I wanna go home."

8

THE NEXT MORNING, THE ALARM RINGS OUT LIKE A
shot and Nita jumps up with a shiver running down her back.
"What? What? What?" she screams out before realizing she's
alone. She rolls over to Louis' side of the bed to shut up the clat-
tering clock with the heel of her palm. "Louis?" she calls out from
the edge of the bed. "Louis?"

When he doesn't answer, Nita thinks he's probably in the
bathroom. She throws on a shirt he left on the floor and walks out
toward the rattling pipes across the hall. The high-pitched sound
fills her ears, making her think Louis is drawing hot water for his
bath. But when she reaches the room, the light is off and no one is
there. Her hand skims the grooved surface of the wall until it finds
the light switch. Nita flips the switch up, then stares at herself in the
mirror. She holds her hands straight out from her side, making her

arms look like wings. She bends her knees and points the tips of her fingers to the top of her head, like a ballerina. Then she twists until she can see most of her back. The tail of Louis' shirt falls to the middle of her thigh and she thinks she might look good in a miniskirt. She moves back and forth, making the shirttail bob up and down, then she holds her hair up over her head. Nita likes the way she looks in that shirt, likes the feel of the tail against her thigh. She turns around and slips a toothbrush into the pocket, like a ballpoint pen. She studies her face and tries to figure if she could look official.

When Nita tires of trying out facial moves, she flips off the light and turns the corner to look for Louis in the kitchen. She pictures him there with a bowl of corn flakes and a napkin tucked into his shirt. But when she reaches the table, she finds only a little slosh of milk on a placemat and a dent in the Naugahyde chair. She can't figure out how long he's been gone. Ten minutes? Fifteen? An hour? He got up before the alarm and rushed off to work. Embarrassed, she thinks, he must've been embarrassed. Good, then he'll learn to stay on his side of the bed and not go scaring me halfway to Houma!

Nita runs a stream of hot water from the tap and wrings out a sponge to wipe the placemat on the table. Then she runs the sponge along the edge of the card table and down the side of the legs. She walks back into the kitchen and fills a large ceramic bowl with water. Down on her knees, she scrubs each tile of linoleum on the kitchen floor. Her hand goes round and round in tight little circles and she dumps out and refills the water three times. Then she spies a crusty brown edge on the stove. She wipes and pushes and scrapes until the crust is gone. But the color stubbornly clings to the edge and Nita wonders, Did someone paint it on that way? There's a brown edge on the range, too, and the fridge, and even the baseboards have something of a yellow-brown line running along the top. She takes a toothbrush to this line and scrubs until the bristles start to break off, one by one at first, then in little clumps like hair. There's no mop in the house, so Nita takes a dish towel to the floor in the hallway and the bathroom. She scrubs and wipes and dusts and shines until the whole apartment smells like a vaporous cloud of ammonia and bleach. The sharp, acrid smell makes her eyes wince and her mouth pucker, but it's not until she runs out of hot water that she stops.

After a cool bath, Nita tries to get comfortable in the Naugahyde chair. She squirms and adjusts and readjusts her arm, then she jumps up to try out the plaid wingback. The fit isn't any better, so Nita gets up and starts pacing around the floor. She walks into the bedroom, then walks out again into the hallway. She thinks maybe the walls are bothering her; there's nothing on them, not a single picture. Or maybe it's the lack of windows. She counts only two and that includes the diamond-shaped one in the door. Then it hits her: she's alone. For the first time she can remember, she's completely and undeniably alone. Just her, just Nita, no one else. No one to boss her around, to tell her to do the dishes. She can leave the dishes in the sink, or she can eat right now if she wants to, right this minute. She can run to the bathroom and sit on the toilet for as long as she likes. She can use all the toilet paper, too. Nita claps her hands in front of her nose as she realizes there's no more school to worry about either, no more classes. No one to laugh when she gets the answer wrong. No one to poke fun at her bare feet, to call her No Shoes Nita. Maybe there's something to married life, she thinks. At least the days could be hers, to do as she wants. She laughs at a thought in her head. It's like she married herself, really. She could be her own wife, or husband, however it goes.

To celebrate this thought, Nita decides to go shopping, or to make groceries as her mother likes to put it. It wasn't often, but when Gilda had a little extra cash she liked nothing better than to head to the store. She always dragged Nita along to show her how to avoid getting ripped off. "Nothing makes me feel so good as a real *bon marché*," she once told her. Then another time she heard Gilda tell a friendly sales clerk, "A good buy is better than a good man—at least when you get home you know what you got!"

Nita thought her mother was a little crazy, but now she thinks it would be nice to stroll down the aisle with a cart full of groceries before her. Louis left her no money and no car, but she can walk to the Piggly-Wiggly and charge the bill to his name. In a flurry of excitement, she spins on her heels and walks back into the bedroom to find something to wear.

Outside, Nita doesn't make it all the way down the rickety stairs before turning around. The heat rises under her dress and circles her throat and she has to stop to remember that it's still only March. Just a few days before it was windy and cool outside, but Louisiana summers never start gradually and never obey the calendar. Oh well, she shrugs, then heads back upstairs for a lighter dress. In the apartment, she calls Louis at work and asks him to call over and okay a few groceries at the store. "Okey-dokey, Boo," he says and she rolls her eyes as she puts down the phone.

At the Piggly-Wiggly, Nita zooms down the aisles with her cart and makes a sudden stop when she sees something exotic. Spaghetti! she almost screams out loud. She's always wanted to try spaghetti. There's frozen pizza, too. The stove won't be fixed for another day or two, but she throws a pie in the cart anyway. Peanut butter, she loves peanut butter with cane syrup and marshmallow cream. She buys cake mix, too, the good kind, Duncan Hines Devil's Food. She buys mixes for brownies and muffins; she buys Jimmy Dean sausage and a carton of eggs. She buys milk and orange juice and something called pomegranate juice, just to see what it tastes like. She buys a loaf of Evangeline Maid white bread and another of Roman whole wheat; she's never tried whole wheat. On one aisle she finds Chun King water chestnuts and bamboo shoots and glass noodles. Glass noodles! She giggles and throws a pack in the cart, then follows it with Hershey's chocolate milk, Carnation malted milk, New York sharp Cheddar cheese, Del Monte french cut green beans, *petits pois,* Konriko rice—long grain and short, bananas, grapes, cherries, Sunmaid raisins in a jumbo box, ground meat, chuck steak, bacon strips, chicken wings, bell peppers, jalapeño peppers, iceberg lettuce, cherry tomatoes, roma tomatoes, and some little green buds in a jar with a label that says Fancy Style capers.

Before she places the capers in the cart, she studies the label and imagines eating the tiny buds, imagines the sea-flowers blooming inside of her. She thinks she might eat anything at this moment; she's so excited by the freedom she finds in the Piggly-Wiggly. It's not until she brings her cart to a halt in front of the checkout stand that she begins to worry. Am I buying too much? she wonders. Am I buying all the things a housewife should buy? Just then, she remembers that she's forgotten to look for a mop, for a new sponge and a box of Brillo pads. She could use more Clorox, too, but the checkout girl has already started ringing the total and Nita's too embarrassed to ask her to stop. "Charge it," Nita says, nearly giggling at the phrase, "charge it to my . . . to my husband's account."

"Are you Mrs. Toussaint?" the girl asks.

Nita nods her head, but the sound of the name disturbs her, so she turns to the curly-headed boy bagging her groceries. "Have you ever eaten capers?" she asks him.

He nods his head yes and reaches for the carton of eggs.

"How about glass noodles?" she asks. When the boy puts down the carton and scratches his head, she laughs.

"Glass noodles," he says. "Now you got me."

When the bags are packed, Nita remembers that she has no car. She asks the bag boy to walk the two blocks back to the apartment with her. The store is nearly empty and the manager says it's all right, so Nita grabs a bag and the boy grabs two and they head out together, laughing about the noodles. At the top of the staircase, she realizes that she has no money for a tip. She invites the boy inside for a moment and runs to the bedroom, where she finds a pile of dimes and a couple of quarters. "I'm sorry it's all in coins," she says. The boy tells her not to worry, money's money, and he heads out the door.

Louis returns home shortly after five to find Nita in the kitchen with a pot of spaghetti on the stove and the smell of fresh tomatoes and garlic in the air. He loves spaghetti, but supper is the last thing on his mind as he slams the door behind him. After Nita called this morning, he gave his friend Bootsy a ring and asked him to head over to the Piggly-Wiggly and just, you know, check up on Nita, make sure she's all right. Though Bootsy is two years younger than Louis, he's much broader and half a foot taller and, in many ways, he seems like the older of the two. He often reminds Louis to keep an eye on his new wife. "Women are tricky little foxes," he says, "every one of 'em." And when Bootsy pulled up to the parking lot, he wasn't surprised to see Louis' wife walking out with the bag boy. He followed them in his pickup until he reached the apartment. When he saw the boy go inside, he called Louis at the office with a report. "Man, she's a beaut," Bootsy said. "You'd better watch her close. Those men'll stick to her like bugs to a blue light. You should've seen that bag boy when he walked her home . . ."

"What do you mean?" Louis jumped in. "Do you think she did anything with him?"

Bootsy laughed and said, "Man, what you think? I got X-ray vision or something? All I'm saying is you better watch her."

"Well, what do you think I oughta do?" Louis asked.

His buddy paused a moment, then said, "Me? I'd let her have it when I got home. I'd go kinda crazy just to let her know I'm not foolin'."

Louis barely made it through the rest of the day at the rice mill. Somehow in his head, Bootsy's suggestion took on the bronze weight of fact. He couldn't believe it; his wife wouldn't let him touch her at night, but she carried on with the bag boy during the day? Louis kept thinking of what he should say to Nita and even went into the bathroom once to practice shouting at the mirror. Finally, he felt he was ready. He clocked out a few minutes shy of five and tore up the wide streets of downtown Crowley, with the thought of his wife and that bag boy burning a hole between his eyes.

When he reaches the apartment, Louis slams the door behind him and Nita's head jerks up from her place over the stove. Before she can say anything, he marches over to the radio and shuts off Camey Doucet's Gospel Hour.

"That's my cousin," Nita says. "You just shut off my cousin."

"I don't give a flying fuck about your cousin," Louis shouts, and even he's surprised at the force of his rage. "Your cousin can kiss my ass. What I wanna know about is the goddamn Piggly-Wiggly bag boy."

"What are you talking about?" Nita starts to shake as she stares at Louis' purple face. She turns off the fire under the pot and steps out of the kitchen. She tells Louis that she invited the bag boy into the house in order to tip him. He glares at her and asks what she tipped him with. She says, "Change from my pocket. What else?" then asks if he had her followed.

"That's exactly what I did." Louis clenches his fist, then smashes it against the table. "I should've known not to let you out by yourself . . ."

"What am I, your pet? You wanna keep me on a leash?"

"You're whatever I tell you you are. You act as if this house was yours. It's not. It's my house and you're my wife and it's time you act like it."

Louis tells Nita that she's putting him in the poorhouse. He tells her that he called the Piggly-Wiggly to find out how much she bought. Then he asks if she thinks he's rich—after all, he only makes ninety dollars a week.

"How am I supposed to pay rent, pay insurance, fill my car with gas, *and* pay a fifty-dollar food bill? Are you out of your fucking mind?!"

"Yes," Nita says as she walks toward the hall, "that's exactly what I'm out of."

Louis paces around the room, then heads to the kitchen to survey the damage. Junk, almost all junk. What is he supposed to do with a can of bamboo shoots? Does she expect him to eat a plate of water chestnuts? Why did she buy two kinds of rice, two kinds of bread, two kind of tomatoes and peppers? Is this the goddamn Noah's Ark of grocery food? And is he supposed to believe that bag boy didn't make a move on Nita? Is he really supposed to believe that shit?

Louis noisily slams a few cabinets, then marches back to the bedroom. When he turns on the light, he finds Nita hunched over the bed, stuffing clothes into a paper bag. Tears run down her cheeks and makeup is smeared across her face and he thinks maybe he's never seen her look more beautiful. Bootsy's warning flashes through his mind, but Louis shuts his eyes and forces out any other picture. He sees only Nita in his head, Nita and those beautiful hot tears on her cheek. He wants to take her in his arms, hold her back against his chest. But he's scared suddenly, scared she'll turn him away. So he just stands in the doorway, trying to think of something to say.

"I'm sorry," he starts, but it catches in his throat and he chokes.

Somehow Nita hears only, "So." She turns on her heels and stares him down.

"So?" she asks. "So? Is that all you can say?"

Louis feels his eyes start to sting and he tastes a bit of saliva in his mouth.

"Where are you going?" he asks her, then works it around in his head to something he could tell Bootsy. "Where do you think you're going?"

"I *think* I'm going away from here, from you, from this rat-trap you call a house. That's where I *think* I'm going."

Before she can say anything else, Louis explodes. He bangs his fist against the wall and kicks at the baseboard with his shoe. "Nowhere. That's where you're going. You're *my* wife, mine!" he shouts at Nita.

The sound of his voice ricochets through Nita's head and what she hears is that this is a fight she can't win. He's right; Louis is right. She's going nowhere—there's nowhere for her to go. She can't go back to her mother's house, not with Buford there, standing guard over the refrigerator and the bathroom door. If she goes back, he'll shout at her every time she has so much as a slice of cheese.

Nita falls silent and Louis takes her silence for consent. He looks at the floor, then at his wife. He tells her that from now on when he's at work, she's going to stay home and take care of the house. If she needs to go somewhere, *he'll* take her. If she needs to go to the store, *he'll* tell her how much she can spend. "And you're gonna start talking to me and stop making me feel like I married my damn self," he says.

Louis starts to kick the wall for effect, then stops. Nita's eyes are darting around in her head and he can see that he's got her. "All right, Boo," he says, "let's eat."

Late that night, Louis wakes up once again to the sound of Nita's crying. He puts his hand out to her face and this time she doesn't push it away. He rolls on top of her, wriggles out of his underwear and begins to tug at the back of her cotton gown. But before he gets too far, she crosses her legs and says, "I can't. It's too soon."

Louis doesn't understand why she won't let him undress her, but he decides to leave her alone. He wonders about his friend's advice: Should he have gone crazy like he did? Should he have shouted at Nita and kicked the wall? Louis reminds himself that he *is* the man, after all, and—as Bootsy would put it—a man's not a man till he sets down some rules.

Somehow, though, this thought fails to cheer Louis. So he decides to try another move. He stretches his hand out until his fingers almost touch Nita's hair. After that, neither of them speaks, but Nita falls asleep with her head against Louis' arm and he thinks, Well, at least it's something.

9

FOR THE NEXT SEVERAL WEEKS, NITA FOCUSES ON ONE
word of her wedding vow: obey. Whatever Louis says, she follows. Even when she feels a fury kick up inside her, a hot wind of
rage, she stays quiet. She answers his questions, she talks when he
talks, but that's all. She doesn't even say anything when they go to
his parents' house every weekend and never visit her mother. That
is, she doesn't say anything until one Sunday when they finish off
the umpteenth pot of gumbo and Louis' mother corners her in
the kitchen.

Usually, when Louis and his father walk out to the front porch
to share a couple of beers and leave the women to clean up, Anna
says not one word to Nita, although they stand side by side washing dishes. Even when they're all seated at the table, Anna does
her best to exclude Nita from any talk. So Nita is surprised when

Louis' mother turns to her and says, "Something wrong at your house?"

For just a moment, Nita wonders if Anna is trying to be friendly. She looks at Louis' mother and can't tell what she's thinking. After Nita finishes wiping the plate in her hand, she quietly says, "No."

Anna plunges another dish into the soapy water and looks not at Nita, but at the curtained window over the sink. "Then tell me, is this how they do it in Jennings?"

Nita is still confused. She can't figure out what Louis' mother is trying to say, so she hunches her shoulders, but keeps quiet.

Anna yanks the gold-rimmed plate out of the water and shoves it into Nita's hands before shouting, "Then, *dis-moi,* are you just lazy or are you looking for a place to sponge a free meal?"

The heat of Anna's words goes straight to Nita's hands, which start to shake as she almost drops the plate. "What do you mean?" she asks.

"What do I mean?" Anna shouts. "What do *you* mean? Coming here weekend after weekend like I have nothing better to do than to cook and clean all day. I didn't watch my son get married just so I could keep on feeding him the rest of my God-given life."

Nita thinks, but doesn't say, Do you really believe I *want* to come here? Do you really believe I like being ignored? Instead, she folds the towel in her hands, then places it on the counter and says, "I'll talk to Louis."

During the drive back to Crowley, Nita says nothing to Louis. She sits with her arms folded across her chest and her face in an exaggerated pout, while she stares at the passing cars and road signs. Louis can't figure out what's wrong with her. She seems to have these spells more and more; she falls into silence, and the silence is anything but quiet. He swears that he can almost see the thoughts twisted up inside her head and he's sure that she thinks too much. He watches as she worries herself into a nervous fit, but doesn't know what to say to her. He's glad, at least, that they're not fighting.

But then, as soon as the door to the apartment is closed behind them, Nita explodes. She tells Louis what his mother said and she tells him as well that she never wants to go back to Iota. A stream of tears falls down her face and she runs to the bedroom and locks the door behind her. Louis sits in the green loveseat he borrowed from his parents, then stands back up. He paces the room, wondering if he should knock on the door or bust it open. He's caught between anger at his mother for shaming Nita and anger at Nita for blaming him. How dare she lock him out? he thinks. How dare she act as if she called the shots around here?

But even as Louis' anger rises, he feels a knot of remorse well up inside him. Maybe all this is his fault somehow. Maybe they shouldn't go to his parents' house so much. He wants to talk to someone, to figure out what he should do. But when he calls Bootsy, no one picks up the phone. He sits back in the chair and imagines holding Nita and lying on top of her, but the thought doesn't much comfort him. It's been several weeks since she let him anywhere near her side of the bed.

Later that night, when Nita comes out of the bedroom, she refuses to eat any of the leftovers that sit in the fridge. Louis worries that she's too thin—she can't weigh any more than ninety pounds—and he wonders if she eats at all when he's at work. Ever since they fought about the food Nita bought, she's only cooked frozen fish sticks and crab cakes with tater tots for dinner. She has one cake or maybe two sticks and claims that she's stuffed. He wants to see her eat more and he wants to see her concoct some of the crazy recipes she planned before. But now she only buys the cheapest groceries she can find and *she* keeps reminding *him* how little he makes. So, in order to get her to eat with him, Louis tells her that they'll make no more than two Iota trips a month. He also consents, against his own will, to take Nita to see her mother in Jennings.

The next weekend, on a hot, sticky Saturday near the end of April, they pick up Gilda and Nita's eleven-year-old sister, Monetta Lou, for a picnic, and Louis is the silent one. He barely speaks while the four of them drive to nearby Lake Arthur park. And when they lay out their blanket and he sees that Gilda and Monetta Lou have brought nothing to eat, he sulks. He almost can't believe it—Nita starves herself at home, but here she is ready to feed not only the two of them, but her mother and sister both. How can Nita expect him to feed her family, Louis thinks, when she knows how much I make? His mother may complain when they visit, but she always has something on the stove. How can Nita's mother come to a picnic and not bring anything to share? He turns to Gilda and Monetta Lou and says, "Looks like we only brought enough for ourselves." Then he stares Nita down.

Nita catches Louis' eye, but decides not to fight him in front of her mother. She says that she's not hungry as Louis quickly devours two whole links of *boudin,* a pack of bologna, several slices of bread, and most of the cheese she packed. Nita scrounged the week before and saved enough for a small ambrosia cake, but she leaves it wrapped in the bag she brought with her. She stares at her mother and doesn't know what to say.

Gilda sits across from her, with her hands folded under her arms. She stares at Louis and her lips press into a tight line. When Louis pointedly looks not at her, but at the sandwich in his hand, she turns her eyes to Nita and opens her mouth as if she was about to say something. But she stays quiet and the silence around them lingers until Monetta Lou slaps at a mosquito on her leg, then shouts, "I'm hungry! I'm hungry!"

Gilda yells, "*Tais-toi!* Don't you know how to control yourself?" and everyone hurriedly stands to leave.

After they drive Nita's mother and sister back to Jennings, Nita turns to Louis and shouts, "How could you be so stingy?"

He just laughs and says, "You should've brought the glass noodles!"

Actually, Louis thinks he wouldn't even have shared the glass noodles with Gilda. He can't stand that woman; that's why he didn't talk to her at the park and that's why he refused to take Nita to Jennings before today. He doesn't know the whole story yet, but he figures she's to blame for Nita's spells. And she's married to this Buford guy who better not *think* of laying a hand on his wife. On the drive home, Louis decides to go to Jennings as little as possible. His mother was right: that town is nothing but trouble. Hell, it's no wonder Nita doesn't know how to shop.

Nita wishes she could talk to someone about Louis, but even her mother refuses to hear how he treats her. When Nita calls after the picnic to apologize, Gilda cuts her short to say that Buford has left again and this time she doesn't think he's coming back. Gilda tells Nita she should be glad to have a husband at all, even if he is a little stingy. A little? she thinks. He wouldn't even give you a sandwich. But before she can say anything, her mother starts to cry and she feels guilty for having complained to her. "What am I gonna do?" Gilda asks. "I don't even have a car." Nita promises to visit her mother again soon.

But the next weekend when she suggests another trip to Jennings, Louis says, "No way." After two more weeks, she asks him again. Louis consults Bootsy, then he again says no. Again and again she tries until finally he shouts, "No! N-fucking-O!"

Nita sulks, but says nothing. She's not at all sure who she married anymore. Not that she ever had any real idea. But she hadn't pictured this bulldog of a husband, this brute whose eyes never leave hers. And she didn't know that her life would become his so completely. He acts like he owns her and won't let her out alone—not to work, not to visit, and certainly not to shop.

From then on, when Nita calls her mother, she says nothing more about Louis. She tries to sound cheery and always promises to visit as soon as she can. But the calls get shorter as she finds less and less to say. And they almost end altogether when Louis sees the long distance bill and explodes. He threatens to disconnect the phone, but she promises to call Jennings no more than twice a month. Who am I gonna talk to now? she thinks. She wishes she had a friend in Crowley, like Louis has Bootsy. Even if they couldn't visit, they could at least talk on the phone.

Nita feels caged and that feeling grows when—even though she avoids Iota—Iota begins to come to her. Louis' father is the first to make an unannounced visit and he happens to arrive on the day she does laundry. The washing machine is broken, so she sits bent over a steel tub for most of the morning, rubbing Louis' shirts together in the soapy water. As Louis Sr. arrives, Nita is trying to pin the shirts to a homemade clothesline while swatting mosquitos off her bare legs. Sweat pours down her face and she has to wipe her hands on her dress before greeting him.

Louis Sr. is decked out in a pair of seersucker pants and suspenders. His hair is slicked back and even though it's hot, he manages to look as if it was both cool and breezy. Nita wishes Louis would dress more like his father, and she wishes he wouldn't pump up his hair in that ridiculous pompadour. She's trying to picture Louis in a seersucker suit when Pop Toussaint puts a hand on her shoulder and asks if she's ready for lunch: he'd like to take her to a place he knows downtown. "Oh my God!" Nita says. "Of course I'm ready!"

She hasn't been in a luncheteria since she married Louis and quit Fiona's. She's excited at the thought of eating out and figures Louis can't object if she leaves the house to have lunch with his father.

When Nita and Pop arrive at Gloria's Place, he runs around the front of his pickup to open the door for her. When they take a table, he stands until she sits, and when the waitress comes, he tells her to order anything she wants. While she looks at the menu, several farmers pass by the table in their overalls and hunting caps. They all nod at Louis Sr. and one of them says, "*Quoi ça dit,* Louis, how's it going?"

Nita is impressed that he would be recognized, even in this little diner in downtown Crowley. She orders a cheeseburger and a *pop rouge,* and she thinks that Louis' father is much more of a gentleman than Louis. He even reminds her of her own father a little in the way that he leans forward as he listens to her, as if he wants to be sure that he hears everything she has to say. Nita hoped to see Hilton once she and Louis moved to Crowley, but has yet to hear one word from him. As she finishes her soda, she worries that he may be in some new kind of trouble. But then she returns her gaze to Pop, who hands her two chocolate Kisses and all the change in his pocket before driving her back home.

The visit cheers Nita and she begins to feel a little better about her place in Louis' family. She thinks that maybe Pop will goad Louis' mother out of hating her. Maybe he'll tell her that it's Louis, not Nita, who's so cheap that he still drives to Iota every other weekend for a free meal. Nita is so cheered that she cooks up a Chinese dinner—glass noodles and all—and she even smiles when Louis pushes away his empty plate, then rubs his swollen stomach and says, "*Pas mal.* Not bad, but I think I swallowed one of those bald-headed Chinamen."

The next morning, Nita is surprised when there's a knock on the door. Could it be Louis' father again? she wonders. Or Hilton? Maybe someone told him where she lives. The thought of seeing her father makes her run to the door with her shoes off and her hair half in curlers. She almost can't believe it when she finds Louis' mother standing in front of her with two other ladies, both wearing the same kind of pillbox hat that sits on top of Mrs. Toussaint's head, and both sporting white kid gloves as well.

Nita stands at the door for what feels like several minutes before Mrs. Toussaint says, "*Mais,* aren't you going to invite us in?" and Nita steps aside to watch as the three ladies walk past her into the apartment.

"Um, make yourself at home," she mumbles to their backs, before dashing to the bathroom where she pulls out the curlers and brushes her hair into a high ponytail. That'll have to do, Nita thinks, as she squints into the mirror.

When she comes out of the bathroom, she sees Louis' mother running a white-gloved finger on the edge of the kitchen counter. There's a dark spot on the Formica that Nita hasn't been able to rub out. She watches as Anna scratches the spot, then sniffs at her glove and claps her hands together. "Caught you off guard?" Anna asks.

Nita hunches her shoulders, then shakes her head no. She tries to think of something to say, some story that Louis' mother might like. But the only thing Nita can think to talk about is her lunch with Louis Sr. "Pop—I mean Mr. Toussaint—came by yesterday," she tells Anna.

"I know," Anna says quickly, before pursing her lips.

"He took me to lunch . . ."

"*I know.*" Louis' mother turns to her two friends and Nita thinks she sees one of the ladies fight back a smile.

"Well," Anna says, "aren't you going to offer us to sit down and have some coffee?"

Nita starts to stammer and thinks that she would kick herself if she could. She's out of coffee and nearly out of milk as well. Louis promised to take her shopping tonight, but what can she tell Mrs. Toussaint now?

"Um, I'm, um, I'm out of coffee," she finally gets it out.

"Well." Louis' mother holds her hands out to the air, then turns to the other ladies. "There's no point in staying for coffee when there's none to be had. *Allons-y!*"

With that, Mrs. Toussaint and her two friends—who were not introduced to Nita—turn on their heels and head out the door. Nita is crushed; she's sure that she's failed some kind of test, and that feeling continues when, two days later, Anna makes another trip to Crowley. Even though Nita now has three kinds of coffee to offer, the visit is just as brief and more awkward than the first. After that, Mrs. Toussaint's visits continue for most of the following week. Each time, she brings a different set of friends, but she always runs her white glove along the counter in the kitchen and never stays for long.

When Nita complains to Louis, he's not at all sure what to do. He's furious that his mother would invade his house and treat his wife like a *negresse*. But Bootsy tells him not to mess in these women's problems, so Louis says nothing to Anna even as he and Nita go to Iota less and less often.

Within a couple of weeks, Anna's trips to Crowley stop altogether and Nita is left alone again in the apartment. She welcomes the silence at first, but then wishes Pop Toussaint would come back and take her to lunch. She sees no one and does nothing but clean all day long. Her sponge goes round and round the counter in circles and the bleach stings her eyes and dries the skin on her hands until finally she feels as though she might go mad. Louis still won't take her to see her mother and he won't even let her go to church during the day.

But, regardless, Nita prays, and as she prays she tries to figure a way out of the cage Louis has built for her. She hasn't let him lie on top of her for weeks. But now she calls Louis to her side of the bed and, each time, she closes her eyes and prays for a baby. Jesus, please let me have a baby, she prays, and please, please let it be a son.

Part Two

1

WHEN HE'S BORN, HE'S PERFECT. TEN TOES, TEN
fingers, again she counts. And blue eyes, perfect! His skin, a rosy
alabaster, and those big ears! Big, bold ears. A strong face. A husky
little body, ten pounds, and she weighed only ninety before. All
the weight she carried around with her, the weight that pressed
against the steel rod in her leg and made her think with every step,
I'm gonna have a baby, I'm gonna have a boy, all that weight is now
in her arms. And he's not crying. There's a sharp smell of antisep-
tic and something almost burnt in the air. There's a rush of people
hurrying in and out of the room and the glare of the fluorescent
light overhead. But he's not crying. Nita looks at her son and almost can't believe she gave birth to him. She licks the tips of her
fingers to smooth the bit of hair on his head, then straightens the
collar on his gown. He's a doll, a tiny doll come to life in her

hands. He's her own sweet emancipation baby, born to deliver her from Louis and that awful house.

In the buzzing light of the hospital room, Nita watches her son's chubby hands open and close as they reach for something to touch: the white cotton field of her dressing gown, the long waterfall of her hair, the soft cave of her mouth. "Look at him grab!" she cries. "His little hands are so strong! And look at his eyes! He knows what he's grabbing, I can tell."

Nita wraps her hands around her baby's, then pokes his nose with the tip of her finger. She runs her palm over the dome of his head and over the cup of his ears, then blows cool air over his face and tries to ignore the rising commotion.

All around the chrome railing of the bed, people crush in to have a look at the new baby. Uncles and aunts, *nanaines* and *parrains,* almost all of them Louis' family. Even Bootsy is there, slapping Louis on the back. No one, it seems, wants to miss the chance to weigh in with an opinion. Their words sound like babble in her head, like what she imagines people saying at a party. But few of the comments are addressed her way. Instead everyone talks to Louis or directly to the baby. Nita tries to nod in agreement to the voices, but she can't keep her teeth from clenching when she hears Anna say, "He looks just like his father. A spitting image." Not for a minute does she believe what her mother-in-law says, it sounds rehearsed and phony and, anyway, can't they all see what she sees? This is her baby, *hers.*

Barely eighteen, Nita can't believe that overnight she's become a mother. She looks at everything around her as if it somehow changed. Her body feels lighter, she expected that, but it feels stronger, too. Is she somehow taller? She thinks that with one good kick she might go sailing out of the room with her baby, sail-

ing away from Mrs. Toussaint and her pillbox hat, away from Louis
and that guard dog look on his face.

"You sure must be proud," she hears someone say to him.
Then Louis' whole face stretches into a wide grin as if he scored a
touchdown or drove his car through a flurry of checkered flags.
Why should *he* be proud? Nita thinks. What did he do? Louis
stares at her and the baby in her arms and she can tell he's thinking that they belong to him.

The steel rod in her leg begins to throb a bit, but the pain
only makes her more aware of how much she can carry. Nita remembers her year in the hospital, the car accident, and the surgery
that put the rod in her leg. When her father visited, he whispered
in her ear, *"Fille forte."* She didn't believe him then, but now her
ears ring with his words, "Strong girl." Nita needs that strength
when she looks at Louis and when the time comes to choose her
baby's name.

Despite the protests of everyone around her, Nita refuses to
name her son Louis III after his father and grandfather. Louis
fumes and even Pop Toussaint seems to sulk a bit. Nita's mother
threads her hands into a knot and wears a worried look on her
face, as if she could tell what her daughter was up to. And Anna
stamps her feet and raises one hand to the air. "You can't do this,"
she says. "A name has to come from somewhere. You can't just
pull it out of the air like it was Mardi Gras!"

But Nita bites her lip and refuses to listen: she isn't naming her
baby for the man she married. She tells no one her real reasons for
refusing to name him The Third; it's a private revenge. Instead,
she smiles at everyone around her and says she doesn't want other
kids teasing her son. She was called names at school and she's
gonna make sure it doesn't happen to him. "Kids can be so mean,"

she says, "I know how they are. They might laugh and call him Louis, The Turd." No, she won't call him Louis. She'll call him Marc. A strong name, a name no one in the room carries.

Once they're home, Nita can't stop looking at her son. She laughs and claps her hands every time he makes a sound. She rolls him back and forth on the bed until he laughs along with her. He's hers, she thinks, all hers. And when he cries out for food, she refuses to feed him from the breasts her husband touched. She boils a bottle and fills it with formula milk she bought the week before. After her baby drains the bottle, she dresses him in a cotton gown with a bow-tied ribbon on the back that looks like a pair of wings. He's an angel, she thinks, perfect.

When Louis first looks at their baby, his face beams and he announces that his mother is right: his son looks just like him. He has the same broad Cajun chin, the same high forehead and sharp nose. What's more, he has the same skin. The same ruddy French complexion and the same stocky body. With a wide grin, big dimpled cheeks, and a smart look in his eye, he's propped up on one arm and a stretch of carpet for his first official photograph. He appears ready to catch a football or a debutante, whichever is thrown his way first.

But even as Louis boasts to everyone around that his son is a real Toussaint, *la vraie chose,* he wonders why the boy keeps looking at Nita and not at him. After all, before the baby was born, he pressed his face to his wife's round belly and directed his son's future: "You're gonna be a football player, just like your father, *hein?* I can tell. Come on, give your mama a good hard kick. Come on . . . that's it! That's my little football champ!"

And after his son is born, Louis lowers his voice to tell him the story of the Cajuns, of Evangeline and Emmeline. But Nita cuts him short and says she doesn't want Marc hearing all those old Cajun tales. She wants him raised on stronger stuff. "All those sad stories," she complains, "and all that music, all that chank-a-chank. It's enough to make a person go crazy."

Nita actually likes the music, Louis knows that. But he can't figure out why she's so jack-bent against tradition. Why can't his son be named after him? Why can't he tell his son the story of Emmeline?

Already, Louis sees that Nita is changing. She snaps at him in a way she's never done before. He doesn't like it and he's glad Bootsy isn't around to see it; but every time he thinks to fight back, he looks at the baby in her arms and figures his wife is just nervous. If she shouts at him when he forgets to pick up more formula milk, he hunches his back and shrugs an apology. She's probably tired, he thinks, from all the late-night sessions with the baby.

Louis watches Nita as she stands over the crib and he sees how his son's face brightens when he recognizes his mama. He wants their baby to look at him in the same way. Instead, even when he holds Marc, he notices that the boy's eyes travel in search of Nita. He doesn't cry, but he's restless in his father's arms. If Louis tickles him, he laughs, and if he blows air into his face, he smiles. But Louis thinks his moments with his son seem temporary, as if some other man asked him to watch this baby while he ran out for a minute.

Louis searches for any excuse to draw Marc closer to him. He offers to hold him when he cries and to help change his diapers. If he wails at night, he tells Nita to stay still—he'll check on the baby. At first, she allows him to hover over Marc, to make faces and wave a set of shiny car keys over his head. She even seems glad to have his help. But baby talk is out of the question, she tells him. "I won't have my son speaking nonsense and gibberish," she says. "Talk to him like a grown-up."

I *am* a grown-up, Louis wants to shout back. He wants to re-mind Nita, in case she's forgotten, that he's still the one who brings home the paycheck, the one who gets to call the shots. He can't help but think his wife is laying down too many rules. What will she tell him next? That he has to wear rubber gloves when he touches the kid? She acts as if raising a baby was a goddamn sci-ence, or some kind of lab experiment he's just waiting to foul up.

But for now Louis decides to do as Nita says. He hasn't seen her this excited since they got married. She talks to Marc with a voice he's never heard from her before. Soft and soothing, but strong, too. As if she was a coach talking to an injured player. Even if she's talking to Marc and not to him, he likes the sound of that voice in his ear. He also likes to watch her excitement every time their son does something new. If Marc gargles or sends his voice up like a siren, her face breaks into a smile and Louis almost forgets that she's just been screaming at him about some new offense.

As he tells it, Louis obeys Nita's rules in every way except one. He decides that if he has to talk like an adult to Marc, he will at least tell his son the stories his father told him when he was a boy.

Late one night, the baby cries out from the crib and Louis gets up to check on him. He makes a few clown faces, then stretches his mouth into an exaggerated smile and wiggles his ears. After the baby stops crying, Louis hangs his head over the railing and, in a whisper, he begins the story of *Evangeline,* the Acadian poem he memorized in school. He tells his son about how Longfellow stole the story and changed it. "And that's just like a damn Yankee, too!" he says.

He tells Marc about how in the poem Evangeline and her fi-ancé were thrown out of Canada with the rest of the Acadians all because they wouldn't speak English or salute the British flag. They wouldn't give up the Catholic church, either, so the British forced them onto ships with almost no food and no clothes but what they had on their backs. Louis tells his son, "At least he got that much right."

Evangeline and her fiancé were put on separate ships, and when they got to Louisiana they had no way of finding each other. Evangeline searched all over the country for her fiancé and finally found him in a hospital somewhere in Pennsylvania, where he died in her arms. "Pennsylvania!" Louis nearly shouts. "Of all the places!"

On another night, Louis tells his son the story his father told him of the real Evangeline, a woman named Emmeline. He tells Marc about how Emmeline watched her family die on the ship and how she had to help throw the bodies overboard. "The Yankee forgot that part," he says.

He also says that once she got to Louisiana, she never left. Emmeline sat under a live oak tree and waited more than ten years for her fiancé to find her. "Now that's a good woman!" Louis tells his son.

After a friend told Emmeline that her fiancé was dead, she went crazy and pulled all her hair out. She died a few days later under the oak, bald and broken-hearted. But what she never found out, he says, was that her fiancé lived only twenty miles away in a little town called Carencro, and he had long before married someone else.

When Louis tells Marc these stories, he knows that his son won't remember them. He knows it's just the sound of his voice that lulls him. But he likes to pretend the boy understands what he hears. He likes the hush that falls over the room and the feeling that, for a little while at least, his son looks up to no one but him.

2

NITA NEVER FINDS OUT ABOUT THE LATE-NIGHT history lessons in the crib. But she watches Louis carefully as he cradles her son and calls him Boo. She cringes when she hears that word—it's enough that she has to endure it herself, but she doesn't want her son called baby names. She also cringes when Louis kisses him and blows air bubbles in his face. "He's a boy," Nita says. "Treat him like one."

The fact of having a baby, a son, is like a doorframe Nita walks through to a new sense of herself. She takes charge of the house and begins to direct Louis in ways that she was too afraid to try before. She tells him she needs a new iron and he buys it. She tells him she needs the car to take the baby to the doctor, and he lets her have it. Then Nita tells him she doesn't like riding in the Falcon with a baby. "It's not safe," she says. "Can't you get a real car?"

She's surprised when he doesn't shout at her, but figures he's just too stubborn to admit that she's right.

Louis doesn't want to sell the Falcon; it was the first thing that was his alone. He's proud of how he takes care of that car. Anna has chided him more than once for buying such a flashy "hot rod," and he thinks how he'd miss revving the engine in her driveway and spinning gravel onto her lawn as he throws the car in reverse. He hates to think his mama will get some satisfaction out of hearing that he sold the Falcon. But he's been staying away from Iota and, anyway, he wants to keep Nita happy, so he calls up a dealer and arranges for a trade. The day before he drives the car onto the dealer's lot, he washes and waxes it by hand. He polishes the chrome fender to a high buff and stares at his reflection. I'm a man, now, he thinks, but the thought doesn't much comfort him. Neither does the name of their new car: Dodge Dart. Rhymes with old fart, he thinks. Bootsy kids him and says next he'll be wearing a cardigan and bifocals.

After Louis buys the Dart, Nita tells him they need a real house, a place with a yard and some room for her son to play. Since Marc was born, the apartment has closed in on her. The holes in the walls seem bigger and, as much as she scrubs and scrubs, she's afraid to let her baby play on the floor too long. She remembers all the project houses where she grew up, the black line of cockroaches that skirted the wall at night and the mice that sometimes darted from room to room no matter what time of day. Sometimes she thinks she hears a rustling in the cabinets or the walls. Suppose Marc crawled onto a roach, or a mouse crawled onto him? Nita can't stand the thought and she can't stand living in this apartment, so she tells Louis again and again that they have to move. At first, Louis doesn't respond. His shoulders go stiff and his mouth flattens out, but he stays silent. Finally, when

Nita calls him lazy, he bursts. "Lazy? Lazy?" he shouts. "I work overtime five days a week. Do you call that lazy? I bust my butt so I can give you what you want! Is that lazy? What do you think I am, anyway? A fucking robot?"

Louis throws his hands down on the chrome table, then he picks the whole thing up and slams it against the floor. Nothing breaks, but the rattle of the legs echoes in the room.

"What do I think you are?" Nita shouts back, but her voice trails off and she can't think of anything else to say, so she just stands with her arms folded across her chest and the steam of her anger rising in the air.

She's angry, but she's scared, too. She hasn't seen Louis like this since before Marc was born and she's afraid of what he might do. Still, she presses him. "We need a house," she says. "We need a house."

"Do I have to spell it out for you?" Louis demands. "No-can-do! We can't afford a fucking house. We can't afford it!" He slams his fist against the wall and a bit of plaster falls to the floor. But Nita won't give up.

"Even if we can't afford to *buy*," she says in a loud huff, "we can rent, but I'm not raising my son in the ratty back-half of somebody else's house."

As her voice rings out, a wail rises from the bedroom and she runs to check on Marc, while Louis stews alone in the kitchen. Damn, he thinks, I can't win, I just can't win.

Within a couple of weeks, Louis finds a small redbrick one-bedroom in a slightly better part of town, but Nita still isn't happy. She tells him it's time to look for a better job, with more money. Louis is not yet twenty-one and has only been at Aucoin for two years; he really doesn't want to leave the rice mill. But Nita is adamant and when Louis claims he can't find anything better, she tells him that, rice mill or no, she isn't going to let her son live on fish sticks and hand-me downs. "I'll go hungry," she says, "if that's what it takes to keep my son fed right!"

The baby comes before everything with Nita, even her own food and sleep. Louis is still making only ninety dollars a week, but she rushes Marc to the doctor's office anytime he cries too long or feels even a little warm. She reads all the baby manuals she comes across and frets over every possible ailment, especially ones with foreign-sounding names like "rubella." Nita follows a round-the-clock food regimen that the doctor set out. All the books and the visits and the formula milk take up a fat share of Louis' pay, so Nita cuts her plate in half: she draws a line down the middle of her dinner and eats only the food on the left-hand side. The other side she saves for lunch the next day. There are nights when her stomach keeps her awake, churning and grumbling. Louis worries that she'll get too thin, but Nita says, "I'm fine! I'm fine!"

Once Marc passes his first birthday, Nita tells Louis that he needs to make some changes. A few weeks before, a woman at the Piggly-Wiggly pulled Nita aside to ask if Louis was a pansy. At first, she didn't know what the woman meant; she just bit her lip and stared at the frosted wig. But when a checkout girl cooed, "Isn't that sweet? Look how your husband mothers that kid!" Nita pieced it together.

Since then, that word keeps rattling in her head. Was the woman right? Is Louis a pansy? Nita can't quite believe it, but she also can't shake the thought. More than anything, she worries about what Louis' fawning might do to Marc. She doesn't want her son to turn into a pansy, so she forbids Louis to kiss the boy good night or to cradle him in his arms. She tells Louis it looks weird to see a grown man fussing over a little boy and that he's getting too old for all that anyway. Nita never saw her father kissing her brother. They shook hands and threw air punches at each other, so why should it be different with her son?

From that point on, Louis shakes hands with Marc before Nita puts him to bed and he carries him on his shoulders or not at all. He wants to hold his son, to kiss his forehead, but thinks maybe Nita is right. He's not a girl and he needs to learn early on how to act like a boy. He doesn't understand, though, why it's okay for Nita to cover their kid with kisses and to whisper "there, there" in his ear every time he bumps himself. He wishes he had a daughter, maybe then he could hold her like Nita holds their son. Maybe then he would have something of his own again.

Louis does have a small triumph when he comes home early one day and Marc opens his mouth to let out his first fully formed words. "Hi, Boo!" he says as Nita groans and Louis shakes his son's hand as vigorously as if he said, "Congratulations! You're my favorite!" But Marc is to him, more and more, like the kid he watches for someone else and even Louis' stories end when his son stops crying in the night.

The feeling of defeat lingers in his head until he gets a small raise at work. His boss, Mr. Aucoin, has noticed the extra hours Louis puts in and has decided to give him full control of the bookkeeping for an extra ten dollars a week. That afternoon, when Louis leaves the rice mill, the Dart shakes with the weight of his foot against the pedal. He usually drives slower since there's a rattle in the hood that he can't seem to find, but he can't wait to tell Nita the news. As soon as he bursts in the door, he spills it all, how he'll have more responsibility, more money. Nita stares at him, then he watches as her lips slowly stretch into a smile. "More money?" she asks.

When he tells her yes, her smile grows a little wider. She claps her hands once in front of her face and he thinks, Maybe tonight.

He even feels brave enough to grab her by the waist and, for once, she doesn't resist. Louis stays pressed against her for just a minute. He lets her scent fill his nose until a startled shriek rises in the next room. Nita quickly pulls away to check on Marc, who's found a way to tug the checkered drapes open and shut.

After dinner, after Nita tucks Marc into bed, and after the lights are out, Louis climbs on top of her and she doesn't say a word. He thinks how he's missed being inside her, missed having her under him. But he's careful not to take too long or to touch her too much. He watches as she bites her lip and he thinks maybe it's good, maybe she likes it. As soon as he's finished, Louis rolls over and falls asleep with the sound of his own snoring in his ear.

Bit by bit at first, but then more and more, Louis starts drinking when he gets home from the rice mill and, as often as Nita lets him, he calls Bootsy over to watch the Saints game on the brand-new Zenith he just bought. Nita doesn't like Louis' drinking or his football buddy, but she says nothing. She's just happy about the extra money he's been bringing home, so happy that she doesn't even say anything when he climbs onto her side of the bed night after night. Louis's always too rough. Always. She has to bite her lip to keep a scream from ripping through her. And he never asks how she feels. Does she want to? Did she like it? But Nita never complains; she just closes her eyes and waits for it to be over.

When Bootsy comes to the house, he gripes to Louis about how broke he is. But he always shows up with a six-pack in his hand and Nita laughs to herself. No matter how small a Cajun man's budget, she thinks, there's always room for a six-pack. With his thick, curly beard and his fuzzy brown flannel shirt, Nita thinks Bootsy looks like a bear, and when he isn't around she calls him "The Grizzly." During commercials, he and Louis walk over to the playpen where Marc sits and throw a few easy punches his way.

She watches as her baby laughs at the sight of them and sometimes claps his hands with excitement. She isn't sure how she feels about Louis and The Grizzly teaching her baby to make a fist; he's only two. But she thinks of her father's boxing lessons with her brother and figures he has to learn sometime, so why not now?

One night, Bootsy tells Louis that Marc is just not getting it. "The kid thinks we're joking," he says. "We're gonna have to teach him how to get serious. Let's move him to the table."

Louis takes a swig from his can of Dixie and looks at Bootsy. He isn't sure his buddy is right when he says that the kitchen table will make a better boxing ring, but he figures he'll show his wife that there are some things only *he* can teach their son.

Louis and Bootsy perch Marc atop the orange and red swirl of the Formica table and Nita watches as her baby raises his hands to the ceiling and shrieks with glee. He looks down at the squares of linoleum, then Nita sees his hands stretch toward the ceiling. He can almost reach the light that hangs by a cord over the table. Marc starts to clap his hands, but then Bootsy says, "All right, boy, here's how it goes."

He throws a fast punch at Louis' chest. Louis is caught off guard, but he quickly recovers. In a Three Stooges voice and with a winding fist, he says, "Why I oughta . . ."

Nita rolls her eyes and thinks, This is what you have to show my son? How to be a clown?

But then Louis tells Marc to make a fist, while holding up one of his own. His son watches him and curls his hand into a ball. "Hold your head up!" Louis says. "Now make a fist with the other hand!"

Once the boy masters yet another balled-up fist, Louis throws a few punches into the air and tells Marc to copy him. Louis beams with pride; he can't believe how fast his son is catching on.

"Do as I do," he says. "Keep your head up. Throw 'em high, boy! Throw 'em high!"

Nita stands at one corner of the table, squinting her eyes. "Careful!" she says, as her baby runs with his fist in the air from one end of the table to the other.

She starts to worry; she doesn't want her baby hurt. Nita finds herself getting angry at Louis. Why does he have to be so rough with Marc? He's only a boy. She decides to tell Louis that she doesn't want Bootsy coming over and turning their kitchen into a boxing ring. She's quickly grown tired of him and the twenty-four-ounce cans of beer he calls tall girls. "Careful!" she repeats. "Careful!"

After a few rounds with Marc, Bootsy orders the kid to aim his fists at Nita, and Louis says, "Throw a good one, now, make it count!"

But with the force of his first half-punch, Marc falls head-first off the table and hits the linoleum with a loud thunk. Nita screams into her hands, then shouts at Louis and Bootsy, "My baby, *my* baby!"

Marc lies on the ground for a moment, not moving and making no sound. Nita's blood races and tears stream down her face. Out loud, she says, "My God! My God!" But then the boy rights himself from the floor and waddles over to her. He has an egg-shaped lump on his forehead that quickly goes from purple to black, but he doesn't cry or scream out in pain. Instead, he covers Nita's face with kisses. Then he imitates her own way of comforting him. "There, there," he says. "There, there, there."

For weeks, Nita tells this story to all her family and to everyone at the corner store. For her, it's proof that her baby is more than a fighter. He's a budding James Dean or Montgomery Clift, a tough guy with a lot of heart. "He's gonna be my little man," she says each time she tells the story. "He'll protect me, for sure."

Louis also likes to tell the story of Marc as a tough guy. He tells the truck drivers at the rice mill how his son has a knack for boxing. But he doesn't tell them that his lessons were cut short and that Bootsy and his tall girls are no longer welcome at the house. Instead, Louis brags about the coming of a new baby. Nita is pregnant and he can't wait. He thinks how perfect his family will be if it has a little girl in it, a new little baby he can hold.

3

WHEN SHE'S BORN, SHE HAS TEN TOES, TEN FINGERS
and everything seems in working order. But Jo has a mark on her
forehead—a brown strawberry which sits at an angle just above
her right eye. She also has yellow skin from head to foot. A jaun-
diced baby, she wails anytime anyone picks her up. She hates being
handled. Her skin rebels against touch by breaking out in red
patches. Her face contorts and too often she spits up on the shoulder of whoever dares to hold her. Her bottom remains in a rash
the entire time she's in diapers. Everything about her seems stubborn and irritated. As Nita puts it, even her hair refuses to grow.
She poses Jo in pictures with a red bow taped on top of her head
where curly locks should be. More than nine pounds at birth, Jo is
too fat for a girl and bears a resemblance to none of the petite
women who crowd into the hospital room to see her. Nita's

mother smiles at Jo, then shakes her head, and says, *"Pauv' bête,* poor thing." But Louis' mother is more blunt. "Look at her!" she says. "She's fat as a *cochon de lait,* a little suckling pig!"

Nita looks down at the new baby in her arms and wonders if there's been a mix-up. Is this angry mewling kid hers? Even if she never speaks it, the thought is there: who does this baby belong to?

Cranky and colicky, Jo refuses the formula milk Nita fed Marc, then she refuses breast-feeding as well. She cries constantly and Nita starts to worry. Marc was so easy. It was as if she knew all his sounds before he was born, knew exactly what he wanted each time he cried. But when Jo's cry pierces the room, Nita doesn't know what to do. She doesn't know what her baby wants. She changes Jo's diaper again even if it's dry. She keeps a fan blowing on the crib. She tries playing Fats Domino from the radio and humming in her baby's ear. Nothing, nothing at all seems to work and an odd feeling settles into Nita's stomach. She doesn't tell anyone this, but she decides Jo doesn't like her.

Still, Nita tries to make her daughter happy. Everytime she cooks, she carries Jo from the crib to the kitchen and lays her on the swirling calico rug. Marc toddles over to his sister and, when she cries, Nita tells him to try tickling Jo's feet. But that only makes her bawl all the more loudly, so he coos into Jo's ear, says, "There, there," and plugs a pacifier into her mouth. Nita watches as Jo pinches up her face and spits out the plastic nipple. Then Marc shrieks with delight, picks up the nipple and puts it back in Jo's mouth. Again and again like a tiny volcano goddess, she spits out the pacifier, and again and again, like a happy little hunter, he puts it back in her mouth. Nita thinks, They're both mine, they're both my babies. How could they be so different?

Even though she has blue eyes and pale, pale skin, Louis thinks his daughter looks just like Nita. "Maybe the color's wrong," he tells his wife, "but look at the *shape* of her eyes and look at that mouth."

She shakes her head no. "If anything," Nita says, "she looks like your mother."

Louis doesn't believe his wife. His mama has blue eyes, true, and pale skin. But look at that mouth, he thinks, I know that mouth. Jo's lips puff up when she pouts, then flatten into a thin line when she's angry—just like Nita's. And—just like Nita—she has a fleck in her eye, a green fleck in the bottom of her left eye. The line of her nose is the same, too. It runs in a perfect slope, then turns a bit at the end. Maybe she's a little too chubby, and maybe she cries too much, but Louis thinks he's never seen a kid with more character. She makes more noise than Marc ever did. Not just loud screams, but soft, plopping noises that sound like duck feet hitting water or a tiny motorboat. She's more active too, squeezing everything in her crib with little pink fists. And when Louis hangs his head over his daughter's face, she may not smile, not exactly, but she stares as if she recognizes him. "That girl knows what she wants," he tells Nita. "We just haven't figured it out yet."

Jo calms down and falls into a quiet glee only when Louis peers through the railing of the crib with a special formula he drives twenty minutes to Lafayette for. Somehow, Jo seems to know he'll do anything for her, that her daddy will drive all around town and into the next parish to find the only milk she'll take. He boils the nipple, screws on the top of the bottle, then feeds her himself. She doesn't let Louis—or anyone else—pick her up yet, but she accepts his milk and stares at him placidly. Louis is glad to call this little girl his and he's proud to be the one who names her Jolyn.

After Jo is born, Nita tells Louis that the little one-bedroom house is no longer big enough. "Are we supposed to sleep four to a room?" she asks. "Like a house full of niggers?"

Louis says nothing while Nita answers herself. "No," she nearly shouts, "no, this is not how we're supposed to live."

He watches as she presses her hands on the counter, as if she were keeping the cabinets from rising up.

"Look at this kitchen," she says. "It's much too small. There's no room for me to cook and watch the kids at the same time."

Louis doesn't even try to fight her. He says nothing while she goes on, "And the tiles on this floor are cracked—I have to get on my knees with a toothbrush just to make sure I get all the filth out. There's no air-conditioning in this house and not a single tree in the yard, not one. The sun bakes these bricks and turns this place into an oven . . ."

Louis begins to think she might go on forever, but then he sees something flash in Nita's eyes as tears start welling up and falling down her face. He doesn't know what to do. He wants to hold her, to comfort his wife. But he doesn't know if her tears are from anger, or if she's really crying. Is she that unhappy? he wonders. Does she really hate it here? Louis puts his hand on her back and feels her shudder beneath his fingers. She doesn't face him, but she doesn't pull away. This house is too small now. He knows that, but he's not sure if he can afford another move. Still he tells Nita, "We'll get a new house, if that's what you want."

Her face doesn't brighten, though. In fact, she looks as if she was stung by an angry mosquito. Louis watches as she nods her head slowly and says, "That's what we need."

Nita wants Louis to take his hand off her back, but she doesn't want to tell him why. There's a sharp pain running up and down her spine and her head is throbbing. She feels as if she had been thrown from the roof to the concrete outside. No, she feels as if she had been thrown from a car. Her back is throbbing almost as much as the night of the wreck. Nita lay in that field more than an

hour before help came, and she thought of her father the whole
time. She thought about how much she missed him. She still
misses him. Nita's tried to find Hilton since she moved to Crowley, but his new wife's number is disconnected and no one's seen
him since the wedding. She wishes she could find her father now.
He'd know what to do for her back. He'd pull out a cast-iron skillet and some old chicken grease to cook up a poultice for the pain.
Then he'd put his hands on her and rub until the heat rose from
her back to his fingers. As soon as he felt the heat, he'd shake his
hands onto the porch and tell her, "*Tout disparu, mon 'ti' chou,* all
gone, my baby."

Since Nita first got pregnant with Jo, the pain's been getting
worse. What was a tingle in her leg with Marc became first a
prickle then a piercing jolt as she carried her new baby. Jo was two
pounds lighter than Marc, but somehow her weight pressed
harder against the rod in Nita's leg. And now that pressure shoots
from her leg into her spine and sometimes all the way to her neck.
But she tells Louis nothing. She worries about the cost of another
doctor, another trip to the hospital. Nita doesn't want to raise her
kids in this cramped place, and she doesn't want her back to get in
the way of a move. So she fights against the scream tearing at her
lips and just nods her head. "That's what we need," she says again.
"We need a real house."

On Saturday afternoons and Sunday mornings after church,
and sometimes on weeknights after dinner, Nita and Louis put
Marc and Jo in the backseat of the Dart as they go in search of a
new house. They drive up and down the wide main street of
downtown Crowley. Nita turns her head to the window to watch
the passing storefronts and the occasional neon sign. She reads the
words out loud to Marc, who calls each one back to her: "Burger
Chef," "Canal Villere," "KAJN Radio," "Rice Theatre." When

Marc stumbles on "Theatre," Nita helps him out. "Rhymes with gator," she tells him. "Like alligator."

Louis stares ahead at the crêpe myrtles that dot the neutral ground and the hundred-year-old oaks that line both sides of the street. The branches of the oaks either stretch or droop—he can't decide which—until they meet in midair to form a canopy. He remembers tearing up this boulevard in his Falcon and thinks how he misses that car.

When Nita sees a sign for a road that looks promising, Louis turns and she tells him to slow down. "I wanna see," she says.

"But none of these houses are for sale," he tells her.

"I don't care," she says. "I still wanna see."

Nita likes it when she spies someone in one of the houses at work washing a car, clipping hedges, or plucking weeds. She likes to imagine what lives other people lead. What they eat, what clothes they wear. She starts to imagine a story behind each front door. The bigger the house, the more excited she becomes. A doctor lives there, she thinks, and he has a tall blond wife with five boys and a trampoline in the backyard. And that's a lawyer's house. He's not married yet, but he's looking for a wife and he's going to take her to New Orleans to see Bourbon Street.

For more than a month, Nita and Louis search block after block of northside Crowley until they find a sand-colored brick two-bedroom on Mockingbird Lane. The house has a newly re-shingled roof and a covered carport, with a row of exotic-looking juniper bushes out front. It faces a fancier Spanish-style white-brick affair and is cater-cornered with the mayor's parents' house. "Perfect!" Nita says. "We'll take it."

The house is more than they can afford, but she can't picture living anywhere else, so she starts pushing Louis again to find a better paying job.

A week later, Nita screams at Louis when she finds that there isn't enough money in the checking account to pay for a new pair of specially fitted Buster Browns that Marc needs to correct his weak arches. "If we can't afford a pair of kid's shoes, how can we afford a bigger house?" she demands.

When Louis hunches his shoulders and says, "It can wait a week or two, can't it?" she shouts back at him, "No! It can't wait—I'll get a job if that's what it takes. I'll work at the corner store, and rock my baby in a buggy if I have to, but *I did not* get married so that my son could go shoeless and I didn't get married so I could live with two kids and a husband in a one-bedroom house!"

Louis makes a steeple with his hands and holds his breath. Then he tells Nita that he's talked to some people at Breaux & Comeaux, a new rice mill that needs an office manager. If he gets the job, his salary will be enough to handle almost twice as much rent. He felt good about his first interview at the new mill, and a second interview has been scheduled for the following week, so he tells her he'll sign the lease on Mockingbird Lane and he'll find a way to buy the shoes as well.

A few weeks later, Louis gets the job and he and Nita drive into their new carport with a load of boxes and blankets. She starts humming when he turns off the ignition, and she tells Marc that there's a song that goes with the name of their street, "And if that Mock-ing-bird don't sing, Mama's gonna buy you a diamond ring . . ." Louis watches Marc clap along to her rhythm and he stares at Jo, who seems to smile in her plastic carrier. I did it, he thinks, I got us this far at least.

In the new house, Louis cradles Jo in his arms and Nita lets him make whatever baby sounds he wants to make. He blows air bubbles with his lips and pats Jo's bald head. He even cleans up after his daughter when, during the middle of dinner one night, Nita walks into her room to find Jo sitting in a pile of her own shit. Somehow she opened her diaper and smeared its contents all over herself and the low stretch of wall in her reach. Jo isn't crying. In fact, to Nita it looked as if she was smiling. But the rank smell hits her nose like the backside of a hand. She tells Louis that she's sure Jo did it on purpose, that her daughter is out to get her. Louis just laughs and fills a bucket with bleach water. "The girl's an artist," he says as he wipes the walls clean.

Jo grows quickly, or so it seems to Nita. The mark on her forehead fades and a few patches of sandy blonde hair grow on top of her head. Her eyes take on a dark blue hue, but her skin remains slightly yellow and Nita thinks she's still too chubby for a girl. Jo is no healthier as a toddler than she was as a baby. If there's a virus in the air, she catches it. If there are measles or mumps, she catches them too. She even manages to catch ringworm from a dog she pets. And if there's an accident waiting to happen, Jo seems more than happy to help it along. She pulls pans from cabinets and topples whole shelves of Tupperware.

When Nita moves all of her kitchen goods to higher shelves, Jo finds her way into the bathroom cabinets where she causes giant Comet snowstorms and Lysol flashfloods. She reaches racks and drawers she isn't supposed to be able to reach and discovers places for hiding that Louis never knew existed. He's fascinated by his daughter as she walks through their house like some kind of baby Godzilla knocking things down. He tells everyone that with her knack for destruction, Jo is either going to lead a demolition derby or she'll be the first female governor of Louisiana. But Nita's patience soon wears thin and she begins shaking Jo and threatening her with the back end of a fly swatter. Louis worries that Nita's too hard with Jo. She was so much easier on Marc. It almost seems as if she expects their daughter to get into trouble, as if she's waiting for something to happen so she can wave her hand around in the air. For as long as they live at Mockingbird Lane, though, Nita's threats have as many holes as the swatter and Jo manages to wiggle through without harm.

4

BY THE TIME JO IS TWO AND MARC IS FOUR, THEY'VE made friends across the street with the doctor's kids, Delilah and Blaise Marcantel. Nita watches them from the window as they play together and she often stands on the front porch and cheers them on in their games, or shows them new ones. When her back is calm, Nita teaches the kids how to play Red Light, Green Light with quick-stop action. She shows them how to be clever and very, very quiet in Hide 'n' Seek. "Don't think too hard when you're looking," she says. "Go to the first place that pops into your mind. And when you're hiding, hold your breath and think of ice cream."

When Nita plays this game inside with Marc and Jo, she always makes sure that she loses. She starts laughing in the bedroom closet and says she can't help it. "My ice cream melted and I had to laugh."

Nita is so wrapped up in the thrill of watching Marc and Jo play with the doctor's kids that she doesn't worry about who's playing with whom. She might scream at Jo when she fights Blaise for his red fireman's cap, or pulls him from the wheel of his tricycle to yank his curly blond hair. But Jo and Blaise are the same age, so it only seems right to Nita that they should play together, while Delilah and Marc are both nearly kindergarten age, so why shouldn't they hug each other and hold hands when they cross the street? In fact, to Nita it seems not only right but perfect that her son should leave behind both his sister and the boy to play with the little chocolate-haired girl. "You should see him," she tells Louis. "He's no dummy—he knows what he's doing. Hooking up with a doctor's daughter!"

Louis tries to laugh along with Nita, but he can't understand what's so great about a doctor's family. What's wrong with the family we've got? he wants to ask her. What's wrong with managing a rice mill? But when he watches her spin around in the kitchen, he forgets his irritation. Though Nita's just turned twenty-two, she looks even younger to him than when they married. Her hair is shorter now and she curls the ends into a flip, which makes her look less Indian somehow. Louis thinks she could be on TV or in a magazine. He stares at his wife and thinks how lucky he is.

He knows he's lucky partly because Dr. Marcantel is always telling him so. If they're both out on the lawn at the same time, Paul makes a point of crossing the street to ask about Nita. Louis was glad when the doctor first said hello. He missed having Bootsy over to the house, missed having someone to share a six-pack and joke about their bosses. Together they made up stories about two bumbling Cajun men from deep in the bayou. Sometimes Bootsy still calls Louis at work to ask if he's heard the one about how

Boudreaux and Thibodeaux went shrimping with a thirty-ought-six? Louis always cracks up laughing and eggs Bootsy on. "Tell me another lie," he says. "Tell me a *ti' cont*." But their calls never last long. They both have to get back to work and you can't exactly crack open a tall girl in the middle of the office.

Louis hopes at first that the doctor might know a good story or two. But when he crosses the street, Paul doesn't ask Louis about his job, the never-ending heat, or even about how the Saints are doing this season. Instead, he runs a finger down his long sideburns and tells Louis in a loud whisper, "If you ever get tired of that wife of yours, just drop her on my doorstep."

Louis knows he should laugh, but he feels his fingers curl into a fist as a thought enters his head: how would it feel to slug a doctor? He barely manages a smile before Paul walks back inside or drives off in his long candy-apple-red Cadillac.

Nita wishes she had an El Dorado like Dr. Marcantel's and she tells Louis that maybe they should visit the neighbors. She has no friends in town and he never takes her to see her mother. They hardly even go to Iota anymore. Nita's never seen the doctor's wife out on the lawn, so she's never had a chance to wave hello. She stares across the street at the huge Spanish doors of the doctor's house and tries to imagine ringing the bell or knocking on the oversized brass plate above the knob. She's afraid, though, of how she might look to Mrs. Marcantel. What do you wear when you call on a doctor's wife? she wonders. What do you say when she opens the door?

Louis won't cross the street, so Nita decides to do nothing either. She remains on her own lawn, watching Jo and Blaise race up and down the length of the driveway while Marc and Delilah draw Crayola faces on blocks of cardboard she cuts up for them. Nita teaches Marc how to make thick lines for all his drawings and to stay inside the lines when he fills in the colors. He looks at her with awe in his eyes the first time he manages to do exactly as she says, and she tapes the drawing to the fridge and covers the edges with gold stars. Nita tries to teach the same to Jo, but her lines run all over the page and sometimes off the page altogether. And the Crayola often ends up smashed in her palm or under her shoe as she runs off to chase Blaise. Nita thinks it's a struggle just to keep shoes on Jo. Like her own sister, Monetta Lou, that girl likes to run barefoot on the hot cement until her feet are covered with mosquito bites and blisters. And she always looks as if she was trying to find a way out of the dresses that Nita sews for her. Nita's glad that it's still only spring and not too hot yet. She can keep Jo outside and out of trouble.

Once summer hits, though, Nita wakes to several queasy mornings and she realizes that she's pregnant again. At first, she's as excited as Louis. She likes the thought of another baby growing inside her, and she hopes for another boy. But she soon begins to worry. Before she's even showing, the rod in her leg starts to shift and her back feels like a dart board every time she stoops or lifts one of the kids. Something else seems wrong, too. She can't name it, but a dizzy sense pops behind her eyes and shoots into her ears. Her head throbs and often she loses balance. Nita tells Louis none of this; she doesn't want him fussing over her, and they'll have enough to worry about with more doctor bills. They'll need to get a bigger place, too. She refuses to raise three kids in a two-bedroom house. Anyway, if she practices, she can breathe her way through the bad moments.

By the time Nita is pregnant again, the town of Crowley has done a bit of growing and the neighborhood has begun to change shape as well. Together, Nita, Louis, Marc, and Jo walk to the new A&P, and to the Dairy Queen, and they also walk to the Ferris wheel and bumper cars of the once-a-year Rice Festival. Crowley now dominates an area of several dozen miles, and people drive in from surrounding parishes to buy their *boudin* from the little wood shacks that line the main boulevard during the festival. The old men in those shacks guard a secret mix of rice, pork, cayenne, and paprika. "Blood sausage is made elsewhere," Louis tells his kids, "but in Crowley it's the real thing: *boudin.*"

Each year, when they walk to the festival, they circle the yellowing marble of the courthouse steps to reach the grandstand. Then Louis and Jo split off to find big blue clouds of cotton candy as Nita and Marc carry flat-headed candied apples on a stick. Electric generators hum like stationary lawn mowers and barkers call out from the shade of their tin-roof buildings:

"Step right up, *cher*. Eat your weight in watermelon!"

"Don't be *honte,* no! Get your fortune told by a bona fide Voodoo Queen."

"Ooo-wee! You talk about good eating, *hein?* This is it! Ya'll haven't had gumbo like this!"

"Two in the hole, I said two in the hole, gets you a stuffed alligator! Three gets you the stuffed animal of your choice and a free round to boot!"

"*Ils sont partis,* and they're off! Neck and neck in the open, it's *Bonne Rêve* and *Clotille's Chance . . .*"

The words of the barkers echo through Louis' head and he welcomes the mix of sounds. As they shout, the harder consonants are sometimes lopped off altogether, or an "H" is added to the next word in order to soften the blow, so that what the barker says sounds like "stuffed hanimal" and "halligator." Extra articles and syllables are added, too, seemingly at random, so that "halligator" becomes "hallimagator" and "tickets" becomes "les tickets."

At times, the Cajun they speak follows a mix of rules from French and English, and at other times it seems to obey no rules at all.

Both Louis' parents speak Cajun, of course, but he doesn't see them often anymore and, when he does, they speak only English to him. They never taught Cajun to him at home and it wasn't taught in school. Maybe Cajun is something that can't be taught or maybe they didn't want him to learn. Or maybe they were somehow ashamed. Louis' father once told him how he was forced into "American" school at age nine, not knowing a lick of English. Everytime he asked a question in Cajun, the teacher made him sit in the corner, with his nose in a circle of chalk. Sometimes she rapped his knuckles with a cypress board filled with holes. Louis Sr. was a quick study, though. He finished near the top of his class and learned to speak English with a thin, if choppy, accent.

When he was growing up, Louis' mother and father often spoke Cajun to each other, especially if they didn't want to be understood, but they never spoke it to him or his brother. Still, Cajun was in the air, on the radio, in the dance halls and jukeboxes, even on the football field, and Louis picked up enough to miss speaking it now. Nita never lets Louis talk Cajun to Marc and he only speaks it to Jo when they're alone. Even then, his phrases get chopped up with English and Louis wonders if words can disappear when you don't use them.

Louis walks past the festival stands with Jo and he feels as if all around there's a secret language being spoken. To his ears, everything with the Cajun barkers is an exclamation or a question mark and Jo claps her hands when they shout at everyone on the street to "Pass a good time!" as if it was something in the air that you could catch and throw to someone else.

After checking out the row of games and food booths, Louis

and Jo usually meet up with Nita and Marc near the bottom of the courthouse steps. Together they walk around the rest of the festival, and Nita lets Marc have the end of her candied apple after he's finished his own. The whizz of rocket whistles and the crack of pop guns are all around them as boys win crystal fish bowls and genuine NBA-style basketballs. Kids scream as the Ferris wheel stops for a moment at the top of its arc. A burst of air from one of the rides twists a swirl of wrappers into a miniature tornado. And always, at the end of the day, the Rice Festival Queen is crowned in a long train of green and gold sequins. Louis lifts Jo onto his shoulders and he squeezes Nita's hand as the queen waves, and he thinks there's no more exciting town than Crowley and no better place than by Nita's side.

Still, with a population just nudging twenty thousand, Crowley remains small and Nita begins to complain that the town is pressing in on her. "You can drive from one end to the other in five minutes," she says. "Now what kind of town is that?"

Nita also complains about the neighborhood. She says the lots are too small, the houses built too close together, and even the rooms in their house are too cramped. She has a painted box her grandmother gave her that opens to reveal ever smaller versions of itself. Every time Nita opens the front door to step inside, she says their house looks more and more like that box. More than anything, though, Nita worries about Mockingbird Lane and what's happening to the neighborhood. Dr. Marcantel and his family moved away practically overnight. Now there's an old Camaro jacked up on cinder blocks where the doctor's El Dorado used to sit, and she saw someone's kid running around in the front yard with nothing but a diaper on. She warns Louis it's time to move. "I don't know what'll happen to these kids," she says, "if we don't get out before the niggers move in."

Louis agrees to the move out of Mockingbird Lane, but Nita can't find the house she imagines, or at least she can't find a three-bedroom they can afford. She can't stay put, though, so she tells him she wants to rent another house until he can get an advance on his salary from work. Louis worries that even with his salary as an office manager, a new house will stretch the budget a little too far. But when he tells Nita this, she stops eating again, or at least she stops eating whole meals at dinner. He begs her to have a little jambalaya or a chicken wing or even a tater tot, and Jo and Marc beg along with him. But she refuses and says she wants them to eat; she'll wait for the new house. Finally, the wait gets to be too much and Nita screams at Louis, "This house is getting me down!"

And she means it in some kind of real way. Barely more than three months after Nita gets pregnant, she has one of her throbbing dizzy spells and falls from a ladder. She lands hard on the linoleum, on her side, and almost immediately she knows it: she's lost the baby. Louis rushes her to the emergency room at American Legion, but her mourning begins before they reach the hospital. As the paramedics lift her onto the canvas stretcher, Nita feels a sharp light burst in her head, followed by a dark swirl in her stomach. Hollow, she thinks, I'm hollow now. And a long wail tears out of her mouth before she passes out.

When Nita wakes, the surgery is over and the doctor tells her what she already knew. The baby is dead; the boy is dead. I knew it, she thinks, I knew it was a boy. She wants to see him, to see her son, but the doctor shakes his head and says no. Louis stands at her side, rubbing her arm and saying something that sounds like Peg. Who is he talking about? she wonders. Who's Peg? Then she hears the doctor say "steel pin" and she understands he's talking about the rod in her leg. When she landed on her side, the rod pierced through the skin, so they took it out at the same time as the baby. Now she has a long line of stitches down her thigh to mark the fall, to mark the loss of her little boy. Louis turns to say something to her, but she covers her face with her hands and cries herself to sleep again.

At home, Nita cries hysterically for several more days. When Louis gets back from work, he finds her curled up in a ball on their bed, her long black hair shooting out across a pillow. He tugs on the end of her nightgown, but she doesn't hear him when he calls her name. He sends Marc and Jo in with a pecan praline, then with a box of her favorite chocolate-covered cherries, but she won't take it. Nita won't eat anything at all, and she doesn't even change her gown. She just keeps shaking her head, saying over and over, "My baby, my baby." Louis starts to wonder if there's something wrong with his wife, and he thinks of calling someone. Bootsy? His father? But he decides against it; she's probably just exhausted, just nervous, that's all.

Eventually Nita leaves the bed and Louis tells her that he's found a rental house in an older neighborhood. The place may not be what she's hoping for, but he figures it'll get them out of Mockingbird Lane until they can find something better. Just before Christmas, they move into the new house and begin to unpack. Nita sees a page of holiday decorations in a magazine and she tries to conjure the sense of winter with fake snow on the windows and tinsel everywhere. She sews a sequined skirt for the Christmas tree and hangs stockings with everyone's name in glitter up on the wall. But as hard as she tries, she can't block out the row of banana trees and bamboo shoots that spring up outside the French doors of their living room, and a trace of summer heat lingers long into December. Still, as Christmas nears, Nita talks more and more about Santa Claus. Her eyes get wide and her brows lift as she tells Marc and Jo how wonderful Santa is and how he'll fill the house with presents and candy and how he'll stuff their stockings with special prizes. "You only have to be good," she says, "and he'll come. You'll see, Santa will come."

5

AS SOON AS WINTER IS OVER, LOUIS AND NITA TAKE
Marc and Jo driving to look for a new house. They ride up and
down the streets of Crowley again, sometimes seeing homes
they've looked at two or three times before. Nita is always fascinated by the houses that don't sell. Are they somehow cursed? she
wonders. Did someone throw a bag of *gris-gris* on the front porch,
or wave a black chicken over the doorway?

One house intrigues her more than any other. A huge creamy
house made of stone with red terra-cotta tiles and chocolate
brown slats running crisscross on all four sides. There's a glassed-
in room over the garage, which makes the back side look like a
carriage house. Two magnolia trees lean toward the driveway and
honeysuckle vines lace their way through the high planks of the
cypress fence. A rainbow-colored snow cone stand sits across the

street and Ruddock's bakery is just a couple of blocks away, so Nita calls the place "The Gingerbread House." She imagines having expensive dinners in the glass room: caviar and escargot, with those long slender glasses of champagne she's seen on TV. So much classier than crawfish and beer, she thinks. There'd be lots of fancy people standing around and maybe even a *negresse* for a maid . . .

"Number Four-thirty-six." Louis breaks into Nita's daydream. "This must be it." Nita peers out of the car and at first she's not impressed with the house she sees. The roof is too green and its peak is way too high, like the old broken-down Acadian shacks that line the bayou roads. But as Nita looks closer, she sees that the house is not at all broken-down. The grass is freshly mowed and there's a new coat of paint on the shutters, which are cream-colored to offset the pink bricks. And the house sits on a corner; that's good luck, or so her grandmother says. Nita steps out of the car and nearly falls into a shallow ditch that runs the length of the lot. Once she regains her footing, she spots a mimosa tree that stands on the side of the house. The branches are heavy with the weight of pink and red blossoms and the trunk leans away from the roof, as if it was trying to make its way to the street. Nita turns to Marc and Jo in the backseat and shouts, "Will you look at that? It looks as pretty as a commercial!"

She clucks her tongue, then runs across the yard to pick one of the soft spindly blossoms. Nita cradles the flower in her hand, then brings it back to the car for the kids to touch. Jo puts her hand out and almost knocks the mimosa to the ground. "Be careful, it's delicate!" Nita says as she draws the blossom back toward her. "The best flowers always fall apart in your hand."

Jo tucks her hands under her arms and sulks. To the floor mat she says, "I wanna touch the flower! I wanna touch the flower!"

But Nita ignores her and turns back to face the house. There's a concrete cylinder that rises from the corner of the lot like a stunted skyscraper. "N. Ave. L" is engraved on two sides of the cylinder and Nita claps her hands in front of her face and says it's the classiest street sign she's ever seen. Louis grins at her delight and honks the horn twice before Nita hushes him with a finger to her lips. "Shhh," she says in a loud whisper, "don't make such a fuss! The neighbors'll think we just escaped from the projects!"

He laughs, but keeps his hands in his lap. "If you want the house, Boo," he says, "it's yours."

Louis's already gotten a raise at his new job and the boss is talking about a promotion, too, so he says he can probably make the down payment on the house. They haven't even seen the inside yet, but Nita's mind is already made up. "Perfect," she says, "it's gonna be perfect."

For a while, it seems she's right. After they move into the house, Louis watches as Nita cooks up a frenzy in the kitchen. She lays out the clear pig's casing for *boudin* and grinds up her own pork and rice. She buys fresh jumbo shrimp and stuffs them with crab meat and bread crumbs. She makes the rich creamy pink sauce for crawfish *étouffée* and chops up the spear-shaped peppers for *maque choux,* a spicy Chitimacha Indian dish with corn and stewed tomatoes. Every night at the dinner table, Nita eats a full plate and serves Louis as many seconds as he wants.

She also teaches herself how to make other kinds of food from magazines like *Southern Living* and *Good Housekeeping.* She learns how to bake her first lasagne and how to fry egg rolls and white corn enchiladas. Louis eats the new food, but doesn't much like it.

One night, he pushes his empty plate away and tells Nita that the egg rolls are just a Chinaman's burrito. "*Mais* me," he says, "all

I need's a good gumbo. Now *that's* good eatin'! This Chink food's probably gonna make my eyes slant or my head shrink."

Nita stares at him for a moment and laughs. Then she turns to Marc and says, "I don't know about you, but if I can't see the world, I'm at least gonna taste it!"

Louis understands right away that his wife sees him as a fool. She almost never laughs at his jokes, and even when she does, she rolls her eyes and pinches her nose as if someone squashed a stink bug in front of her face. If he makes a fart joke, Nita plugs her ears and runs from the room. "I won't listen to that kind of talk," she says, "it's filthy!"

Louis wishes his wife weren't so serious, so proper. She seems constantly worried about what other people think, which he doesn't understand since they visit no one and no one visits them. Sometimes, she makes him think of his own mother, the way she always has her hands in a bucket of bleach or a sinkful of soapy water. He wonders if she laughs when he's at work, if she throws down the mop and runs outside to dance in the ditch.

Though Nita never stops cleaning, there are days, whole days, when she almost forgets she's married to Louis. In the morning, when the heat outside is not yet visible against the cement driveway, she stretches her arms out and twirls with the kids to kick up their own tiny series of breezes. "A monsoon!" she tells them, without really knowing what a monsoon might be (it's a word she heard her father say once in a joke that had something to do with a raccoon). "A monsoon!" she yells, and Marc, and even Jo, yell along with her, "A monsoon!" And in the dizzy excitement, Nita sometimes forgets that these are her kids, that she's not a kid herself, twirling in the breeze.

But there are other days, longer days, when Nita finds it hard

to leave the bed and make it to the kitchen. The sight of Louis in
the morning unsettles her. She wishes he weren't so clownlike, so
goofy. She watches as he talks and talks, but says nothing to her.
More often than not, what he says falls to the floor and she leaves
it lying there, not wanting to pick it up. She doesn't want to hear
about Boudreaux and Thibodeaux and their adventures in the
bayou. She doesn't want to talk about Bootsy's rifle or Bootsy's El
Camino. Louis never excites her with a new topic or a new idea.
He never says, What do you think about a trip to Mexico? Or even
a drive to Grand Isle? He never offers to rub her back, crick her
neck, or make breakfast for a change. Once, she saw a man brush
a woman's hair in a commercial and thought, Louis's never
brushed *my* hair.

And all he does is eat. Five or six eggs, a tall stack of pancakes,
half a pack of bacon, and sometimes that's not enough. Louis
grabs a pecan roll or a piece of divinity for the road. He's grown a
potbelly that he rubs like a magic lantern before rising from the
table. He seems proud of the extra weight, as if he won it in a contest, or surprised, as if he discovered it lying around his waist for
the first time this morning. But Louis' belly disturbs Nita. She
thinks of the men in the projects who walked around with their
pants hung low on their hips and their shirt unbuttoned or riding
up past their navel to reveal a hairy watermelon. Nita always
swore she wouldn't end up with one of those men. Now she listens as her husband sits in his La-Z-Boy and complains of "Dun-
lap" disease to the kids. "My belly," he tells them, "it done fall over
my lap."

When Louis enters their bed at night, with his pajama top undone, Nita sees those men in the projects and turns her head
toward the wall. As he slides off his bottoms, she pictures the red
elastic marks around his waist and his swollen belly and hairy

chest that look more and more like a gorilla's face to her. Her eyes tear up, sometimes, as she searches for an excuse: "I'm tired" or "*Please,* not tonight." If he pushes, she relents. But then she lets her mind wander to escape his hard touch, his quick hand.

Louis thinks Nita is still upset about the miscarriage, so most nights he doesn't push. He lies next to his wife in bed and watches the rise and fall of her back as she sleeps. Two kids, he thinks, she gave birth to two kids with that pin in her leg. In the hospital, he wanted to tell Nita how sorry he was that he hadn't noticed the trouble with her back. He wanted to say it didn't matter that she lost the baby, that they still had Marc and Jo, and each other. But he was silenced by her tears and her endless crying in the night. Even now, Louis's not sure what to say when he sees a glistening in the corner of Nita's eyes. What can I say? he wonders. What does she *want* me to say?

Soon, Nita becomes restless again. She complains to Louis about Mrs. Vidrine, a plump old lady who lives two doors down in a wood house that shed its paint and several rows of shingles years ago. From time to time, some of the shingles fall to the ground and Mrs. Vidrine's husband throws them in a *pirogue,* an old dugout canoe cut from the trunk of a cypress tree, that he keeps in the backyard. When the pirogue becomes full, the shingles lie where they fall, like blank dominoes scattered across the front yard. Outside, the old lady wears giant floral moo-moos, and bread wrappers around her shoes. And she's always hollering from her house to Nita, "*Viens-wa-ci, chère!* Come over! Come over!"

But Nita doesn't like going over to her house. A smell of mothballs and damp wool hangs in the air, and Mrs. Vidrine only wants to talk about what life was like on the bayou *aux vieux temps.* How it was better before Huey Long, that crooked carpetbagging governor from way upstate. ("Of course he was from upstate," she tells Nita, "practically a damn Yankee!") Yes, it was better before he laid down those highways and the cars started rolling through and everyone started speaking English. *"C'était meilleur,"* she says again and again, *"Meilleur mille fois."*

Half the time, Nita has no idea what the old lady is saying. Her voice gets thick and scratchy as she slips into Cajun. Then her husband walks in to sit on the visquine-covered couch, and place his long hands next to Nita's leg. His fingernails are long and sharp, too, like her stepdad's, and a line of grease clings to the creases in his neck. Nita can't help thinking that this is what she was trying to get away from, that she moved into this neighborhood only to find a little piece of Jennings half a block away. After a while, she stops answering when Mrs. Vidrine hollers across her porch. She just waves and turns back indoors. Nita also forbids Marc and Jo ever to go into the old lady's yard, warning in a low voice, "She's not clean." And she warns Louis that houses are like apples; it takes just one rotten house to spoil the whole neighborhood.

But it's not just one, Nita realizes after a long walk with the kids. There's also a row of houses five blocks away that she says is so run down, "it might as well be the projects." Nita says those people ought to take a tip from her and do a little redecorating. She's put silver-and-gold-flocked wallpaper in the living room and has wainscoted Marc's bedroom. She's also added frosted globes and dimmers on all the lights throughout the house, and painted and retiled the bathroom.

"And I did it all by myself," she reminds her kids, "with almost no help from your father!" Nita bought magazines to search for ideas, then told Louis what she needed from the hardware store. She made most of the changes while he was at work and Marc and Jo played outside. Sometimes she called Marc in if she needed help with a sheet of wallpaper, or if she wanted to move the plastic visquine she used to catch the paint drippings. As her hand glided up and down with the paintbrush, she started to feel something that she hadn't felt since the miscarriage: she could do almost anything, if she tried, and she could do it without Louis' help.

Now that Nita has the house looking the way she wants it, she tells Louis that she hates living so close to such beat-up shacks. And she doesn't want Marc hanging around the boys who live there. "They're too rough," she says. "They play in the street like a bunch of little hoodlums."

Louis thinks Nita is exaggerating about the neighborhood. After all, a psychiatrist from American Legion hospital lives across the street. Louis met him one morning when he left early for work. He also heard the school principal and a C.P.A. live nearby. No, Louis is sure that Nita is exaggerating until she tells him about the moving van that pulls up one afternoon, full of furniture and a whole nigger family ready to move in a few houses down. "I counted five kids," she says, "five."

"Damn niggers," Louis says, before agreeing that it's time to sell. Even though he hasn't paid off the house yet, he tells Nita they might make a little money since Crowley is still growing and she put so much work into redecorating the place.

The day before a final deal on the house is to be signed, Nita makes a tray of pecan pralines and heavenly hash for Marc and Jo. She carries the tray outside and onto the front porch. "It's Mosquito Patrol Day," she tells the kids. "We'd better eat these up before that nasty old truck comes rolling through." Nita presses her lips together and makes a buzzing sound and Marc and Jo buzz along with her. The marshmallow from the hash is gooey and the kids laugh as they stretch it out in long twisting lines.

Although it's late fall, the air remains hot and humid, and Nita feels a delta of sweat forming on her back. Mosquitos buzz around her head and she slaps at the ones that bite her neck. They always seem angrier than usual on Mosquito Patrol Day, as if they know that black truck is coming with its yellow and gray clouds of pesticide. And they always cling to Nita's neck and the sweet-orange of her *Toujours Moi* perfume.

Before the kids finish their pralines and hash, a cool breeze blows into the yard, followed by a series of stronger and stronger winds. And after supper, it cools down so much that most everyone on the block sits on their porches or walks to the edge of their lawns. Nita lets Jo twirl outside in the wind and she serves Louis glass after glass of iced tea. She tells Marc that the house will be sold tomorrow and that with the money they'll get a better place. "This night," she says to Louis, "is like a sure sign that the deal will go off without a hitch."

After they go to bed, the winds quickly build to a low roar and finally to a high whine. Louis wakes up several times and hears the branches of the mimosa tree scratching against the window, as if the tree were trying to get into the house. Around midnight, the winds beat against the screen and he wakes up again. The metallic screech sounds like a train running next to their house, with its wheels scraping off the bricks. The high pitch hurts his ears and he covers them with his hands. He starts to call out for Nita, but before he opens his mouth, the buzzing, black funnel of a tornado rushes by their window. He hears the groan of wood and an explosion that rings out like a giant echo. Then the bottom of the funnel lifts into the air and rips the roof right off the house.

When Nita wakes, the first thing she sees is all the mud and dirt splattered on the wall. She's sure that she's done something wrong and that her stepdad is going to be furious, until she sees

her robe on the floor and she realizes that she's in Crowley, not
Jennings. Nita almost feels relieved, but then she looks up to see a
thick bunch of branches swirling over her head, where the roof
used to be. The winds whistle and she thinks she hears someone
screaming. There's a space in the bed next to her and Nita starts
to tremble. Where's Louis? Where's Marc and Jo?

Louis has gone down the hall to check on the house. But before he makes it to the end, the tornado dips back down to sweep
through the living room, kitchen, carport, and breakfast corner,
sucking half their house into the air before smashing it to pieces.
This isn't happening, Louis thinks, it's not happening, as he
presses his hands against the walls of the hallway and a cold sheet
of rain falls on his face.

In the bedroom, Nita looks out the window and watches as
the tornado shreds the top of the mimosa tree. The branches
crack as they're sucked into the air. Then the trunk is plucked out
of the ground and hurled past the window. The juniper bush from
the garden flies by, too. Then it flies back and twirls in the air before being snapped to bits.

Nita's crying by the time Louis reaches the room. She's crying
and calling out his name. "I'm right here," Louis yells, "I'm right
here." He puts out his hand and she takes it. Everywhere around
them, there's the high brittle sound of glass shattering and wood
splitting. And through it all, they both hear a fast angry buzz.
Across the street, telephone wires and utility lines sway and snap
and the crackle of live electricity explodes in their ears as they run
toward the kids' rooms.

Marc is scared and shivering with his head under a pillow
when they reach him. He ducked before the window burst and
smashed against the opposite wall. Little shards of glass cling to
his skin, but none of the cuts are deep. Nita hears her own

strained voice as she screams with excitement, "Thank God! Thank God!" And Louis lifts Marc off the bed before she takes him in her arms and presses him to her body.

The next sound Louis hears is Jo's voice crying from her room. She's hurt, he thinks, she's alive, but she's hurt. He runs with Marc and Nita down the hall to find Jo curled in a ball under her bed. A stream of tears runs down her face, and she holds a few tufts of hair in her hand, but she's not hurt. Louis kisses her cheeks and Nita puts Marc down to wipe Jo's face. Louis says, "We're all here." Then, as if he can't believe it, he shakes his head and says again, "We're all here."

6

HAND IN HAND WITH MARC AND JO, NITA AND LOUIS work their way though the house, stumbling and sometimes dropping to all fours. Even when they stumble, they try to keep their hands together, as if the tornado was going to drop down again to suck one of them into the air.

Louis leads the way toward the place where their living room was. The floor of the hall is covered with overturned tables and broken bits of glass, and they crawl over a twisted mattress and a TV that's been hurled into the doorway. They walk barefoot over scattered Tupperware and over drenched curtains and a toppled fridge. They step around one half of the plaid couch and crawl over the La-Z-Boy that sits in the middle of the room, on top of the hurricane door. They crawl over a coffee table, past garden tools, and under a canopy that covers the spot where the back door used to be. Not one of them suffers a scratch as they make it over the mangled threshold.

Every other house on the block is wrecked by the tornado— except one. It stands in perfect shape and doesn't even have a busted-out window. "Passed right over us," the Castilles say as they welcome Nita and Louis. To Nita, as soon as they enter, it seems as if the tornado never happened. Mrs. Castille leads her to a stone fireplace, then treats Marc and Jo to hot cocoa with mini marshmallows and gives them heavy wool blankets to wrap their feet. She tells Nita that she feels like a nurse at Dr. Castille's hospital. "Of course I don't have a clue as to what a psychiatric nurse might do." She laughs out loud and Nita laughs with her, though she doesn't really understand what Mrs. Castille means.

She doesn't know why exactly, but she feels easy with this woman. She looks at her blonde teased-out hair, at her small pink lips and silk robe, and remembers that she herself must look frightening. Nita's hair is matted to her head, she has no makeup on, and her terry-cloth nightgown is tattered from all the crawling around. She feels embarrassed, so she lets her eyes wander around the kitchen. She sees copper pots and copper pans and giant copper spoons hanging from the roof, from some sort of floating chrome island. Mrs. Castille has a separate hutch to showcase all the dishes she bought in the twenty-eight states she's visited. "It's supposed to light up," she tells Nita. "Course nothing electric is gonna light up tonight!"

Mrs. Castille doesn't talk like the old Cajun ladies she knows, and she doesn't sound anything like Mrs. Vidrine. Nita's not surprised when she finds out that Mrs. Castille is from Texas. "Beaumont," she says, "though that's practically Louisiana."

And Mrs. Castille works for the phone company, even though she has a twelve-year-old son. Nita's never met anyone from

Texas, and she's never met any woman who worked. "He doesn't mind?" Nita asks her. "Your husband, I mean."

"Oh Lord, no," she says, "he thinks if I didn't work, I'd probably go crazy!"

Every few minutes, Dr. Castille opens the door to grant a tour of the Miracle House to awestruck neighbors. Nita watches as the men walk through the house in a hush, with both hands cupped behind their back. They try to laugh off the tornado and tell stories about the tornados and hurricanes their parents lived through. "I'm talking forty-foot waves," she hears Louis say as he tells them about his parents and Hurricane Audrey.

Some of the other men talk about Hurricane Camille, which swept the Mississippi coast just a couple years before and tore through a hotel famous for its annual hurricane parties. They laugh and say, "If we had known this was coming, we would've thrown a party!" Then they shake their heads from side to side and manage to say "Thank you" or *"Merci"* to Dr. Castille before walking back out toward the street.

To Louis, the women seem anxious. He watches as they try to calm each other. Some of them smooth their hair in the hallway mirror and tell each other not to worry, then carry cups of cocoa to their kids. Louis wanders into the kitchen for a cup of cocoa for himself and asks Nita if she's seen Marc and Jo. "Your daughter's nodded off on the couch," Mrs. Castille says, "and your son is with Paul—my son—in his room."

Louis thinks maybe he should check on Marc, but decides against it. Instead, he walks over to the couch and stares at Jo, who's wedged herself between two cushions. *Pauv' bébé,* he thinks as he rejoins the men to ask if they've heard about the time Boudreaux and Thibodeaux were caught in a hurricane on the bayou with nothing but a toilet seat and a pair of ladies' gloves . . .

Louis! Nita thinks and almost says, these people are from *Texas*. They don't want to hear about Boudreaux and Thibodeaux.

But Louis goes on with the story, and by the time he's finished, a circle of men are slapping him on the back and Louis' face is red from laughter.

Most everyone on the street has family who live nearby. After warming up at the Castilles', they drive off to spend the rest of the night at a *nanaine*'s or *parrain*'s house. Even Mrs. Vidrine passes through the kitchen to say she's going to stay with family on the southside. But Nita and Louis have no family in Crowley, at least not that she knows. She still hasn't found where her father's living, and she doesn't want to drive to Iota in the middle of the night. "I don't want to wake your mother," she tells Louis when he asks what they should do.

"But, Boo," he says, "we have to do something."

"Stay here with us," Mrs. Castille offers. "The kids are resting, but none of us will be needing more sleep tonight."

Nita thanks Mrs. Castille and says maybe they'll stay just until morning, since daylight is only a few hours away. When Dr. Castille closes the door behind the last of the neighbors, he and Louis take up the two rockers in front of the fireplace. Then Mrs. Castille takes out the plates from the hutch and tells Nita about all her travels.

In the morning, before they can even figure out a way to call Iota, Louis' parents drive up in Mrs. Toussaint's four-door emerald-green Mercury. Nita is not at all surprised when Mrs. Toussaint barely says hello, but she is surprised by her excitement at seeing Pop. When he steps out of the car, Pop Toussaint flashes his big smile and throws a silver Hershey's Kiss her way. "*Mais,* I'll be jack-damned," he says, "I guess this is one way to see my kids."

Nita laughs and carefully slides the Kiss into the one pocket on her nightgown. Then she turns to watch as Mrs. Toussaint crosses

the street to busy herself in assessing what's left of the house.
Louis' mother shakes her head from side to side as she picks up a
warped Tupperware container. Its lid was pierced in the tornado
by a twig and she tugs on one end as if she might find a way to
mend the damage. Everywhere, there are scattered mud- and rain-
drenched clothes, and bricks with pine needles sticking out on all
four sides. Nita thinks the bricks look like petrified porcupines,
but she's afraid to say so, afraid that Mrs. Toussaint will think she's
not serious or that she's somehow responsible for this mess. Nita
is relieved when Louis decides not to comb through the house today. "Let's just get back to Iota," he says, "before we all pass out
like possums in the heat."

As they pile into the Mercury, Nita turns to thank Mrs.
Castille and realizes, for the first time, that the house is lost and
that they have no new place to go. She's angry at Louis now, angry
that he didn't listen to her, that he didn't sell the house sooner.
What are we gonna do for money? she worries. What are we
gonna do with a demolished house? And what will I do in Iota?
How long will we stay with Louis' mother? She falls silent as Pop
switches on the radio and they drive off to the high-pitched sounds
of an accordion and Cajun words fill the air around them. *"Comment
moi je va faire?"* the song asks. "How will I do? Always alone."

It's been a while since Nita's been to her in-laws' house, but
she sees right away that nothing has changed. The wide lawn still
spreads more than two acres around the house and looks as if it
was just mowed. Azalea bushes still gather in neat half circles in
the back of the house and a brick planter runs alongside the shell
driveway, which lies under the shade of a sprawling magnolia tree.
Inside, every inch of the house is still scrubbed, wiped, polished,
and rubbed to a high glossy sheen. There are ivys and ferns growing on marble stands, each plant trimmed and sprayed with a kind

of artificial dew. There are shelves and shelves of what Mrs. Toussaint calls her "Depression Glass and Curio Collection" and there's a row of antique china cups in the dining room, some marked Made In Occupied Japan.

Though the place is bigger than anywhere Nita's ever lived, the rooms quickly close up as Louis and Pop haul box after box from the wrecked house into the living room, dining room, and even the closed-in front porch that Mrs. Toussaint calls her "*foyer.*" Every time they put a new box on the floor, Nita and Louis' mother sit side by side with a bucket of warm bleach water between them. They scrub and save what they can—a toaster, a tin colander, a pile of T-shirts and socks—but they say almost nothing to each other. Even though none of what they wipe belongs to Mrs. Toussaint, Nita is especially careful not to break anything. She feels a pair of blue eyes on her hands as they go round in circles, and she feels the silence grow until it's no longer silence, but a low, steady roar.

Louis hears a low roar, too, but for him it's the sound of his father's silence. Louis Sr. cracks joke after joke with Nita and with the kids. He tells stories about a giant *crapaud,* a frog that lives in the gully behind their house and that he claims is so big he could eat a rabbit. He pushes Marc and Jo through the yard in a big blue wheelbarrow, and he lets them take turns sitting on his lap as he mows the acreage around the house with a small tractor from the farm. But he almost never talks to Louis' mother, and when Louis and his father drive to Crowley to pick up another load of boxes, they sit in silence, listening to the hum of the tires on the asphalt and the dueling fiddles on the radio.

"What's wrong, Pop?" Louis wants to ask. "What's wrong?" But he can't ever get the words into his mouth, so he turns to watch the rice fields and the barbed-wire fences as they rush by the window.

Only when they walk together in the one-street "downtown" of Iota does Louis' father seem like his old self. He flashes a big smile at the ladies in the post office. He shakes hands, slaps backs, and everyone he meets seems anxious to hear a word from him. "Louis," they say, "*quoi ça dit!* What's going on!"

His father may hesitate a moment, but then he reaches in and finds some story, some short little tale that makes even the older ladies laugh into their gloves. If Louis Sr. meets other farmers in the drugstore, someone dogged by a loan from the Farm Bureau or a good crop of beans gone bad, he lets his hand fall on their shoulder before telling them, *"Lâches pas la patate!"* (Louis always laughs to himself at the sound of the phrase. To the farmers it means, "Hang in there!" but the words actually say, "Don't let go the potato!")

Louis wishes his father could be this easy with him. Instead, he watches as Louis Sr. takes Marc by the hand for a ride in the Ranger, or for a tour of the white-washed oak trees and monkey-grass planters in the backyard. He buys Marc a new pair of Dingo boots and a straw cowboy hat to match his own. He even teaches the boy how to mop his forehead with a handkerchief when it's really hot, while he shouts *"Poo-yie!"* to everyone around.

Nita may not be crazy about all the Cajun her kids are picking up while they're in Iota. But she's glad Pop Toussaint takes to her son so easily. She doesn't even mind when he tries to show Marc how to shoot blackbirds out of a tree. Pop bought him a BB gun, but the boy is still too small to hold it on his own. So Pop crouches behind him to prop half the gun on his shoulder and wrap his finger around Marc's on the trigger. Nita cheers when a bird finally falls to the ground, and Mrs. Toussaint shrieks behind her, but says, "It'll be blackbird dressing tonight, if you shoot enough of those little vultures down!"

Pop impresses Nita most when he takes her and the kids on a tour of the farm. "Five hundred acres," he tells her, and she can't even picture what five hundred acres might look like. As they drive along gravel and limestone roads, she points to different spots on the land. "Is that yours?" she asks. "And how about that over there?"

Pop laughs and says, "Yes, *chère,* that's mine too." He gives M&Ms and Kisses to Marc and Jo, and always at the end of a drive he hands Nita a Kiss and all the coins he keeps in a tiny leather wallet.

Nita is proud of how Marc acts in Iota, following his paw-paw around, clopping his new boots on a rubber mat anytime he comes in or out of the house. Like a little man, she thinks, *my* little man.

But no matter how hard she tries, Nita can't keep Jo out of trouble. She topples a bougainvillea plant from its ceramic base on the back porch and, more often than not, she spills whatever she's eating all over Mrs. Toussaint's maplewood table. In the mornings, Nita struggles to get Jo in a dress. The girl shakes off her clothes to run through the house in her shorts or in a pair of quilted panties before Nita can catch up with her. "That's a *fille bête,* right there," Mrs. Toussaint says, not to her, but to the pot on the stove. "If you don't learn how to tame her, she'll grow into a little beast for sure."

She worries that Mrs. Toussaint is right. Each year, Jo seems to get wilder and wilder. Only two days ago, she broke a rocking horse that Pop gave to Marc. She bit the legs with her baby teeth and snapped one leg completely apart from the base. Louis actually laughed when he saw the tiny broken leg in her hand. He called her a "rodeo queen," but Marc burst into tears and Louis' mother hauled Jo outside for a beating with a fig branch. Jo's cries pierced through the bubbled panes of the window and Louis stormed out of the house for a drive in the Dart, while Mrs. Toussaint glared at Nita as if *she* was the one who broke the horse's leg.

Louis can't stand how his mother looks at Nita, and he's grown tired of her orders. Anna's started speaking to Nita now, but only to give her a command: move that chair out of the way, tell Jo to eat on the floor, move the broom side to side when you sweep, not back and forth—it's bad luck! Anna treats Nita like a maid, like a nigger woman for hire. She controls everything in the house and Louis' Pop does nothing about it. He just murmurs in agreement if she demands that the trees be whitewashed again or the roof be changed. *"Mais oui,"* he says as he cracks open another can of Dixie.

Louis almost can't believe it when he walks in the house after work one night to find Anna complaining to Pop about his wife. "She doesn't even know how to fold a towel right," he hears his mother say in a low, tight voice. "She leaves the ends hanging out, not tucked like they ought to be. She never puts my silver back in the right order, and I caught her wiping a cast-iron pot with a rag—a *cotton* rag—when everyone knows that a rag'll ruin the seasoning and leave your gumbo tasting like lint!"

Louis feels his ears begin to burn as he walks from the door to the kitchen. He's seen how hard Nita's worked while they've been here. He knows she's tried to do whatever Anna says. He's tired, damn tired of his mother's constant complaints. Nothing ever satisfies her, Louis thinks as he grips a large ring of keys in his hand.

Anna doesn't hear him walk up behind her, or if she does, she ignores him as she goes on, "And she can't control that girl, that *fille bête* runs around this house as if she was on a *courir de Mardi Gras!* What is she chasing all day long? Nita lets her act like she was some dirty river Cajun's kid, some *ya-ya*'s daughter. *C'est tout*— I've had it!"

Anna starts to slam her hand on the counter, but before she does, Louis' hand flies over her head as he throws the ring of keys against the kitchen window and a sharp cracking sound fills the air.

"She's *my* wife!" Louis shouts. "And Jo is *my* daughter—"

"And this is *my* house!" Anna shouts back, and that fact hits Louis' face like a fist. Everything he has to say, everything he's wanted to say to his mother rises up to his eyes and he starts to cry. He looks to his father for help, but Louis Sr. stays silent. So this is what she did, Louis thinks as he stares at the man whose name he carries, she silenced you. Louis imagines his father in that hospital bed, a whole year of not talking. "A nervous breakdown," he heard someone whisper at the time, and he tried to picture nerves actually breaking in his father's body, snapping apart like big black cables stretched too far.

She's not gonna silence *me,* Louis thinks, even as he stares at Anna with nothing but the heat of rage on his lips. "I've found a place," he announces suddenly, "I've found a place and we're moving out." And for the second time, Louis makes plans to leave his mother's house.

7

THE PLACE LOUIS FINDS IS A BRAND-NEW THREE-
bedroom house on the southside of Crowley. The house is made
up in a Spanish style, with sepia bricks and twin arches stretching
from the beveled wood and wrought-iron of the front door to the
curving half-wall of the two-car garage. The Spanish motif was
forgotten at the roof line, though. With its high peak, long slope,
and dark green tiles, the roof looks as if it was lifted by the tornado from an old Acadian cottage and then dropped suddenly into
its current spot.

Although it now faces the manicured mounds and artificial
lakes of Crowley's only golf course, the stretch of land under the
house once served as the low-lying bank of a small gully that people in the area call Bayou Bend. The bends were forced out of the
bayou, though, and the land was cut into tight, square lots, most

of which sit empty. The new neighborhood is expected to take off, Louis tells Nita, but it hasn't happened yet.

Giant water oaks, fat sugar pines, and a couple of magnolia trees still crowd the empty lots, and Spanish moss hangs from branches like stretched-out lace doilies or a string of petrified cobwebs. Nita likes the deserted feel of the street and the fact that there will be no nosy Mrs. Vidrines or crazy neighbors peeping out of their windows and inviting her kids over to play. "Just imagine," she says as she twirls in the fluorescent glow of the kitchen, "we'll have the street to ourselves and our own personal golf course, too." To Nita, the Bayou Bend golf course means a step up from their old house and, to Louis, that step seems to carry her to a new place of contentment.

She cooks again, making all Louis' favorite dishes, even all the Cajun food he loves. In the morning, he follows the smell of Steen's cane syrup to the kitchen as Nita makes *pain perdu,* lost bread, the way it's supposed to be made, with thick slices of stale bread, eggs, nutmeg, milk, and lots of sugar. He watches as she dips the slices of bread in the bowl, then drops them into a pan sizzling with oil. The bread fries up crisp on the outside, forming something of a crust, and stays soft and gooey on the inside. "You talk about good eating!" he says, as he reaches for another slice. "This is it!"

Louis' salary has grown more comfortable, so at first he doesn't complain when Nita fills the cabinets with what he says is enough food to survive two nuclear blasts, in addition to another tornado or hurricane. Nor does he complain when she throws herself (and his checkbook) into decorating the new house. She orders jade-green deep-shag carpets for the floors and a long curving sectional sofa that she calls "Mediterranean." She buys ceramic cherubs and paints them gold and orders a marble coffee table and a hutch for the living room. "Green and gold," he hears her tell Marc, "that's our color scheme. Green and gold, the color of hope and sunshine!"

The color of money and money! Louis thinks, but doesn't say. He's glad he insured the last house so well, and that the buyers didn't back out after the tornado. Of course, he didn't get full value on the place, but he still made what he considered a nice profit. So why not let Nita have a little fun?

Louis likes watching her eyes grow wide as the doorbell rings and a catalog-delivery man hauls in another shrink-wrapped package or a long carboard tube. She starts humming Fats Domino songs as she rips into box after box. If she's really excited, she sings a song that raises Louis' brow and fills his ears. "I know time goes by so slowly," she sings, "and time can do so much. . . . Are you still mine?" He tries to catch her eye as the words tumble out of her mouth, but she looks away, and for all he can tell, she's singing to the wall.

Nita once heard her father sing that song to her mother. "Unchained Melody," he called it, a song he'd heard on the radio in New York. The tune sticks in her head as she polishes the glass drops on the electric chandelier in their bedroom. She twists a plastic knob and the metallic candles flicker high and low. Nita nods her head in approval, but decides the window needs a valence and the walls need flocked paper. "Then this room will really glow!" she tells Louis, and he tries not to add up the cost in his head.

Within a few months, Nita has the house looking so good that Louis decides to invite his parents for a visit. Though he's been avoiding Iota and he's still angry at his mother, he wants to show off the house and his wife's handiwork, so he plans a barbecue for the very next weekend.

When Sunday comes and the green Mercury pulls up to the driveway, Marc and Jo race outside to wave at their paw-paw. Louis watches as Pop hands a full bag of Kisses to each of the kids, before reaching back into the car for a rhinestone-studded shirt for Marc and a pair of metal roller skates for Jo. Pop clicks his fingers in the air, then magically draws a tiny silver key from his ear. "For the skates, *'ti' chère,*" he whispers to Jo.

As Marc gazes at the stones in his shirt and locks his fingers in his paw-paw's hands, Louis turns to look at his mother, who is already taking a self-guided tour of the long S-shaped flower bed in the front yard. He's surprised to find her approving of what she sees. "White verbenas," she says. "I've always loved white verbenas. And you have junipers, too!" Then she squints her eyes and asks, "You're giving them enough water in this heat?"

When Louis says yes, she just nods her head and continues her survey, swatting away mosquitos, but not stopping until she inspects every bud on every plant in the bed. By the time she's done, Pop and the kids have already gone inside the house and Louis' shirt has a ring of sweat around the neck and each arm. Anna pats at her forehead with a kerchief in one hand and shoos away a mud dauber with the other. When the wasp bounces off her gloved finger only to circle Louis' nose, she laughs out loud and he laughs with her. Let it be easy, he thinks, let it be just like this.

But when Anna enters the house, he sees her face pinch up and her feet jump back as if she just happened into a roomful of sour milk. *"Poo-yie!"* she says. "What's that smell?"

And Nita, who's been standing in the kitchen stuffing alligator meat into casing, instantly feels ashamed. Too much ammonia, she knew it even before Mrs. Toussaint said anything. Nita got so worried when Louis told her of the barbecue that she scrubbed nearly every inch of the already clean house. She tried lighting a votive candle earlier, but a cloud of ammonia still hangs in the air and now Louis' mother stares at her with a look that says, *You* married *my* son?

Mrs. Toussaint claps her hands together once, then leads herself on another tour, this time examining Nita's work in each room of the house. "Eww!" she says again and again. "So much gold!" And although Nita doesn't answer, Mrs. Toussaint asks about every lamp in the living room and every painting on the wall, "Now why did you put that *there?*"

Later, when Nita goes to the bathroom, she finds a row of painted harlequins reversed and a lamp moved from one side of her bedroom to the other. She's furious that Mrs. Toussaint would touch her things, but worries that maybe Louis' mother is right, maybe she doesn't know how to decorate or clean, maybe she doesn't know how to do anything at all.

As everyone gathers around the table for Mrs. Toussaint to say the blessing, Nita worries that the alligator sausage will be too tough and that the "dirty rice" will be too salty from the ground meat, too soggy on the bottom, or too full of onion tops. Did she take out the biscuits in time? Did she put enough bacon in the purple hull peas? Nita is so worried that she barely notices Pop helping himself to plate after plate and loudly munching his approval. But she does notice the triumphant look in Mrs. Toussaint's eyes when she stares at the seam in Nita's dress and catches a small string that's come undone. Louis' mother leans over to twist and yank the string between two fingernails. "Should've used a crossstitch!" she says, with her finger to the ceiling. And Nita suddenly feels like she's in school again, with a crowd of kids laughing at her bare feet.

After supper, Mrs. Toussaint places both hands on the table and announces that it's time to go. While his wife tugs on her gloves, Pop slips a Kiss and a pocketful of coins in Nita's hand and whispers, "Your house looks *belle, chère, très belle*." Then he pats Louis on the back and says out loud, "*Mon fils,* you've got one hell of a real Cajun cook!"

Louis is relieved when the Mercury pulls out of the driveway and Pop honks goodbye. All throughout supper, he kept staring at his mother, trying to hold her eye. He's furious at Anna and can't figure out what she has against his wife—no, he *knows* what she has against Nita, but it makes no sense to him. Why can't his mother see how amazing his wife is? She can stuff *boudin* or fry an egg roll, lay a carpet or hang wallpaper. On her own, she learned how to découpage and cut out patterns for the kids' clothes. She's a good cook, a *great* cook; he doesn't need his father to tell him that. And, well, she has those dark eyes and that soft little mouth that he wants to kiss much more often than he does.

At night, now, Nita doesn't resist Louis. She lets him roll onto her side of the bed, even though she still dreads his touch and the pained look that crosses over his face. She's grateful at least that it's always over in a hurry and that he sleeps like a drunk man. She lies awake while everyone else is asleep, picturing a certain room of the house and thinking how she might improve it somehow, maybe add another mirror or paint the gold to silver. These maneuvers calm Nita and keep her from thinking about her back, which has started to throb again.

That throbbing is sometimes so intense that she can't see anything but a blazing light between her eyes. If she's mixing a batter or scrubbing the floor, a jolting nerve can shake her until she thinks she's falling. Even if she's sitting on the ground, her feet quiver and her hands tense up before flopping about in search of something to grip. Nita squeezes a scrub brush or a wooden spoon until the light dims and the pain passes out of her back. In those moments, she's sure that everything in her life is wrong, that everything she's done—*is* doing—is hopelessly wrong. She married the wrong man, moved to the wrong city. Even her kids seem wrong somehow. And Nita's mood, the weight in her head, never lightens until she pictures her father touching her, calling her by her full name, Bonita, Bonita Ray.

Nita tells Louis none of this, of course. He would just fuss over her, calling her Boo and Baby, and—worse—he might tell Pop and Mrs. Toussaint. Nita doesn't want Louis' parents thinking she's some nutty swamp Cajun, full of complaints and mysterious ailments that no real doctor ever heard of. The steel rod in her leg is gone; there's no reason why her back should hurt or why that light should pop behind her eyes. She's glad, though, that the phantom pain never lasts for long and that she can hide it from Louis and the kids.

If Marc and Jo are nearby, Louis pretends not to notice Nita's bad moments. He cracks a fart joke or tells the kids a *ti' cont* about wolves who can not only swim, but who paddle through the bayou in stolen pirogues. But if the kids are outside or in their rooms, Louis watches Nita as she grips the countertop and arches her back like a cat. He longs to help her in some way, but can't figure out what to do, how to touch her, what to say. So he falls into silence and studies the curled tab from the beer in his hand. As the local news enters his ears with the weight of fuzz, Louis thinks maybe he can talk to Nita in bed, maybe he can press himself against her back and rub the place where she hurts. He thinks this until Maria Placier, the blonde anchor, stares at the camera to say, "Good night, Acadiana," and he heads off to bed alone.

Later, when Nita crawls under the covers beside him, Louis tries pressing against her. Sometimes she lets him hold her for long stretches; whole minutes tick by as he breathes in her sweet-orange smell. But she squirms away if he holds her too long or if he rubs a tender spot on her back. And during the day, she talks more to Marc than to him. So Louis turns his attention more and more to Jo. When he comes home from work, Jo runs into his arms and he twirls her over his head. Then she leads him by the hand into her room, where she shows him whatever sprawling mess she's managed to create for the day. Louis praises each tiny disaster. He shakes his head and says, "Now, don't tell me a three-year-old *'ti' fille* did all this by herself?" as he stares at a half-collapsed pile of Lincoln Logs or a mess of Pick-Up Sticks scattered across the floor.

Jo looks at Louis with doubt in her eyes. She seems to need her father to realize the bayou shack or cow barn she's made. As he puts it, she's already a skeptic, certain only that whatever she's tried to do has come out wrong. So Louis's careful not to correct her. He doesn't try to show her how she could build a stronger base for the shack, or how it's better to find two logs that match than to snap one in half. Instead, he smiles at his daughter's work and calls her his little architect.

Louis is so caught up with Jo that he barely notices the nearly perfect drawings Marc makes. And he never even plays with the boy, so Nita takes it upon herself to teach her son what he needs to know. She props him up on the toilet in the morning as she teases her hair out with a comb. She talks in a low voice to Marc, as if he was her secret confidant, and makes him cover his mouth while she sprays a sticky cloud of Aqua Net. After Nita steps into one of her pink and blue pantsuits, she relies on his opinion: "A scarf or the velvet choker?"

While Marc hesitates in a moment of grave consideration, Nita squints at the mirror and catches sight of her son's perfectly pressed pants and the high buff on his Buster Brown shoes. She turns around to run a finger through his hair. And while she waits for him to speak, she's struck by his blue eyes. A deep, watery blue that stares back at her without blinking. Nita recognizes something in her son's eyes and feels a warmth settle just beneath her skin. This boy is mine, she thinks, and even if the thought reminds her of the boy she lost, she can't resist a smile in the face of Marc's seriousness. "So," she asks again, "what's it gonna be?"

With a furrowed brow, he says, "The choker?"

"The choker it is!" she answers back. Then, in a low voice she tells Marc she's decided to give him prekindergarten lessons. "You'll get a head start," she says, "you'll be one step ahead of the other kids."

Nita reads to Marc and has already taught him the alphabet and all of his numbers up to one hundred. But now she starts giving her son tests from a book she bought on spelling and reading. She stands him before a blackboard in the kitchen and calls out words for him to spell. Then she reads stories to him from a stack of Golden Books: *Dumbo, Bambi,* and *The Blown-Around Room.* She makes him answer questions about the books, and when he gets one wrong she puts an *X* on the board and makes him listen to it again. "Listen close," she says, *"listen."*

Marc catches on quickly, so quickly that Nita begins to imagine that her son will not only make it all the way through high school, but on to college too. And then maybe he'll study to be a doctor, she thinks, or a lawyer. And maybe he'll move to a real city, some place with a mall like Lafayette or even New Orleans . . .

Then, bang! Almost without fail, Jo knocks down some remote shelf and breaks up Nita's thought. That girl never wants to sit in on the lessons with Marc. Instead she plays with her logs and sticks until she gets bored and finds something to climb. At some point, she falls or the thing she climbs on falls, and out from her mouth emerges a long and angry wail. Nita tries to calm Jo, to make her sit still, but she always squirms away. Finally, the crashes and the crying become too much for Nita. She slaps a ruler against the blackboard or slams a book to the floor. "That does it!" she screams, as she chases her daughter from room to room. When Nita catches her, she shakes Jo into silence, then plants her in a corner on her knees. Her cries become loud sobs, which don't subside until Louis comes home. Then, she calls his name over and over again, "Daddy! Daddy!" Nita is almost certain that Jo throws these tantrums on purpose, that her daughter is trying to make her break.

When he finds Jo on her knees, Louis picks her up and holds her in his lap. He doesn't ask what she might've done wrong or why she's upset. Instead, he tells her a story about a French-speaking crawfish from Bogalusa, before he tickles her into laughter.

Louis wonders why Jo's so wild when he's gone, and he thinks Nita is too hard on the girl. She's made charts out of construction paper and posted them on each of the kids' doors. Each chart has a calendar on it and each day has a box. If she decides Marc and Jo have been good for the day, she gives them a gold star or a yellow smiley face. But if they make a mess or break something, they get a red-devil sticker. Marc's door practically glitters with all the yellow and gold on it, but Jo's door is covered with row after row of red-devil faces. She's only three, Louis thinks, there's no way she can be that bad.

I try, Nita tells herself, I really try to make that girl behave. Nita buys her daughter the kind of clothes she only dreamed of when she was a kid. She buys Jo buckled white shoes and lacy white tights that clip to her panties. Nothing I had was white, Nita thinks, nothing. All her clothes were handmade from the same old yellow *cotonnade* her mother bought from some lady in Jennings.

"Made in Louisiana," the old lady liked to remind her mother, "harvested right there in Alexandria." Nita refuses to buy *coton-nade* for Jo. Even when she can't afford a more expensive store-bought dress, she buys satin and lace and real cotton and sews a dress with seams and a hem so perfect that no one would know it didn't come off a rack. Jo's clothes practically gleam from the closet, and Nita tries to curl her daughter's hair like a Victorian doll's. "Hold still," Nita fusses as she brushes out the tangles. "Hold still," she says, until Jo kicks her and races from the room.

Jo runs from perfume bottles and hair spray as if they were cans of Raid, and she always dirties whatever dress Nita chooses for her. If there's a puddle outside, Jo sits in it. Once she even raised the lid to the toilet and stepped into the bleach-scented wa-ter with her patent-leather shoes. She splashed around until the lacy trim of her dress puckered and her tights sagged. Nita chased her through the house and out the back door and stopped shout-ing only when she heard a door slam across the street and a light popped behind her eyes. "Now you've done it!" she hissed at Jo. "Now you've really done it! That lady's gonna think I'm as crazy as a mosquito in the dead of winter!" Then she grabbed her daugh-ter's lace collar and tugged her into the house.

With Marc's clothes, Nita follows Pop Toussaint's lead. She buys him quilted cowboy shirts with Sears Toughskins jeans. And she dresses him in Dingo boots with small silver harnesses. One afternoon, a photographer spots Marc in the Piggly-Wiggly and asks Nita if she would let the boy pose for him in his Western wear. His picture will go in the newspaper, he says, and Nita gets so excited that she forgets what she's been shopping for.

The day of the photo shoot, she polishes Marc's boots and straightens the cowlick in his hair with a little hair spray, and tries to ignore Jo's constant crying. As the photographer aims the camera at Marc, Nita's son looks straight ahead with a carton of milk next to him and a tiny plastic horse. When the shoot is finished, the photographer claps his hand on Marc's shoulder and tells Nita, "Perfect!" And when the milk ad runs the next week in *The Crowley Daily Advertiser,* Nita thinks, At least I have this much, a perfect son.

8

THE SAME WEEK THAT MARC'S AD APPEARS IN THE PA-per, Nita discovers a line of crumbling old pinewood apartments jacked up on concrete pilings less than half a mile from where she lives. Without hearing it from anyone, Nita knows right away that she's stumbled on a row of project houses, and she's not the least bit happy about it: What was Louis thinking when he bought this place? Didn't he know he should check out the neighborhood first? She's glad the apartments are concealed by a bramble of bamboo, banana trees, and cat-o'-nine-tails, but what if some nigger kid finds his way onto her front porch? Or, worse, what if Marc and Jo find their way into the projects? Get snatched up by some outlaw with a sawed-off shotgun?

Then——sitting right across from the projects——Nita spies an old abandoned cemetery. As she puts it, all those broken-down graves and overgrown vines send a shiver down her back. She whips herself into such a worried frenzy that she can't wait for Louis to come home. She calls him at work to tell him it's time to move.

"Are you kidding me?" Nita hears Louis' voice rise into the receiver. "We just got settled."

"*You* may be settled," she says, "but I'm not. I can't be, not knowing there's a row of niggers and a cemetery just around the corner."

"They're not around the corner, Boo," Louis says, "they're half a mile away."

Boo, Nita thinks, *Boo.*

"And we can't afford to move again, not with everything we just put into the house."

"Then I'll get a job," she decides and declares at the same time, "I'll go to work if I have to, but I will *not* stay in this nigger-infested neighborhood and I will not have my kids running around some project street!"

At once, Louis feels torn between his anger at Nita for speaking to him like this, especially when he's at work, and his anger at the fact of the projects. He's never seen a nigger family around, but if one showed up in Bayou Bend, he knows there'd be a run from the houses and all the prices would drop like a drunk man in the Louisiana heat. Still, he can't afford a move and there's no way he's gonna let his wife work. Louis remembers what Bootsy once told him, "Only Yankees and niggers put their wives in the field!" And he readies himself to tell Nita exactly that, but his boss enters the room, so instead he says in a tight whisper, "I've gotta go. We'll talk tonight."

Nita is too frustrated and angry to cook supper, so she defrosts four meat pies she made earlier in the week, along with leftover *maque choux*. I'll show him, Nita thinks as she sets the table with fury. I'll show him. I'll get a job and make my own money. I'll get us out of this place, maybe even out of this town. Though at first she was glad to get out of Iota and back to Crowley, the little town has started to squeeze itself around her again until she thinks she might choke. Nita wants out of Crowley, out of Acadiana. She wants to live in a new place, without accordions and sad music and old ladies telling each other old stories in French.

As soon as Louis walks through the door, she hits him with her plan. "I'll work at the phone company," she tells him, "just like Mrs. Castille. But I won't stay in this house. I won't."

Louis takes a long breath. After Nita called, he sat at his desk stewing. Did she even realize how much money he'd spent on the new house? Did she know there was no genie in the bottle, no voodoo queen paying their note every month? Nothing seems to make Nita happy, not for long at least. He's tired and doesn't feel up to this fight, but he folds his arms across his chest and gives her a sharp look. "I'll tell you one thing," he says, preparing the line he's practiced all afternoon, "I am *not* a nigger and I am *not* a Yankee and no wife of mine is ever gonna work."

"I'll work," Nita says, "I'll get a job. Even if I have to scrub other people's floors or wash cars, I'll find a way to get us out of this place!"

Suddenly Louis knows just what to say. He slides one hand in his pocket and rubs his fingers against his keys as if they were a deck of marked cards. He lets his chest fill with air before letting his words loose. "Then tell me, who's gonna drive you there? *Who?* 'Cause it won't be me!"

To hammer his point, Louis slams two fists on the counter and stares Nita down with flared nostrils, waiting for her retort.

But Nita has no answer, no comeback. Even before the slam of Louis' fists, she felt her plan slip out from under her. She hadn't thought about the car. In her mind, the job came easily; there was no need to go out and get it. But Louis's right: they still have only the Dart and she can't work without a car of her own. She's trapped in this house, just like her mother, with nothing but cooking and cleaning and kids who'll soon be in school. Marc starts kindergarten in the fall and what's she gonna do then?

Nita decides to run away. She'll take the kids and leave Louis with the cooking and the laundry and the vacuum cleaner. She'll call her mother in the morning and figure out a way to get to Jennings. But for now, she stops speaking to Louis.

"Good pies," he says after supper, glad that the fight was short and that for once he won. But Nita just pulls her lips tight against each other and stares into tomorrow.

The next day, she finds her mother at home and in a rare good mood. Buford walked out on her again several weeks ago, but— *grâce à Dieu!*—he's back, and now he's got a job as an oil hand, working seven on seven off . . .

Nita holds her breath and thinks, Buford! I forgot about Buford! She can't go back to Jennings, not with *him* there. She can practically hear his scratchy voice cawing in her ear, *"Mais,* what's wrong, *chère,* can't make it on your own? Gotta come running back to Mama?"

But if she can't go back, where can she go? Nita thinks of her older sister, Vina Lee, who has a house in the Mermentau woods. Then her mother begins a long story about how Vina Lee tried to kill herself, ran her husband's pickup into a pine tree and now he's left her, but it's really for the best since she always thought he had *le sang maudit.* "More than once," Gilda says, "Vina Lee came home to find a dried frog right on top their bed, and I don't have to tell you what *that* means!"

Then Nita's mother goes on to talk about Monetta Lou, Nita's younger sister, who plucks her eyebrows and wears miniskirts so short that she gets sent home from school practically every day. She has two boys over, Ti-Joe Gautreaux and Mike-Bob Robin, they go into her room for hours and play that nigger music and when Buford hears it he gets so *fâché* his face turns purple. . . .

Nita puts the warm end of the phone against her neck and remembers why she stopped calling her mother. Gilda always launches into a litany of complaints, and if Nita tries to break in with a complaint of her own, Gilda shushes her. "Be glad you *have* a husband," she says, before she goes on to talk about how she's been having those spells again and how her ears sometimes ring . . .

When Nita finally hangs up the phone, the throbbing in her back becomes so intense that she crawls into bed and stays there until Louis comes home. At the sound of the door, she rises to peel a sinkful of shrimp. But she blocks out the sound of Louis' voice in her ears, that prickle at the base of her spine, and instead she pretends she's a chef in a four-star restaurant somewhere in Texas, Houston maybe. If she tries hard enough, she can block out the sound of Jo's screams, too, and the word buzzing in her head, "Daddy! Daddy!"

Not all of her days are bad. In fact, Nita often plays games with Marc and Jo when Louis's at work. Together, they play Simon Says, I Spy (her favorite), and Red Light, Green Light. If the mosquitos are quiet and a rare breeze kicks up outside, Nita takes Marc and Jo for a long walk by the golf course, where she tells them fantastic stories about all the places she's never been. Marc's eyes light up when she describes a city or a country outside Louisiana, and even Jo pays attention to the sound of the Spanish names that Nita learned from her father: *burrito, cerveza, corazón; di-ablo, Dios, margarita.* She smiles when Marc calls her "Margarita Nita," the ring of the words so much softer, *cleaner,* than Cajun.

Nita even makes a game of scrubbing floors and washing walls. She arms Marc and Jo with toothbrushes and spends hours showing them how to scrub room after room of baseboards. "Up and down," she says, "not back and forth. Pretend that you're brushing the wall's teeth."

And when Jo shouts, "Walls don't have teeth!" Nita sucks in her lips and gums out her response, "Then how do they talk?" She laughs and Marc and Jo laugh along with her, and the high sound of their voices fills the room.

But more and more of Nita's days end with her back throbbing, her head pressed against a pillow, and the curtains drawn. At night when Louis lies next to her, she stiffens her limbs and holds her breath, trying to make him think she's fallen asleep. She can't bear the thought of his weight on top of her, his red face and quick hard jabs between her legs. She gives him no reason now; she just pulls away from his touch or ignores his hand on her leg. If I keep my eyes closed, Nita thinks, he'll go away.

But Louis doesn't go away. He stays next to Nita with his nose pressed to her pillow and the scent of her hair rising and falling with his breath. Louis worries that he's scared his wife somehow. Was he too hard on her? Maybe he shouldn't have yelled and slammed his fists. Nita still makes breakfast and supper and packs his lunch, but she barely talks to him now. In fact, she hardly looks at him. Even when he pushes himself inside her, she clamps her eyes shut or looks past him at the ceiling or the wall or the closed door (he's never sure exactly *what* she's looking at; he only knows it's not him). Her silence pulls at him until he aches and decides he must be doing something wrong.

To Nita, it seems as if Louis' only real concern is Jo. He dotes on that girl until Nita begins to worry. She thinks Louis' mother is right: Jo is a wild girl and Louis's only making her worse. During the day, Nita tries to keep both Jo and Marc inside the house, afraid they might run into trouble if she lets them out alone (she pictures them falling into a ditch, being bitten by a water moccasin or cottonmouth snake, or running smack into two men, hulking black men with nets). "You never know what kind of crazies are out there," she says, "just waiting to pounce on two little kids!"

But as soon as Louis comes home, he lets Jo run out into the yard, where she searches for stray golf balls from the putting green across the road. He watches as she tries bouncing those balls on the front porch or stuffing them into the crawfish holes that dot the front lawn like dirt chimneys. Louis loves watching Jo run in circles with her arms spread out. A smile breaks out from the corner of her mouth, and he thinks that his daughter looks like a doll-shaped version of Nita. Even though he knows his wife can't stand to see Jo dirty, he lets her play with Zsa Zsa, the neighbor's balding Pomeranian. He lets Jo cradle the tiny dog in her arms, rub the blue satin ribbon on its head, and he laughs as it slobbers and sheds its hair on her dress.

Nita shrieks when—again and again—she sees her daughter's red velvet dress coated with dog hair. And she feels her blood surge when Jo walks to the skinny bayou that runs behind the house and steps right into the muddy edge as if it wasn't there. Jo's white patent-leather shoes are forever coated in black bayou gum, and Nita has to scrub her tights by hand to get the stains out. But when Nita tries punishing Jo, putting her on her knees in a corner, or grounding her inside, Louis tells her to get up, that it's okay, that she's done nothing wrong.

One afternoon before Louis gets home, as Nita makes a batch of gooey pralines for Marc and Jo, she hears the hurricane door bang shut and she knows Jo's run outside again. She slams the wooden spoon against the counter and runs out to the front lawn and, when she steps out into the buzzing heat, she can't believe what she sees: Jo has raised her skirt over her stomach and her hands are shoved in her panties. Nita's own hands shake and she fights back a scream. She can't believe Jo would shame her like this, that she would run around the front yard with her skirt up and her stomach hanging out like some project kid, some little *negresse* with pigtails and a potbelly. Why can't that girl behave? *Why?*

Already sweating from the heat, Nita feels the taste of salt at the corner of her mouth. "Get in this house!" she yells at Jo. "Get in here and tell me exactly what kind of filth is going on!"

When Jo walks into the kitchen, Nita screams, "What the hell are you doing with your hands down your panties? And in front of all the neighbors, too!"

Jo stays silent, which only makes Nita's fury boil higher. "Answer me! Answer me!" she screams before bringing her hand down hard and fast against the girl's cheek. As soon as Nita feels the sting in her own palm, something inside her snaps. She's gotta teach this girl a lesson! She runs toward the bedroom, searching Louis' chest of drawers for a belt, but then a memory flashes in her head and she runs back to the kitchen to pull out a ten-pound sack of rice from the mill where Louis works. Nita drags a knife across the top of the sack, just as Buford used to do. She tilts the sack forward, spreading rice on the floor next to Jo. Then she makes her daughter strip to her panties to kneel on the hard kernels. "And you can stay there!" she screams. "Until your father comes home!"

Throughout all this, Jo pinches up her face and remains silent. But as soon as Louis walks in the door, she lets loose a long wail and races for his arms. She cries and cries while he plucks the rice kernels from her knees and Nita thinks, I give up, I just give up.

The next day, as she boils water for spaghetti, she spies Jo in the living room scratching at the place between her legs again. Nita shouts, "That does it!" She throws down the tin colander and screams at Jo to get in the kitchen. Then she shakes Jo and shouts, "When will you learn? When will you learn how to act right?"

Nita wraps her arm around Jo's waist, then lifts her up and holds her hand over the boiling water on the stove. She thinks of Louis and how he's always letting Jo off the hook. She feels that light burst behind her eyes again and her spine twitches from her neck down to the small of her back, but she doesn't let go of Jo.

"Hot!" Jo cries as she tries to fight her way out of Nita's arms, "It's hot!"

The steam from the pot rises and the water gurgles loudly as Nita shakes her head back and forth, screaming, "Filth! Filth! Filth!" Nita's hair falls from the weight of the steam and sticks to the side of her face. She can feel her makeup begin to run, and the thought of black tears streaming down her face only makes her angrier. Her voice rises and she yells "Filth!" once more as she shoves Jo's hand into the water. Jo screams and her face twists up in pain and her cheeks are covered in tears. "Please, Mama!" she cries. "Please!"

Nita takes Jo's hand out of the water and presses it against the girl's panties. "Don't ever let me catch you touching yourself again!" she shouts. "Not ever!"

Then she opens the door to the freezer and puts Jo's red hand against the chill of the ice tray. But her hand keeps sticking, and Nita finally lets it sit under a stream of cold water in the sink.

A few minutes later, Louis walks in the door from work. He sees Jo on the floor crying and thinks, Not again, not *again*. He looks at her hand, which is still red and now swelling and he feels like he's going to cry, too. But he doesn't cry and he doesn't ask Nita what happened. He just presses his hand to his eyes and, in a low whisper, says, "We've gotta get her to the hospital."

Louis drives the Dodge Dart as if it was his old Falcon. He ignores red lights and stop signs and keeps the flashers on. His hands turn white as he grips the wheel and his jaw keeps moving back and forth. He says nothing to Nita and she says nothing to him. The only sound in the car is the high pitch of Jo's sobbing, then the low echo of Marc's sobs along with hers.

When they get to the hospital and check into the emergency room, a nurse asks what happened. Louis looks at Nita, then with his lips tight against his teeth, he says, "My daughter burned herself." When the nurse asks how old Jo is, Louis quietly says, "Three." But when she pulls out a form and asks him to complete it, he slams his hand on the counter and says somebody better see his daughter *and quick*.

Right away, they're shown to a curtained-off area and Louis lifts Jo onto the single bed. She's still crying and he stares at Nita and shakes his head. Nita bites her lip and puts her hand up against her mouth. She taps her foot against the floor and the silence around them keeps getting bigger.

Louis is only slightly relieved when the doctor enters to examine Jo's hand. After a quick look, he says the burn is second degree. The doctor gives Louis some salve, which he rubs on Jo's hand when they get home. He sits Jo in his lap, coos in her ear, and sings a few bars of *"Saut' Crapaud"* about a frog who burned its tail in a fire. *"Prends courage,"* Louis sings, "be brave and your tail will grow back."

Even while he sings, he's furious at Nita, furious that she would hurt Jo like this. But he's afraid to say anything because if he opens his mouth, he'll let loose a raging storm: he'll shout at his wife until he turns purple and there's already been enough shouting in the house. No, he doesn't want to shout, but he doesn't want to talk either. So he just pulls Jo closer and continues the song.

Despite Nita's warning and despite the burn on her hand, Jo keeps scratching between her legs. Nita catches her doing it again and again until she finally decides to bring her to another doctor. Louis leaves Nita the car and hitches a ride from one of the other men at the mill. All day, his thoughts run in tight little circles, tracing the outlines of his wife and daughter.

That night, Nita tells Louis that Jo needs surgery. "She's too small," Nita says. "She can't pee right, so it burns and makes a rash between her legs."

Also that night, Nita cries, not to Louis, but alone in the shower. She thinks of the burn on her daughter's hand and scrubs her own skin until it's raw, scrubs it as if she was scrubbing the kitchen counter or a dirty baseboard.

Jo goes into the hospital the next week for an hour-long operation. Nita holds her daughter in the room before surgery. She pushes Jo's hair out of her eyes and says, "I'm sorry, baby." She kisses her on the forehead and looks at Louis.

"I was in the hospital before I married your father," she says. "I was stuck in that room for almost a whole year."

Then she turns back to Jo and says, "You'll be all right, you're my little girl."

As soon as she's back home, Nita serves Jo all her meals in bed. Every supper for a week she makes Jo's favorite: fried shrimp with creole mustard and Mexican corn bread with ketchup. Jo likes to stir up the two sauces and mash her shrimp in with the corn bread and Nita lets her be as messy as she wants.

For weeks after, she plays with Jo in the living room, or sometimes on the porch outside. She teaches her daughter to play Hopscotch and jump rope and she reads her nursery rhymes as well. Jo repeats one to Louis about an Itsy Bitsy Spider and one about a girl who was made of sugar and spice and everything nice. Her eyes widen when she tells Louis that rhyme and she says, "Me, too. Mama says I'm made of sugar and spice."

AFTER MARC ENTERS KINDERGARTEN, NITA FEELS A hole well up inside her. He's only gone for half a day, four days a week, but while he's gone she feels lost. She tries plunging her hands in a bucket of bleach to wipe down the windowsills or reading Golden Books to Jo, but she ends up chasing her daughter through the house, out the front door, and halfway onto the golf course to smack her for some new offense: a broken bowl, black stains on the carpet, a ripped-up pair of tights.

Before the end of the school year, Marc wins highest honors in Mrs. Broussard's *Maison de Memoirs,* the best kindergarten in town, and Nita bakes a seven-layer dobérge cake topped with a sizzling sparkler. But even as she beams at the picture in the paper, the shot of her six-year-old boy with a rolled-up diploma in his hand, she feels an odd surge in her head. What'll she do when he's in school all day long, every day, when she's trapped in this house, when he doesn't even need afternoon lessons anymore?

Nita's bored, bored and restless, and she thinks again of getting out of this town, this house. Maybe a trip away would cure the throbbing in her back or lift the cloud that's settled in her head. But Louis never wants to go anywhere, not even Iota and certainly not Jennings. She asks him to take her on a vacation or a weekend trip, but he tells her no again and again. Finally she jerks her hair up with her hands and screams, "I'll go mad in this house, do you hear me? Mad!"

When Nita asks Louis for a vacation, he flinches. He doesn't want to tell her no and he definitely doesn't want to tell her why. After all the decorating and redecorating, and after all the hospital bills, his checking account is as dry as a pile of burnt rice chaff. He could afford a trip to Iota or Jennings, it's true, but he doesn't want to go near either place. Anyway, what's wrong with Crowley? he thinks. What's wrong with where we're at?

Week after week, month after month, Nita hits him with her request and he finds himself struggling not to snap at her with a hot tongue. But then once—and, as he puts it, against his will— he loses it completely.

Louis comes home from work on a sweltering Friday night, after a long afternoon spent out of the air-conditioned office on a loading dock. The foreman was shorthanded, so Louis climbed on top a Caterpillar forklift to push burlap sacks filled with short-grain rice from one end of the warehouse to another. By the time he finished, even the back of his knees were dripping sweat. Yet when he walks in the front door, dinner is not on the table or on the stove, and Nita shouts at him, "The kids have eaten, but if you're hungry try boiling an egg!"

Louis stares at his wife, but says nothing. He can feel his throat tighten and his eyes cloud over, but he says not one word as Nita swears she's not cooking again, not in this house, and not until she gets beyond the Crowley city limits. When Louis still doesn't answer, Nita softens a bit. "Please," she says, "please, can we go away?"

Here it is, Louis thinks, the moment he's prayed for: Nita pleading with him, Nita wanting something, anything, from him. Here's the moment he wishes he could put his hand out to her hair, whisper, I'm sorry, Boo, I'm sorry. But the heat of the day, the heat of the warehouse, hasn't left him. He feels it crackle on his skin as he smashes his hand against the wall and kicks a leg out from a chair before screaming, "No! No! And *fuck* no!"

That Fuck No! reverberates throughout the house for weeks after. Nita stops speaking to Louis, and he can't even get near her in bed. He wakes, showers, and leaves the house before she wakes now. He stays late at work, bucking for a bonus, a raise, a promotion, some way to give Nita what she wants. When Louis comes home, he finds supper on the stove and Jo at his feet. But if he tries to catch Nita's eye at the table, she turns away. He feels as if a thick sheet of visquine hangs between him and his wife, as if they are separated by a shadowy plastic curtain.

In fact, Nita only seems happy when Marc brings home a new report card. Every six weeks, the boy scores a string of A's, and Nita fills the kitchen with pecan pralines, heavenly hash, and long squares of divinity fudge. She runs in circles though the house, cheering and shouting as if their son ran forty yards to win the homecoming game, or as if she herself won the column of A's in a raffle. Louis likes watching Nita's excitement grow as her eyes once again trace the vertical lines on the report card. He likes watching her mouth open like a small purse as the laugh of a little girl tumbles out. Louis likes watching his wife until he remembers that her laugh, her cheers, have nothing to do with him really. He's not even sure if he could make her as happy as this, if he could give her what Marc delivers without fail.

The joy Nita finds in Marc's report card almost keeps her from thinking about the trouble with her back—that throbbing, that low traveling pulse never goes away now—and about the trouble with Jo. The girl seems to get worse and worse with each passing week. Nita finds her running outside in her panties for all the neighbors to see, or sitting in the backyard, scooping mud into her mouth as if it was a fistful of fudge. More than once, she's had to wash Jo's mouth out with soap—at five, she already answers Nita with a sassy tongue. If Nita tells her to take a bath or go to her room, Jo just tucks her hands under her arms and screams, "No!" "I don't wanna!" or "Shut up!"

She makes faces at Nita, too, ugly distorted faces, with her tongue hanging out and her nostrils flared like a tiny bull's. Marc never made faces at her; he never bit her either. Yet when she backs Jo into a corner to get her dressed, that girl scratches, claws, and bites her way out of Nita's hold and into the next room. She runs away from me, Nita thinks, my own daughter runs away from me.

And Louis doesn't help any. He's always telling Jo what a sweet girl she is, calling her an angel, his *jolie blon'*. He never calls Nita *jolie,* never says anything to her about how she looks. She might as well stay in a bathrobe and leave curlers in her hair, she thinks. Why go through all the fuss when the only man who looks at her doesn't even notice?

Sometimes, the two troubles mix, Nita's throbbing back and Jo's wild streak, and the lights in Nita's head buzz and snap until she finds herself screaming at Jo with the tail end of a leather belt in her hand. Was she hitting her with the buckle? Was she hitting her with the tail? The leather is warm and her hands sting and for whole minutes she can't remember exactly why she's been spanking Jo, what made her go for the belt. The TV, the radio, the pattering rain outside all fall mute. The only sound Nita can make out is Jo's high-pitched scream in her ear, "Mommy! Mommy!" and her own low sobs. When Jo lets her, Nita takes the girl in her arms and together they cry until the sound of the rain returns and the burn in their skin begins to cool.

Nita and Louis haven't gone to church in weeks, maybe months. They never talk about it, but Sundays come and go now without the ring of St. Michael's iron bell or the drone of Father Préjean's voice floating overhead. Still, Nita prays. She prays to feel right again, for her back to ease up, for her head to clear. She prays, bent over her side of the bed, always the same prayer: please let me find a way out, let me find a way, a way . . .

In the middle of one of her prayers, the phone rings and when Nita picks up she finds Marc's teacher on the other end. Nita's thoughts are still so tangled, she blurts out, "What's wrong? What has he done?" before she realizes it's Marc the woman is talking about. Nita speaks calmly to the teacher, carefully pronouncing her words and trying not to sound like some Cajun hick. Yes, Nita says, she knows how well he's doing. Yes, she'd be happy to come in to discuss placing him a year ahead. But even as she speaks, she feels her blood race and her face flush with pride.

After Nita hangs up the phone, she stares at her son as if he was a visitor from out of town. Or a package containing a handwritten answer to her prayers. My boy is that smart, she tells herself, One whole *year* ahead of the other kids! Nita thinks again about Marc in college, Marc as a doctor or lawyer, Marc as a senator, Marc as the governor or even——why not?——the President! She may be stuck in this house with a man she can hardly bear the sight of, she may not be able to work or go to school, but her boy is going someplace——she's sure of that.

Instead of moving Marc ahead, though, Nita decides to move him out of Betsy Ross altogether after she meets another mother in Marc's classroom, the mother of the boy who places right after Marc in every test and quiz, a black mother sitting with a black boy on her lap.

"A nigger!" Nita shrieks at Louis when he comes home from work. "A little nigger boy in the same classroom as our son!" Louis is surprised to find Nita speaking to him again, but he quickly gets caught up in her rage. "A nigger?" he asks as he shoves his hands in and out of his pocket, "a nigger?"

Though Louis' anger is almost as deep as Nita's, though he steams with the same fury as his father (who's told him more than once that niggers took over New Orleans and that they'll take over Crowley and Iota, too), though his hands are nearly raw from the tight fists he makes and unmakes, Louis also finds that he's glad to share something with Nita, glad that they can throw themselves at the same brick wall. He doesn't even argue when Nita insists on moving Marc from Betsy Ross to Our Lady of the Immaculate Heart, though now he has to scramble to find money for tuition and a uniform. "Goddamnit!" he shouts, hoping the force of his words will impress his wife. "A nigger? Next to my son?"

As Nita and Louis expect, there's not a single black student in all of Immaculate Heart. Still, Marc doesn't last long at the Catholic school, or at least Nita doesn't let him stay long. After he comes home one day with a red face and a purple mark on his arm, she discovers that one of the nuns smacked her son with a stalk of sugar cane just for correcting her spelling on the black-board. "No one," she tells Louis, "and I mean *no one* hits my son!"

Louis doesn't want to see his son hit either, so he agrees to move Marc back to Betsy Ross. But he can't figure out why Nita gets so upset about a nun smacking their son once when she smacks Jo almost every day. Louis's not around to see it, but when he comes home and calls for his daughter, he's not surprised to find some new mark on her arm, a bright purple welt next to a fading yellow bruise. Even on the hottest days, Nita dresses Jo in ankle-length skirts and long-sleeve blouses to hide the marks that scatter down her legs like swollen mosquito bites, or run down her arms like a row of bursting stars.

Jo even briefly stops talking to *him* when Nita enrolls her in kindergarten class six months later. She doesn't answer when Louis comes through the door and calls out hello. She doesn't laugh when he takes her in his lap and sings one of the old Cajun songs he knows: *Pauv' petit' Momzelle Zizi, elle a un bobo, un bobo dans son petit coeur,* Poor little Momzelle Zizi, She has a bobo, a bobo in her heart. (When Jo doesn't laugh, Louis thinks, *Bon!* A silent wife *and* a silent daughter. What am I gonna have to do? Learn sign language?) And Jo leads the kindergarten teacher—not Mrs. Brous-sard, whose entrance test she didn't pass—on daily runs through the backyard, around bushes and trees, and once through a hole in the fence. What is she trying to get away from? Louis worries. Where is she trying to get to?

When he's home, Jo causes no trouble that he can see. Or at least not the kind of trouble that calls for a beating with a belt, a branch, or whatever else Nita might grab when he's not around. Louis wants to ask his wife if she's embarrassed, if that's why she puts Jo in long sleeves. But he's afraid to anger her, or to stir up his own anger. He's also afraid to face another day—or week, or month—of silence. Some days, Louis is furious at Nita. Furious. But as soon as she steps behind the stove and ties an apron tight around her waist, as soon as he catches sight of the green fleck in her eye, Louis' fury loses direction and he becomes so confused that he doesn't even see where it's heading.

The first time Louis snaps at his son, he realizes too late that the boy didn't really do anything wrong. One night after dinner, Marc drops a bowl on the floor—by accident, Louis is sure—but the sound of the crack runs right through Louis' ears, as sharp and loud as if the bowl broke over his own head. "What the hell is wrong with you?" he shouts at Marc. "You think money grows on a goddamn tree? Who's gonna pay for a new bowl? *Who?*" Louis can hear his own voice in his head. He even thinks, What am I doing? *My mother* used to say that! Still, he has to walk out of the room to stop himself from smacking his son.

Louis doesn't hit Marc and he doesn't yell at him often, not while they live at Bayou Bend, but that's only because the boy never seems to do anything worth yelling about. Which leaves Louis wondering, What kind of kid is this? He's a boy: it's his job to get in trouble, to race around the house as if he was being chased by a mad swarm of mosquitos, to run outside in search of the nearest pit of oozing, oily mud. He should fail at least one test; he should stink in at least one subject. Instead, the A's pile up on Marc's report card like a stack of gold coins and Nita stares at their son as if he were a walking, talking column of white light. She's never shouted at Marc, not once. She's never whipped the boy, never even shaken him by the shoulders.

Soon, Louis finds that he nearly explodes when his son lets loose with a daily and endless series of questions. After every TV show, after every meal, on every drive through every part of town, down every aisle of every grocery store they enter, Marc poses one question after another: "Where does the light go when you turn off the TV?" "What makes the cake stand up in the oven?" "What's KSIG?" "What's a taco?" "What's cracklin'?" "Why do people eat the pig's toes?" "Why does the door open when you step on the black square?"

"Who cares?" Louis wants to yell. "Who gives a coon's ass about what makes a cake rise, what makes a door open?" Is the cake good? Does the door work? These are the things that matter, he wants to tell his son, don't bother with the rest. But he knows Nita would glare at him, just as he knows already that Marc is no longer his son, no longer his to guide, not in any way that really matters.

Usually Louis holds back: he tries to tune out Marc's voice, tune out all the questions. But one night just after he gets home from work, Louis doesn't hold back. As soon as he takes off his shoes and reaches for his slippers, the doorbell rings and Louis is surprised to find his father standing there, with a straw hat in his hand and without Louis' mother. Pop's hair is slicked back and Louis notices for the first time a streak of gray just over his father's left ear.

"Mais, quoi ça dit?" Pop says as he wipes his hands against the kind of one-piece zip-up suit that Iota farmers love to wear. "Cajun overalls," Louis once heard his father call them. Even in those overalls and even with that gray streak in his hair, Pop looks sharp and Louis is excited to see him. But before Louis can answer his father, Marc throws out a circle of questions and Louis slaps at the buzzing sound of his son's voice in his ear. "What? What? What?" Louis shouts. "Why? Why? Why? Stop it! Just stop it with all the frickin' questions!"

As soon as he finishes, Marc's eyes well with tears and Louis feels his own ears turn hot. He struggles for something to say, some apology, until his father speaks up.

"Can't learn nothing without asking, can you?" he says, "*Laisse-lui,* let him ask, let him ask." Then, instead of reaching out to Marc, Pop puts his hand out to Louis and squeezes his arm. His father's never touched him like this, and right away Louis wonders, "Is something wrong? Is Mama all right?"

But as they walk to the kitchen table, Pop tells Louis that everything's fine, *tous ça va,* that he's merely come with an offer.

"How'd you and Nita and the kids like to join your *mère* and me on a trip to Astroworld?" Pop says. "My treat?"

Louis stares at his father, not knowing what to say. He hasn't seen his parents in how long? Months, at least. Now, Pop wants them all to pile up in a car and drive to Houston, of all places. Actually, Louis thinks it's funny, that his father would finally take his mother on a vacation, and that it would be Texas! He thinks maybe they should go, just so he can watch his mother's face cringe. "Pee-yew!" he can hear her say as they cross the state line and she pinches up her nose.

Louis looks across the room at Marc and Jo, who are already jumping up and down, and he looks at Nita, whose eyes are practically glowing. He doesn't want their first vacation to happen this way. He wants to pay for a trip with his own money, to plan it himself. Louis worries about Nita, worries that his mother will treat her like a nigger maid who's lucky to be along for the ride. He worries about all this, but when he turns back to face his Pop, only one word makes its way out of his mouth.

"Sure," Louis says, and Nita takes the kids' hands to form a spinning circle on the carpet, and for the first time in a long while, he feels as if he made the right choice, as if he did the right thing.

As soon as Louis says yes to Astroworld, yes to a trip out of town, Nita feels her heart speed up and her hands fly into the air. She knew it, she knew the first time she saw Pop Toussaint that he would be the one to make everything all right. Nita thinks how a vacation will soothe her back, how it'll take her mind off Jo. And Texas? Texas! She'll finally make it to at least one place her father told her about. "Everything's big in Texas," he said, "even the toast." Nita imagines slices of bread bigger than a cast-iron pot, bigger than a cutting board or a kitchen table. She imagines Texas millionaires walking the streets of Houston with shiny boots and ten—no, twenty—gallon cowboy hats. She imagines rows and rows of gleaming stores, miles of shopping and restaurants. Not just Cajun food or steaks either, but places where you can order real Chinese egg rolls and Mexican enchiladas served on steaming plates. Places where a mariachi band strolls down the aisle, singing and shaking those painted sticks. And then there's Astroworld, all the rides, the roller coasters and carousels, the candied apples and the late-night shows. Nita is so wound up about the trip that she doesn't even worry about Louis' mother, or about how she might wear the cost of the trip over her head like a crown of thorns. No—as Nita puts it—her only worry is that she might not make it through the night without exploding from excitement.

By Friday, Louis's already approached his boss and set up the trip to Astroworld for the end of the next month. And Nita's packed and unpacked twice just so she can be in practice when the time comes.

In bed that night, Louis decides to try reaching out to Nita's side, to put his hand on her pillow, and when he does, she doesn't pull back or turn her head away. Instead, she turns to face him and a little light from the table lamp gets caught up in her hair. She even opens her mouth a bit and he wonders if he should kiss her. He puts his hand forward to touch the place where the light falls on her forehead, but before he reaches it, before he can bring his lips to hers, the phone rings.

As Louis draws his hand back from Nita's side of the bed and rises to find the receiver, he curses out loud. "Damn!" he shouts. "Damn!" He fumbles for a moment, then hears a muffled cry: his mother's voice cracks over the phone line and already Louis knows what she's about to say.

"It's your father." Louis can barely hear his mother's words. "He's been hurt." His ears go dead to the rest: something about an eighteen-wheeler and a drunk driver.

Louis's not even sure whether he says anything to Anna before he hangs up, whether he asks if she's all right. No, he can only hear the rattle of the Dart as the razed fields of rice and the burnt stretches of unused land run together. As Louis races to Iota, he's thinking of nothing but Pop's hand on his arm and how at this moment he wants to slip inside his father's embrace.

Before the phone rang, before Nita decided to let Louis touch her, she heard a low, steady humming in her ears. She heard that same sound the night Pop came to offer a trip away. And though she says nothing to Louis in the car, she knows what that sound meant. Already Nita knows it, she knows that Pop is dead.

Like her *grand-mère,* Nita can suddenly see what lies ahead. She can see the funeral home: the carefully arranged flowers, the hundreds of farmers lined up for a view of the closed coffin. She can hear Louis' shriek as the lid is opened for a moment and he gets a glimpse of his father's mangled body, of his distorted face. She can see Anna's face too, stern and fixed at the funeral home, but her lips keep quivering and her head won't stop shaking. Nita can see her own hand wrapped in Louis' as they walk away from St. Joseph's. Marc and Jo walk on either side of them and Nita sends a prayer out over their heads. More than ever, she wants out of Iota, out of Crowley and Acadiana. Let us find a new town, she thinks, a new city, a place where we can start again.

Part Three

1

BEHIND THE WHEEL OF THE MOVING VAN, LOUIS
fidgets in his seat. He can't get comfortable driving with such a
long trailer behind him, and he can't shake the sound of his father's voice in his ear. The day of the funeral, as Father Robichaux
swung a gold orb with incense and muttered a few Latin words
over the casket, Louis bolted up from the pew. "Pop!" he shouted.
"Pop!" Louis was certain that his father had just whispered something, some advice, some warning in his ear. What was it? he
wanted to ask him, What'd you say? But the sad eyes all around
said no one else heard the voice, and his mother's gloved hand on
his own told him to sit down now, behave.

Louis looks over at Nita, who's kept her eyes glued to the side
window for the whole drive. "Happy, Boo?" he asks her, and when
she says yes, he can feel the heat in his ears cool and his hands

loosen up on the wheel. Still, he worries if they're heading in the right direction, if they've made the right choice. (What if Pop was trying to tell him not to move, to stay put in Crowley?) Louis's lined up an apartment ahead of time, but he doesn't have a job or even a lead on one. There are no rice mills in Lafayette, no tall silos or long corrugated tin warehouses. There's only oil, and what does he know about drilling? About rigs and derricks?

When Louis worries out loud, Nita tells him not to fear: a big town means big jobs. She has no doubts about the move, not a single one. After all, she's done research; she's read the article in the *National Enquirer* about all those Lafayette millionaires with helicopter landings in their own backyard. With all the new malls and galleries and boutiques, the article called Lafayette "The Cajun Riviera" and said it was the hottest hot spot in all of the South. "In fact," she tells Louis, "there are already almost a hundred *thousand* people living there."

Maybe it's still in Acadiana, and maybe it's still full of Cajun rednecks, but Nita won't mind. Louis'll get a job with an oil company and soon they'll be making more money than they ever could've made in Crowley. She'll finally be living in a place that's not only on the map, but in a magazine, a place where people actually move *to*, not just some old town where people are born and die.

The thought of the word *die* unsettles Nita and she turns back to face the white dots of the highway and the huge billboards that rise up from empty fields to proclaim "Lagneaux's, The Crawfish King" and "For the Best Cracklin', the Best Boudin, Best-Stop!" Even better, she spots signs for McDonald's and Domino's Pizza and for all kinds of fast food she's only seen on TV. "You can get anything in Lafayette," she tells Louis, sure as if she lived there all her life, "anything at all."

Inside the city limits, Nita cheers each turn Louis makes and Marc and Jo cheer along with her. "We're almost there," Louis says as he swings onto the exit for *Pont des Moutons* Road. Tall sugar pine trees and low, squatting azalea bushes circle the uphill drive from the road into the parking lot. A row of lagustrums clings to a crisscross wooden fence, and even through the windows of the van, Nita can smell peat moss and sweet olive in the air. "Belle Chase Town Houses," she reads the sign out loud. Impressed with the sound of the place, she pictures crystal chandeliers hanging in every room, a sunken den and huge vaulted ceilings.

But when Louis turns the key, Nita sees no sunken room, no crystal anything. The walls have no wallpaper, no wainscoting, not a lick of color. The carpet is a withered mottled-brown shag with eerie dark spots that she already knows will never come out. By raising her hand and standing on her toes, she can almost touch the ceiling, and a musty odor remains long after she opens the windows and throws bleach around. Still, it's a two-story, she consoles herself, and it's *not* in Crowley.

Nita soon finds other consolations. There's a tennis court behind the last row of town houses and a bench next to a small artificial pond. She doesn't know how to play tennis, and she never sees anyone on the court (she can't even imagine anyone running around in the Louisiana heat swinging a racquet over a net), but she likes the thought of the green court and the yellow balls, the chance that someday she might see someone in a white sweater instead of a pair of ragged overalls and a cutoff T-shirt.

On weekends, when Louis's not out looking for a job, Nita takes the car to La Promenade Mall, where she buys rainbow-colored snowcones for Marc and Jo and walks from store to store, passing her hand over genuine silk blouses and custom-made tote-bags, leather miniskirts and bellbottom jeans. Nita wraps a hand-

dyed scarf over her head and bats her eyes at Marc. "Excuse me,"
she says, "but do you have a date for the prom?" He laughs and she
laughs along with him, but then she puts on a cowgirl hat and with
her finger shoots the price tag on a pair of cork-heeled clogs.

Nita can't buy anything in this store, not one thing. Even if she
could, where would she go with a miniskirt? Louis never takes her
dancing or out to eat; he won't even come to the mall. For just a
minute, Nita wishes she wasn't twenty-four, wasn't married to
Louis or anyone at all. She wishes she was back in high school and
some boy really was asking her to the prom. Nita can see him
standing before her, hiding a rose—no, a dozen roses in a gold
box, the ones on long stems that cost a bundle. He holds the box
out to her and pops the question. "Yes," she says out loud, then
looks down at the kids. "Let's get out of here."

Nita doesn't mind Belle Chase, not really, and she doesn't
complain, at least not until Marc and Jo start school again and she
finds herself staring at the spots on the floor or watching cars
come and go from the lot outside. Other women step into sleek
Cougars and Volaré station wagons, and she can practically hear
the commercial as they drive away, see the road and adventure before them. In the morning, when Louis leaves for his new job at
Leblanc Mechanical—not an oil company, and nothing that will
ever make them rich—Nita quickly feels the walls close in and the
air grow thin around her. She can't stand being trapped alone in
this tight little apartment, day after day, five days a week. She
wants her own car, some way to get out. But when she tells Louis,
he stares at her as if she just asked him to spin moss into gold.

Louis wishes he could buy Nita a car, he does. But then again
he likes having her home, likes knowing when he walks through
the door he'll smell the briny shrimp that Nita peels in the sink,
or hear the sizzle of flour and oil hitting the pan to make *roux* (or

even the loud pop of her chink noodles in a wok). I work all day, he thinks, all day. Don't I at least deserve to know where my wife is?

Anyway, where would Nita go? To the mall? Louis can't understand why she wants to drive through all that traffic, through all those stoplights just to stare at a bunch of things she can't afford to buy. He's gone shopping with her once or twice, but he can't stand the look on her face as she picks up some glittering top, presses it against her body, only to flip the price tag over and drop her mouth. Louis wants to buy the top, wants to buy the car, wants to give Nita everything she sees. The fact that he can't only makes him shrink into his clothes and turn his head back to Crowley.

It didn't matter what kind of money you had in Crowley, he thinks, no one seemed to have all that much anyway. But here, even the men dress like roosters and crow all day about the black, shiny money rising in pools beneath their feet. Oil and money are everywhere in Lafayette: nearly every bank and every office building has a giant drill bit or miniature derrick rising from its lawn or cement lot. And even downtown is called "The Oil Center." Louis doesn't want to work in oil; he misses the good-natured farmers with their crumpled, dusty cowboy hats and their jokes about Texans and Cajuns. ("What's the difference between a Texas redneck and a Louisiana coonass?" he heard a farmer ask once, and three men piped in unison, "The Sabine River.") Louis's only pushing papers at a bottom-feeder company, some place that supplies tools to the contracting firms that the oil companies call. But the way the men swagger into the office to boast and brag makes Louis cringe, and the way his meager salary feels when he gets home makes him wish he'd never left the rice mill, never left the five-mile strip of Crowley. All of it is enough to make Louis burst, and finally he does.

One afternoon at Leblanc Mechanical—in his office—at his desk—Louis starts to cry. He cries longer and harder than he did at his father's funeral, pressing his face into his hands until the tears fall onto the blotter below and his boss knocks on the door to see if there's a problem. "No," Louis tells him, "no, sir," but he gives Louis the afternoon off anyway.

On the drive home, Louis floors the Dart and feels the wheel shudder under his grip. He feels his face flush, too, as the city around him melts into a blur of traffic lights, neon signs, and a nonstop streak of cars. When he walks through the apartment door, right away Nita asks what's wrong.

"What's wrong?" Louis shouts before punching the wall with his fist. "I'll tell you what's wrong!"

But then he can't think of anything else to say. He doesn't want to tell Nita how much he hates Lafayette, hates his job. How he wants to go back to Crowley and how much he misses his father. He stands there, staring at his wife, at her chicory-colored arms crossed over her chest, rising and falling with her breath, and his anger sinks back into him.

"Pop . . ." is all Louis manages to say before Nita reaches out and does something she's only done once before. She slides her hand inside his and whispers, "I miss him, too."

Louis wants to lean over and tell Nita how beautiful she is, how he loves that green fleck in her eye, the color of her legs against a white skirt. He wants to wrap his arms around her and press his lips to the slope of her nose, the curve of her chin. He wants to pull her down onto the couch, lie on top of her in the daylight. But he's afraid to lose this moment, so he just squeezes her hand and nods when she asks if he's hungry.

As Nita throws oil and salted cornmeal in a hot iron skillet to make couche-couche, she thinks of Pop and that look on his face when he offered a trip to Astroworld. Then, she thinks of her own father and how before he left the wedding reception, he pulled her onto his lap and wished her *"une belle vie,"* a good life ahead. That was the last time she saw Hilton. Before she knows it, she's crying into the cornmeal and Louis's lips are at her neck.

She doesn't want to turn around, doesn't want to feel his stomach pressed against hers. But Nita feels sorry for Louis, she knows he misses Pop, so she doesn't resist when he reaches over to turn off the fire and take her hand.

Louis pulls Nita not to the couch, but to the bedroom upstairs where the light burns too bright and she has nowhere to look but at him. Her own tears quiet down as she stares at his round belly and at the strange patterns the hair on his chest makes. When he presses his mouth to her ear, she sees that already he's growing hair on his back, too. Sweat pours from his sideburns onto his cheeks, and she thinks how everything seems too big up close, as if they were staring at each other from opposite ends of a microscope. Louis pushes his way inside her and she lets her mind wander back to her father. Where could he be? Is he back in jail? Is that why he hasn't called? Soon, Louis rolls off and Nita thinks, At least it was fast.

But for Louis, it isn't fast, isn't slow, isn't anything but frozen. As he enters Nita, he tries to catch her eye and sees that she's looking past him. What's she looking at? he wonders. How can he make her look his way? What does she want? But then he knows; he knows what lies between him and Nita like an invisible sheath: she wants a better house, a better life. And she doesn't want him. The knowledge chills Louis and the fire within so quickly that he has to force himself to finish and not let the tears fall in front of her.

That night, Nita stays in the kitchen long past dinner, making giant popcorn balls with Steen's cane syrup for the kids and long squares of magic cookie bars for Louis. She doesn't complain when he climbs on top of her again before he bathes and *before* he brushes his teeth. But this time she notices that Louis doesn't finish, that he can't finish. He says nothing to her, just rolls over to hug a pillow.

Night after night, week after week, now, Louis tries to enter Nita, but it's always the same. As soon as he's inside her, his mind wanders back to work or bills or to what Nita wants and he's soft again. Damn, he curses in silence, goddamn!

Louis stops trying after a while. He goes to bed before his wife, lets himself drift away long before she climbs the stairs. Nita certainly doesn't complain when Louis stops touching her; she's grateful for the rest. But she balks when he comes home from work with a six-pack, then a twelve-pack, draining each bottle of beer when she's still trying to save a little money for a better apartment or maybe a house of their own, or maybe, *just maybe,* a trip away.

At first, Nita turns her attention from Louis' drinking and back to Marc and Jo. Her son still comes home every six weeks with a straight-A report card and now he's been cast as Thomas Jefferson in the school play. "A President?" she screams out. "You're gonna play a President!" That week, Nita buys Marc a stack of books on the lives of the Presidents, and together they read at night about how Abe Lincoln made his own lamp and writing board, and how the wife of John Adams hung clothes out on the White House lawn. "If people like that made it to Washington," she tells Marc, "just think how far you can go!"

As for Jo, Nita knows exactly where that girl is going: straight to reform school. Already, in second grade, she's cut class, sassed two teachers and a vice-principal, run off with a boy who stole his father's pack of cigarettes, and forged Nita's own signature on a report card filled with two C's, three D's, and one bright flaming F! When Nita whips out the belt, Jo doesn't even bother to run. She takes beating after beating with clamped teeth and a wide grin on her face. And to make things worse, as soon as Nita puts Jo down on her knees, she gets back up to sit in Louis' lap. And he lets her stay there, holding his beer, listening to him sing or tell a joke between commercials. More than once, she hears Louis say, "That went over like a turd in a punch bowl!" And Nita grimaces or holds her nose before walking out of the room.

Finally, after dinner one night, she tells Louis she's had it.

"It's the seventies!" she screams, "not the fifties! You can't keep me locked up in this house like some nigger slave, cooking and cleaning for you the whole week long and never going anywhere. I want a car. I wanna take a class, learn to paint, something besides soaking my hands in dirty dish water all day!"

But Louis's had it, too. He's grown tired of Nita's constant complaints: the apartment's too small, the carpet stinks. Marc needs new boots, Jo's ripped all her stockings again. We need a new curtain for the shower, a new set of pots for the kitchen, I want a car . . .

"You want a car!" Louis shouts back. "Then why don't you buy a goddamn car? Why don't you go out, sit in some hot office all day long so you can come home and listen to me holler about all the things *I* want. I want a hot rod, not that old Dart. I want a Trans Am or a Firebird with a V-8 engine. Who's gonna buy one for me? Who's gonna buy *me* a motherfucking sports car? Who!"

Nita glares at Louis, then aims back, "You won't let me work! You won't let me have a car so I can *go* to work. I'll gladly make my own money. Gladly! But I will not sit here and watch you drink away my son's college fund and tell fart jokes all night long!"

Nita raises her hand to slam her next point on the table, but before she does a sharp pain shoots from the back of her neck down her spine, then up again. She's had pains like this before, but they've always gone away as fast as they've come. But now the pain doesn't leave. It keeps rising up and down her back like a hot bullet ricocheting from her skull to her hips. "And you . . . ," Nita shouts, "you . . ."

Bam! Louis watches as Nita falls backward to the floor. For a moment, he thinks she's faking, thinks she's trying to make him crack. No one falls that hard, he thinks, no one falls backward. But when he looks down and see Nita's body flat on the floor and the kids crying at her side, he knows it's real: he's lost her. First his father, now his wife.

"Get up, Mama, get up!" Marc and Jo shout. But Nita can't move, can't lift herself from the floor. The throbbing that runs from her neck to her hips has spread like an electric tree throughout her back. Her shoulders, neck, head, and every inch of her arms are at first scorching hot, then she feels nothing at all. She can see Marc and Jo, see their mouths moving and their eyes filling with tears, but she can't hear them. In fact, she can't hear anything until Louis stoops over to look into her eyes. "I can't move, I can't move," she keeps saying, not at all sure that her words are coming out in the right way.

But Louis hears her and his heart races as he runs for the phone. Ambulance, ambulance, he thinks, trying to remember who to call, Acadian Ambulance. And in the long ride to the hospital, he swears over and over that if she makes it, if Nita makes it, he'll be a better husband, he'll give her a better life.

2

WHEN NITA WAKES, SHE FINDS HERSELF STARING AT a white cinder-block wall and a curtain around her bed. There's a tube shooting from her arm into an upside-down bottle over her head. She hears voices on the other side of the curtain, low and foreign. French? Is someone trying to talk to her in Cajun? Everything around looks smeared, fuzzy, like the bad reception on the mounted TV above. A minute or two passes before Nita figures out what's going on: she's in a hospital and there's someone in the bed next to her. It's a woman's voice she hears. *"Mais, tout sera bien,"* the voice says. *"Pas 'pas mal,' pas 'comme çi, comme ça,' mais* bien. *Moi, je le sais!"* Nita can sort out most of what she hears: Everything's going to be fine, not okay, not so-so, but fine. She hears the voice again and again in her head, a sharp, pointed voice that she's heard before.

Nita then hears the clink of heels against linoleum before the curtain slides back a bit and she sees the face behind the voice. That blue pillbox hat, those white gloves. Anna, she thinks, Louis' mother. What is she doing here?

"Well!" Anna cries out, as if Nita was her own daughter, not some girl from Jennings who married her son. "You're awake."

Nita doesn't know what to say. Maybe she's dreaming, maybe the doctors gave her too many pills and she's imagining Louis' mother standing here. But then Anna keeps talking. "You'll have to take better care." She wags her finger, scolding Nita. "You had everyone *pleine de peur,* all worried and nervous."

"Louis," Nita tries not to slur her words, "where Slouis? Where'sa kids?" Her head feels stuffed with marbles. Her own words rattle between her ears and she can barely make out what Anna says, something about the man in the next bed. He knew Pop's father or brother and lost a leg working on a rig offshore.

"Go back to the farm," Anna says, "that's what I told him. Leave that black, slimy filth alone. Oil kills, but soil never hurt anyone!"

"Lou," Nita tries again, "where's Louis?"

"At work, *bien sûr!* Someone's gotta work to pay off these bills. They're certainly not gonna let you stay here for free. I don't know why you had to come to Lafayette, anyway, why you had to move so far away."

Thirty minutes, Nita thinks, it takes half an hour to drive from Iota to Lafayette. Why is Anna lecturing her? Why is she even here?

"I guess Crowley wasn't good enough for you. I guess it wasn't enough I lost Louis' father." Anna covers her mouth with a trembling hand, as if the words stung as they crossed her lips. "You had to do it. You had to take my only son and grandkids to another parish, too!"

"Please." Nita tries lifting her hand to stop the rush of words. "Please," she says, as Anna's face becomes a blur again, a swirl of pink and white.

The marbles in Nita's head are gone now, but they're replaced by the battering sound of Anna's voice. She wants to shut off that voice, shut off those words. Where's her own mother? Why isn't she here? Maybe she's gone to find Hilton, to find her father. He'll walk in any minute, strutting like a cowboy, holding a field of flowers and a mountain of gift boxes. She hears him say, "*Ma 'ti' fille,* my little girl," then he sings an old Hank Williams song as she falls back to sleep with the lull of his voice in her ears.

While Nita drifts in and out of dreams, she thinks she hears someone crying. But when she wakes again, she sees only Anna, hunched over searching for something in her purse. Suddenly, she feels as if she should offer Louis' mother a cup of coffee, or a praline on a silver-lined plate. Nita hasn't really talked to Anna since Pop's funeral and she thinks she should've called her, should've made Louis drive the half hour on I-10. "Sorry," Nita wants to say, but before she can get the word on her tongue, Anna turns around.

"Up again?" she asks, then turns to face the TV before Nita can answer. Nita stares at the wall of Anna's back, wishing she had something to say, something more than "Sorry" or "Please."

Though Anna stays the remainder of the afternoon, and the rest of the week, too, coming in the morning with a patch of quilt to sew and leaving when Louis shows up after work, she says nothing much more to Nita. They sit just a few feet apart in the same half-room, under the same buzzing fluorescent light, and barely speak. Sometimes a laugh track from an afternoon rerun fills the screen, and Nita's grateful for the canned sound, the cued moment when she can let out a laugh of her own, however nervous or loud it might be.

Every afternoon shortly before 5:30, Anna stands up, with her purse clutched tightly to her side, waiting for Louis' entrance. As they say goodbye, Nita watches Louis kiss his mother once on each cheek, which she thinks odd, more than odd, weird or foreign, or yes—Nita admits—*queer*. Another voice floats into her ears as she remembers the woman in the Crowley Piggly-Wiggly, how she cooed at her son in Louis' arms. "Look how he mothers that boy!" the woman said, and Nita hears again the meaning between the words, lying still as a rifle in the grass. Of course he called his mother, Nita thinks, of course!

Actually—as Louis tells it—he doesn't call Anna first. He calls Gilda, but the operator says the phone is disconnected. Even if she answered, though, he knows she'd have some excuse: Buford won't let her drive to Lafayette, Buford left and took the car, she's having spells again and can't leave the house. Nita's mother didn't even come to Pop's funeral. Hell! Louis thinks, as angry as if Gilda actually refused to look after her daughter, at least my mother picks up the phone when I call!

Maybe it's not easy for Nita, sitting alone in this room all day with his mother, but he's grateful to Anna for watching his wife, for making breakfast and dinner, cleaning the house, and seeing the kids off to school everyday. So he kisses her on each cheek, once for himself, once for Nita. And after his mother leaves, he lets himself stare for long hours at his wife while she falls back to sleep. If she wakes, he thinks, she has nowhere to look but at me.

Asleep on the hospital bed, Nita looks like a schoolgirl—with her inky black hair in pigtails and not a drop of makeup on her face. She looks like the girl she must've been right before Louis met her, playing jump-rope and Hopscotch. Then he remembers the accident, or remembers Nita telling him about the accident, about being flung from her brother's car, and the reason she's here now: one vertebra practically disintegrated, two more fused to-gether like hot rubber bullets left too long in the sun.

When Louis finally takes Nita home, when he pulls the Dart into the apartment lot and points out the kids standing next to a brand-new Plymouth Volaré wrapped in ribbon, she twitches in her seat, then throws her hands against the dash. "We got a new car?" Nita shouts. "We got a Volaré!"

"Not we," Louis says. "You. It's yours, Boo, that car is all yours!"

"Mine?" Nita asks, and her lips stay open and her eyes go wide, as Louis dares to pull her close, to press his face to her neck. He can't hold her long, though. Her arms swing out and her legs pump up and down against the floor before she pulls the han-dle and races down the cement to meet her kids and Louis' best idea ever.

Nita hugs Marc and Jo tight to her side—letting her nose fill with their scent— but she can't wait; she has to get behind the wheel of the car now. When she sees the keys dangling from the ignition, she turns the engine over and pulls the shift into reverse. As the long hood of the Volaré draws back, she catches sight of Louis and the kids cheering her on. But she doesn't wave or honk the horn; she wants to feel as if she's done this forever, as if it was only natural for her to drive away—alone—in her very own car.

What Nita notices first is the silence. There's no one in the car but her. She's totally and completely alone and she can't remem-ber a time when that was true. Even in the hospital, Louis or his mother sat next to her night and day. But now there's no one to tell her which way to go: right, left, or straight ahead. She can make a U-turn if she wants, or just sit back and watch the speedometer climb. Nita lets one hand fall from the wheel to rub the cool velour of the seat. She hears Ricardo Montalban for just a moment, singing the commercial in her head: "Volaré, Vo-Oh!" Then she fiddles with the radio until she catches an oldies station playing Irma Thomas, "The Soul Queen of New Orleans." I could go there, she thinks, I could turn left onto I-10 and drive all the way to the French Quarter.

Away from Belle Chase Town Houses, away from Moss Street and *Pont des Moutons* Road, away from Louis and the kids, Nita watches as the city of Lafayette opens up. She flies down Evangeline Thruway, Kaliste Saloom, Eraste Landry, dodging in and out of cars on each of the long twisting roads. (Once she overheard a woman at the mall say that instead of designing streets for Lafayette—like they do in any other sensible town—they just poured asphalt right on top of old cow paths.) Nita's driven before, of course, but she feels a new power under her fingers and a rising urge to push the accelerator pad to the floor.

As she turns onto College Drive, she grips the wheel tighter. She could be one of the students at USL, driving to school for her afternoon class. She could park near the campus lake, under a live oak to keep the car cool. Nita imagines waiting for a boy, one studying to be a doctor. She laughs as he bumps his huge stack of books against the window, then reaches over to open the door.

Nita passes the tall white columns of the university president's house, the strange round coliseum, the skinny little bayou arm that runs through this part of Lafayette. But she's not interested in the gray cypress trees or the white oleander blossoms. She's headed straight for the downtown oil center, to zip up and down the square blocks where the fancy ladies shop: Abdalla's (which features a genuine crystal chandelier over the entrance), Lafleur's (where they drape even stockings on padded satin hangers), and *La Boutique* (with its spiral staircase leading up and down from the changing rooms). She pulls into one of the lots and lets the engine run while she watches boys in pressed navy uniforms haul stacks of boxes from the store to the trunks of waiting Cadillacs, Continentals, BMWs, and Mercedes. One day, Nita thinks, one day . . .

Then she puts the car in drive to make her way back home. No, not home, she decides, back to that apartment, that town house, that spot midway between Crowley and the next place. If only Louis was smarter, she thinks, more ambitious. If only he knew how to flip the switch that would turn their apartment into an in-town estate, their cars into a pair of Rolls, or at least Volvos. If he could choose the right job, instead of settling for whatever picayune thing comes his way. If he weren't so lazy, so satisfied with where he's at, maybe she wouldn't have to drive over old cow paths or watch other women shop. Maybe she could make that turn onto I-10, drive to New Orleans or Houston, or even California.

When Louis spots the Volaré making its way up the drive, his face breaks into a smile and he feels the warm thrill of watching Nita park his first truly important purchase. His wife, wrapped in silver. His wife, in a brand-spanking-new car. It has to be new, he told the salesman. Nothing secondhand, not even mint, and no demo would do (if he was gonna go in debt, it might as well be all the way). And while he resisted a few add-ons—8-track tape player, automatic windows—he knew Nita would want velour seats, AC, and power steering. The guy at Acadiana Motors— Fungus was his name—even threw in some *lagniappe,* a little something extra on the house: a steering wheel padded in genuine Naugahyde.

Louis's proud of the Volaré, proud of the deal he made and the news he's yet to break. He's up for a new job, courtesy of one of the blowhards who's been coming to the office every day. Choppy Landry, cousin to the guy who runs Mammoth, a big-deal oil com-

pany with platform rigs all over the Gulf, has taken a shine to
Louis and told him about a position at the company's headquar-
ters in Lafayette. Louis's nervous about the interview. What do
you say to a corporate VP, he wonders, much less a CEO or CFO?
Might as well be a room full of UFOs for all he knows about the
petroleum field. But Louis considers what Choppy said, how the
square root of oil is always six figures long, and he thinks about
the bills already on his desk (the hospital, the rent, utilities) and
the bills yet to come (the car note, insurance, gas). Then there's
Christmas ahead, presents for Marc and Jo, so Louis swallows
hard and readies himself for the short walk to his new career.

A few weeks later, Louis' mother nearly bursts when he calls
to invite her to a celebration gumbo, but not from joy. She clicks
her tongue into the receiver, then scoffs at the idea. "Gumbo?" she
cries. "In this heat!" Anna reminds him that gumbo weather doesn't
start until after the first freeze, "And that's never in November, I
don't know what Nita's thinking!" Anna also reminds Louis that
working in oil is nothing to be proud of, nothing to celebrate. In
fact, he should be *honte,* ashamed to work with such filth. But,
"Comme tu veux," she agrees to come anyway.

When Anna arrives at Louis' town house, they avoid going inside. Instead, Louis follows his mother to the small flower bed and
each of them fall to their knees, plucking up ragweeds and stray
St. Augustine grass, and furiously raking the black Louisiana soil
over and under, as if they might clean up the mess between them
or might even uncover some memory, some crucial moment from
their time together with Pop. After they pull every possible weed
and water every plant, Louis still finds little to say to his mother,
but he feels easier next to her and he's almost grateful when she
saves her one jab at Nita for long after the gumbo, and after the ice
cream with pecan pralines.

Before Anna steps into the green Mercury, before she waves a final goodbye, she pulls two wax paper–wrapped pralines from inside her purse, one each for Marc and Jo. Then she loudly tells Jo the secret to her recipe. "It's all in the way you boil and stir the sugar," Anna says. "Gently! Gently! And it's gotta be dark Louisiana cane. Not that sandy Hawaiian grit your mother keeps on the shelf!"

Louis watches as Jo shoves the whole praline into her mouth and Marc tucks the candy safely in his pocket. They both smile and wave their hands before the headlights of the Mercury. But Nita says nothing to him or Anna, she just draws her mouth into a tight little line and stares straight ahead.

Nita doesn't complain. She's still too thrilled with her car and with Louis' new job to say anything about his mother snubbing her——not just with the candy, but all throughout dinner, too. Maybe Anna doesn't actually say anything about how Nita keeps house, but she lays her white gloves on the table just where her hands can rest on them, as if she suspected a colony of germs might explode under her fingers. And she sniffs at each spoonful of gumbo while looking about the room for something out of place.

Anna talks to Louis, of course, about the ongoing saga of the Iota farmers (some family always seems to be losing their land to someone else, the IRS usually), and she talks to Marc and Jo about their school. But she says nothing, not one word to Nita. Even when Nita asks how Pop kept out of tax trouble, Anna just turns to the kids to tell them that *their* farm is doing nicely, *merci bien,* and that——in fact——she's fixing to buy more land next to an old graveyard on the bayou side of Ti-Mamou.

But, no, Nita doesn't complain. Not when his mother drives away, and not later when he climbs on top of her again. Louis's been relentless since she's back from the hospital. Every night, every single night, as soon as the lights are out, he stretches one hand under her head. She can almost count the beats until he moves the other hand to her legs. Then, with hardly even a kiss, he pushes himself between her thighs. He moves back and forth in quick, jerky motions. Sometimes he stabs so hard and fast her eyes tear up. Everything around her—the alarm clock, the faucet, the fridge down the hall—seems to make some kind of noise, like a low murmur in her ear. Nita can see Louis grimace, as if someone was choking him, and she wonders why he wants to do this, why he wants to try again when—again and again—he doesn't finish, can't finish. After he turns to the wall, Nita wonders, Should I tell him it's all right? That it doesn't matter? But soon a new thought creeps into her mind. She tries pushing the word out of her head, but night after night, the question returns with the murmur of the clock, the buzz of the fridge. Is Louis queer? Is her husband a queer?

3

HE'S A MAN WHO CAN BUY HIS WIFE A CAR, HE'S A man who can make his wife happy, that's what Louis tells himself as he arches his back over Nita. He's got a new job and soon, with a bigger salary than he's ever had before, he'll be able to give her what she wants: a new house, a real house in a neighborhood, with a yard and a two-car—that's right—a two-car garage.

Louis lets his eyes wander over Nita's face, searching the closed lids of her eyes, her pouty lips, her dark cloud of hair. But he turns away before she catches him looking at her. He's afraid of what she might see in his look, and this fear unsettles him. Before long, he loses his rhythm, his focus, and he's back to the knowl-edge that Nita's not happy, that no matter what he does, what he buys, she'll always want more. Why can't she be satisfied with what we've got? he thinks as he rolls over to face the wall. Even after Louis bought Nita the Volaré, the very night he brought her home from the hospital, he could tell she wanted to be someplace else, not lying under him, not feeling his weight on top of her.

Eventually, Louis stops trying to enter Nita. At night, he dares a kiss on her cheek and maybe lets his arm fall across her shoulder, but he doesn't climb on top of her, doesn't let his hand wander to the only place he wants to be.

Still, he won't stop trying to give his wife what she wants. When she complains about the apartment, about the tight little kitchen, the spotted walls, and what she calls "that angry-looking carpet," Louis sets out to find a new house.

He counts himself lucky when he finds a place through a drilling engineer at work. The house is not even finished, it's that new, and the contractor—Ti-Pro Arceneaux—is willing to let Nita in on the final touches. The price only sweetens the deal: just under seventy grand for over 2,200 square feet of living area. A huge backyard with a chain-link fence, brick flower beds up front, a covered patio with a sliding glass door, three bedrooms, a kitchen with something called a "floating island," a living room *and* a den, not to mention a breakfast nook and a built-in dishwasher, trash compactor, and garbage disposal. Maybe it's not in a new neighborhood, or on a cul-de-sac. But Louis's never seen so much *lagniappe* in a house, and when he tells the men at work how much he paid, they slap him on the back and say, "Coonass, you practically stole that place!"

Louis likes being called coonass, likes the reminder that he's a real Cajun, not one of these imported Texans or Yankees who run most of the oil companies. He also likes the rush of pride when they slap his back and he allows himself to think maybe the house will change things after all, maybe he'll find Nita looking at him one night across the patio table. Maybe she'll put her hand on his leg and they'll kiss right there, in the dark.

At first, Nita's disappointed. After all, the new house is only a mile away. What kind of move is that? she wonders. But when she sees the long, curving flower beds, the Spanish arches over each window, the wrought-iron on the door, and picture windows in the den, she's as thrilled as if they were moving to a completely different city. She almost can't believe it when the contractor lets her pick out her own carpet—a deep, plush red like they have in ritzy hotels—and her own wallpaper in the den—a mural with a Mediterranean "vista"—*and* her own lighting—chandeliers, not crystal, but still, chandeliers in every room except the kitchen. She even has mini-chandeliers installed in both bathrooms.

Nita's so excited about the new place she decides to call her mother. But when she dials, the operator announces—in what Nita considers a mocking tone—that her mother's number has been disconnected. She calls back and hears the same recording twice before she lets herself believe it: first she lost her father, and now her mother, too. She starts to worry that maybe something has happened, maybe her mother's in some kind of trouble.

But Nita pushes those thoughts aside and decides to drive to Jennings. After all, she's got her own car now. She can leave when Louis goes to work and make it back before the kids get out of school. She pictures finding her mother home and taking her to lunch. They can go to some little café with checkerboard curtains, and when the bill comes, she'll pick it up. No! It's on me, she'll say. Louis's got a new job, *in oil.* Won't her mama be proud? Maybe she can treat her to a movie, too, at the old Bijou theater. Together, they'll ask around town about Hilton: Has anyone seen him? Does anyone know where her father's staying?

When Louis tries to talk her out of the trip, Nita figures he's jealous. That's right, she thinks, I can just hop in the car and go. And go she does. She drives so fast that she makes the hour-plus trip to Jennings in just over thirty minutes. As she turns onto the narrow street where her mother lives, Nita stares at the house she last saw not long after she married Louis. For a moment, she wonders what might have happened if she stayed in the house a little longer. Would she have met some other guy on a different double date? Would she have married some other man, someone who'd know what she wants before she even asks?

Nita decides to talk to her mother about Louis, about how he disappoints her again and again. But when she steps out the car to knock on Gilda's door, she finds that not only is no one home, both the front windowpanes are cracked and a pile of mail crowds the slot between the screen and the busted plywood door. Nita scoops up the mail and looks around until she spies a neighbor, Mrs. Theriot, waving hello from the project house across the street. *"Poo-yie!"* Mrs. Theriot shouts, "but it's hot!"

Nita can see a ring of sweat under the old woman's arms as she fans herself with a fat gray banana leaf. She remembers being afraid of her when she was a girl, afraid of the black chickens she hung from her front porch and the strange smells that came from her kitchen. But I'm grown-up, now, Nita thinks, so she forces herself to wave back. "Yes," she says, "yes, it's hot." And saying so makes her shield her eyes with both hands before she asks Mrs. Theriot if she knows where her mama's gone.

"*Mais,* she went to Mermentau to live with your sister," the old woman answers, looking surprised for a moment that Nita didn't know, before she returns to the tub of snap peas in her lap.

Mermentau's not far, not more than ten minutes or so. But The Cove—where her sister lives—lies away from town and deep in the woods, and Nita dreads driving into a part of the parish even her father seemed to fear. Nothing ever moves in Mermentau, he once told her. As he put it, even the river would sit stagnant if not for the Gulf of Mexico tugging on it. And in the Mermentau woods, on the other side of the murky waters of the river, there are still pockets of Blackfoot Indians. Their numbers are far too small to claim a reservation, so most of them live together in The Cove, in some kind of patchwork settlement on ground that no one has ever been able to tame.

Vina Lee's house sits at the end of a narrow gravel road that slithers off the country highway. The road looks like a slug's trail, like a path made with a lot of effort, but very little direction. It cuts left a bit, then right, then jerks out once more before finally disappearing under the wheels of Nita's car. The house also has an odd look. It leans forward on concrete pilings, as if it was straining to get away from the river's choke-hold. But the pilings sink into the ground, giving notice that the house is going exactly nowhere. Tinfoil blocks out the front windows. An old pie tin lies facedown on the cement steps and several empty milk jugs are scattered across the yard. Nita thinks she can smell the stagnant air and sour milk, even through the windows of the car. She sits behind the wheel, staring at the slope of the porch, thinking how she could fall back into a place like this if she doesn't watch it, if she doesn't keep pushing Louis forward.

As Vina Lee bursts through the screen door and down the front steps, Nita sees that her sister already looks like one of the old ladies at the Pentecostal church in Jennings. She wears a denim skirt, no makeup, and her hair up in a towering bun. Her face looks blank, but her eyes glitter as she approaches the Volaré.

"Look at you!" Vina Lee yells at Nita, waving both hands over her head. "Look at you! Just like a movie star! Bonita Ray, *chère,*

look how pretty you are! Look at this car! Good Lord, y'all must
be making it all right!"

Right away, Nita feels both proud and embarrassed, as if she
stole the car and the makeup and got away with it. She's no movie
star, she knows that, but she's at least acting some part and she
struggles now to remember her lines. "Hi," she tries to say as ca-
sually as if she saw her sister only yesterday, "how's Mama?"

But Vina Lee ignores the question as she ushers Nita inside to
sit at the table before the one good fan. Her voice drops to a loud
whisper as she complains how much the bunions on her feet hurt
and how her back—"from that accident, you know"—still gives
her trouble. As Vina Lee talks, Nita squints into the room next to
the kitchen and makes out a figure slumped over on a couch. The
couch is covered in strips of visquine and propped up on one side
with a phone book and a short stack of plywood. Nita can still
hear her sister's voice in her ear, something about how her husband comes and goes like a Louisiana rainstorm, with a lot of
worry and no warning. He stays gone for weeks on end, too, hunting duck and deer long past the season and leaving her no way of
getting to town. But as she talks, Nita stares straight ahead at the
figure on the couch until she's sure of who she's looking at.

"Mama?" Nita asks quietly, afraid that maybe Gilda's sleeping.
But her mother just turns her head for a moment, then stares back
at the TV, as if some vital announcement was being made, or as if
she might find more comfort in the blue-green glow of the screen
than in looking Nita's way. "Mama?" Nita asks again, not sure if
Gilda recognizes her. "It's me."

"One of her bad days," Vina Lee says. "Some days she'll only
talk Cajun, other days she won't talk at all."

Then—without missing a beat—her sister goes on about
what a handful her boys are, and now Mama's laid up like this. It's

all going to kill her, she's sure, and that's why she needs these pills. But her prescription's run out—"Sweet Jesus!"—and the light bill is due and does Nita think help will ever come her way?

Even when Vina Lee stops talking, the air around seems charged with her complaints. Once or twice Nita tries to break in. She raises her hand, but forgets what she wants to say. Still, she keeps her hand open, hoping any minute the thought might return and she'll only have to close her fingers to catch it. Finally, Nita clicks her tongue against her teeth and asks, "What happened?"

With that, her mother jerks her head up and shouts, "What happened? What happened? He left again, Buford left. This time he took the car, took everything out the closet, even took his slippers. He's not coming back, *Je te dis,* I tell you, he's not coming back!"

Gilda starts to sob into her hands and Nita wonders, What to do? Should she hold her mother, take her home to Lafayette? But before she can decide, Gilda runs to the back bedroom and slams the door shut.

Vina Lee picks up where she left off, as if nothing unusual was happening, as if it was normal to see her mother lock herself in a room. Then Nita remembers it *is* normal. She remembers how Gilda made her stay home from school to clean the house, to deal with the bill collectors and the welfare people. How anytime Buford (or one of her other husbands) left for more than a day, she hid herself, telling Nita that she was *laide comme un cochon,* ugly as a pig, that no man would ever want her, not for long, so they might as well pull the curtains, lock the doors.

Like a mosquito in the background, Nita hears her sister drone on about life in Mermentau and Jennings: their younger sister, Monetta Lou, plucks her eyebrows off completely, then paints them back in a high black arch. She also tries to kill herself once a month. Vina Lee says she does her best to ignore the little cuts and the bourbon on her breath, but last week Monetta Lou rammed her husband's Econoline van into a pine tree. "And Claude?" Vina asks, without waiting for an answer. "*Pauv' bête!* He's even worse . . ."

Nita's sister goes on about how their brother shacked up with a Yankee girl, how she's turned their house into a nudist colony—their two girls walking around in the backyard with not a stitch on, not even a pair of panties or a halter top. Then there's *Tante* Verda who's become certain that a *loup-garou,* a werewolf, lives in the bayou behind her house. She sleeps with a rifle and eats so much garlic no one can stand to be near her.

Through a side window, Nita sees a pack of boys—Vina Lee's sons—running by with their shirts off and mud smeared across their bodies like Indian warpaint. They come and go quicker than her eyes can follow, but without looking she can see their bowl-cut hair, their bad teeth, and the bad road that lies ahead.

Vina Lee tells Nita that Ti-Joe, her oldest son, is already caught up with the law, writing hot checks and wrecking some stolen car when he's not even old enough to drive, and if that's not enough . . .

Her voice batters away in Nita's head until she thinks she might scream. Even though the fan blows, the air is unbelievably still. It's the objects that move in this heat. Vina Lee's stove, her tabletop, the calendar on the wall, all seem to waver as if they were made of gas or as if everything was lit by a flame. A line of sweat clings to Nita's lips and, she's sure that some part of her makeup is already running down her face. I have to get out of this house, she decides, I have to go. She reaches inside her purse, pulls up a checkbook, and writes out in a thin cursive script, "One Hundred Dollars and No Cents." Vina Lee is still talking when

Nita rips the check along the perforated lines. "I can't stay," Nita says, "but maybe this'll help."

Her sister presses the check to her chest, then brings it to her lips. "You are blessed," she tells Nita, "blessed!" And in that moment, Nita believes her. I *am* blessed, she thinks, I'm lucky to be away from here, away from all this. She looks at her sister and thinks how she's already becoming their mother, already nursing her misery (and everyone else's) like a wet rag against a sore tooth. She keeps holding the rag up to the light to see if there's blood, if the pain has left a mark. Either way, Nita knows, she'll be disappointed. Either way it won't be what she expected.

Before she makes her way out of the house, Nita walks down the hall to knock on Gilda's door. "Mama," she says, softer than she means to, "Mama . . ."

But Gilda doesn't answer, or at least she doesn't answer in any way that Nita can understand. She just mutters something in French. *Fou?* Nita wonders. Is her mother saying it's crazy? What's crazy? Or who?

As she steps into the Volaré and turns the knob for the AC on high, Nita decides it's the place that's crazy. Who wouldn't go mad living like this? Who wouldn't want to curl up on the bed, with this heat beating down and no way to cool off? Maybe we can move up north, she thinks, maybe I can convince Louis to take me where there's mountains and snow and no one's ever heard the words *"Pauv' bête."*

Once again, the highway clicks under her wheels, the exits zip by. Only now, it's home that Nita looks forward to, with Jennings and The Cove farther and farther behind. She doesn't think of Louis, not as her destination. She thinks of her kids, Marc and Jo. She thinks of going back to school, getting her diploma, finding a job. She remembers Mrs. Castille on the night of the tornado, how happy she seemed with her job at the phone company and her twenty-eight plates from different states. Nita drives into a cloud, drives into a burst of rain and wind, and sees her own freedom, her own happiness in the distance, like a flash of lightning. She decides to chase it.

4

WILL HE LET HER GO TO SCHOOL? WILL HE LET HER
get a job? No frickin' way, Louis thinks. He barely has Nita as it is;
he doesn't want to lose her completely. Already, he regrets buying
her the Volaré. He didn't know she'd disappear so quickly, drive
all the way to Jennings and leave him with leftovers. He also didn't
know she'd zip along the highway so fast that she'd get a ticket on
her first trip out of town—$100 to add to that damn check she
wrote her sister. Is he running a welfare camp? Louis wants to ask.
Exactly how many mouths is he supposed to feed?

He tries saying it softly to Nita: I don't want you to work, I
don't want you to study, he repeats in his head. I just want you
lying under me, I just want you needing something, anything,
from me. Tell me what you want, I'll buy it. Whatever it is, I'll
find a way. But I don't want some man ogling you from across a

counter or behind a desk. You're my wife, and I intend to keep it that way.

All this Louis tries to say, but when he opens his mouth only one word makes it out: "No!" He almost can't believe the force behind the word, the heat that charges off his tongue. He slams his fist down on the table and shouts again, "No! No! And *hell* no!"

Louis flattens his hand on the table, tries to smooth his anger. But when Nita glowers at him, something inside breaks.

"Goddamnit! There's no way I'm gonna let my wife work!" he shouts. "There's no way I'm gonna come home to cellophane-wrapped meals and notes taped to the fridge! I didn't buy you that car so you could go chasing all over Acadiana looking for God-knows-what. I bought you that car—"

His voice breaks. He needs a glass of water, a cool glass of water, but he goes on.

"Goddamnit all to hell! I want you at home where I know where to find you. Cook, clean, take care of the kids, that's the only job you have, the only job I want you to have. Understand!"

I should stop, he decides, I should stop right now. But the words come in a rush, explode and practically push their way out of his mouth.

"I'm the man in this family, I'm the one who makes the money, no one else! *Comprends?* Got it?"

Louis stares at Nita and thinks maybe she's gone deaf. Her face is red, purple really, and her chest is beating hard with her breath, but she doesn't say anything. She just keeps squeezing her hands and shaking her head. Then he watches as a light snaps in her eyes.

"Yeah, I got it!" Nita shouts back. "I finally got it. You wanna make me into my mother. You wanna lock me in this house like some kind of prisoner until I go crazy!"

Before Louis knows what's happening, Nita's hand is in the air. He thinks for a moment that she might hit him, that she might bring her hand hard and fast against his cheek. He almost wishes she'd do it. At least then he might break through the ice around her. He might know once more what it's like to feel her skin against his. She might even hit him so hard he'd bleed, then she'd fall into his arms, beg forgiveness, press her vanilla-scented neck to his ear, her small hands to his burning cheek.

But Nita doesn't hit Louis, not yet. Instead, she picks up a pink glass bowl his mother gave them and slams it to the ground. He stares at her, not knowing what to do next. Why is there always such a big ditch between what he means to say and what he ends up saying? Why does he always screw things up so completely?

At work, he knows just what to say at any moment. A call comes in—one of their men may be in trouble on a rig offshore—and Louis doesn't hesitate. The right words pop out of his mouth and he gives directions so fast and so well that he's been bumped up from district to regional manager. He's even been given his own pager and he almost welcomes the random midnight call, the crisis he can step in and handle.

But Nita, how should he handle Nita? Louis looks at her wet eyes, at her clenched fists, and wishes he could take back even half of what he said. Now she won't talk to him for at least a week. Now the air around him will freeze and he'll feel like a ghost, unnoticed in his own house.

He's not a man, Nita thinks, he's a monster. What kind of man would curse his wife? What kind of man would want to keep me locked up, buy me a car and tell me not to use it! Nita can feel the hot tears push their way out of her eyes. She wants to scream in Louis' face for hours, to lock him in a closet for days and make

him feel as caged up, as nearly mad as she sometimes feels. She
wants to make him know how silence throbs in the house when
the kids are in school, how Jo screams in her ear as soon as she gets
home. But she says nothing to Louis after the bowl breaks. She
doesn't even stoop to pick it up. Instead she forms a plan. If he
wants a maid, she decides, if he wants a nigger woman, he's gonna
have to pay for it.

A few weeks later, Nita demands and gets her very own charge
card. Louis's making enough money that she can drive to the Oil
Center and—instead of sitting in the car—she can get out and
walk straight through the enormous glass doors of Abdalla's or
Lafleur's. She can spend hours walking up and down the stairs to
the changing room at *La Boutique,* trying on sunflower dresses,
halter tops, and designer denim. And when she's through, she can
look at the clerk and say, "I'll take it."

The MasterCard slides from Nita's hand and soon her closet
fills with Gloria Vanderbilt jeans, thigh-high suede boots, fringe-
sleeved jackets, and wraparound dresses in silk jersey. Nita likes
the look the salesgirls give her when she walks in; she's there
to buy and they know it. They circle her with new ideas: Have
you thought of matching ruby shoes for that nail color? Have you
thought of a hat to go with that medallion belt? She likes how they
make her feel smart for choosing the right dresses, saying no to
the mossy-looking gray ("Too old lady," they say, "too country
come to town") and yes to the vermilion-striped rayon ("That fabric is so *in,* look how it grabs you in just the right places!").

Nita also likes the way men stare at her as she makes her way
back to the car. Some whistle, others blow their horn. They all
make her feel something Louis never has.

He's always at work now, anyway. He doesn't come home until after dark, and then sometimes he jumps out of bed at two or

three in the morning to answer a call. He's gone so much that Nita starts to feel like one of those single moms she saw on an episode of *Donahue*. Louis doesn't even pay attention to the kids anymore, at least he barely notices when Marc scores another string of A's, or when he wins the first writing award in his class, then goes on to win the district and state contest, too. He's only in middle school, but Marc's room fills with tiny trophies, certificates, ribbons, and awards for poster contests, spelling bees, and social studies projects. Even so, Louis has no time for the boy. He never lifts a bat or tosses a ball his son's way. He never races Marc to the mailbox or shows him how to hold a hammer or a screwdriver.

No, it's left up to Nita to teach their son what he needs to know. She flashes cards to him in the morning while they eat breakfast. She coaches him from the mirror while she takes rollers out of her hair, slides gloss over her lips. His subjects get harder and harder for her to follow as he's placed in advanced classes, then in a special program for gifted and talented students. Still, she pushes herself to keep up with Marc, to memorize every multiplication key, to know every capital of every state, to hear the accented syllable in every vocabulary word. As they curl up on his bed, poring over diagrams and notes, she almost feels as if she was in school, as if she was a student herself.

Maybe Louis won't let her work. (He says they'd have to hire a nigger woman to look after the house, and doesn't that mean she's right, she's doing a nigger woman's job?) But she's not about to let him get her down or hold her back; she's not about to let him keep her—or her son—from getting somewhere.

Over and over again, Nita maps out her son's future: the Ivy League schools, the diplomas on the wall, all the zeros next to his salary. She dreams so much and so often about what might happen to him that she almost can't believe it when he's invited to spend the night with a doctor's son. "Francis D'Aquin, Dr. D'Aquin's boy?" she asks. "*He* invited you over?" She throws a couch pillow in the air, then squeezes Marc's hand in hers. "Yes," she says, without even thinking of Louis, "of course you can spend the night with the doctor's son!"

Though Louis doesn't want his son sleeping at some stranger's house, he decides not to fight Nita. He figures he's already won the only fight he's ever gonna win. She won't leave the kids to a babysitter or the house to a maid, but she'll never ask what color to paint the cabinets or how long to let Jo stay on her knees. She makes each decision as if he wasn't standing right next to her, as if his tongue long ago fell out and shriveled to a raisin.

No, he won't fight Nita anymore. But he doesn't understand her excitement, doesn't understand why she's so willing to drive halfway across town to leave their son at some house they've never even seen. Nita won't let Marc run outside unless she can follow behind. And the minute he gets a grass stain on his trousers or a scuff on his shoes, she chases him back in the house to scrub up and listen to an endless list of verbs and dictionary words that Louis can't imagine anyone ever having a use for. What good will it do that boy to know the imperfect past tense? How in the hell will he ever use a word that's as long as a centipede on the page?

Louis thinks Nita fusses too much over Marc, always straightening the curls in his hair, adjusting his collar. Half the time, she won't let him leave their front yard. She worries about kidnappings and stray men lying in the front ditch with a shotgun. Nita's constant worry makes no sense to him, since the only kidnapping he's ever heard about was of the neighbor's balding Pomeranian. And even then he figures it wasn't a kidnapping, but a mercy killing. "That damn dog was so old," he tries to joke with her, "it looked like a pickled armadillo."

Nita ignores Louis, it's true. But the moment a doctor's son calls, she irons Marc's underwear, starches every shirt he owns, and sends him off without even meeting the mother or the father. Wherever they live, if there's a doctor nearby she talks about their family as if they were royalty. Louis may have moved Nita to Lafayette, he may have bought her a Volaré and a brand-new house, but that's not enough and he knows it. Nita's not a doctor's wife and their son is not a doctor's son. He watches as she stuffs a small vinyl suitcase and wonders if those two letters really would change everything, if she'd be happy as a Mrs. M.D.?

On the drive to the D'Aquins' house, Nita thumps her fingers against the steering wheel and sings her favorite Fats Domino tune, "I'm gonna be a wheel someday, I'm gonna be some-body . . ." She looks at the boy on the seat next to her. Her son with his strong face, his bright blue eyes, and neat hands folded in his lap. Reading signs out loud, naming out-of-state license plates, he belongs to her, she thinks, and wherever he wants to go, she'll take him, no matter what Louis says.

When the car reaches the doctor's driveway, Nita stares in awe at the sprawling ranch-style house and at a woodblock sign hanging from the eave that announces, "The D'Aquins." There's a white Cadillac in the open garage, a flagstone sidewalk, and a row of towering cat-o'-nine-tails that separates the house from the smaller homes next to it.

Nita's glad she left Jo at home with Louis. She can picture that girl wailing in the backseat with red eyes and some new stain on her dress, intent on finding a way to make Nita scream at her in front of the doctor's wife. Instead, Marc sits silent next to her and she only fears how her Volaré looks in the driveway. She considers backing up and parking down the street, but then the door opens and a woman steps out in a silk business suit—with a tie!—something Nita saw at Abdalla's, but passed up. She feels suddenly awkward in her yellow sundress and decides not to leave the car. Even when Mrs. D'Aquin walks up to invite her inside, Nita stays put.

As Marc runs off with Francis, the D'Aquin boy, Mrs. D'Aquin looks right through the rolled-down window, right at Nita, and says, "We've heard a lot about your son. He's the bright one, isn't he?" For a moment, Nita can almost hear the sound of applause around her. She's done this much right: she's made sure her son is the bright one.

But as the doctor's house fills her rearview mirror, Nita fixes on the glinting chrome of the Cadillac in the driveway, the glittering pebbles in the sidewalk, and the towering shadow of the doctor's wife walking back inside. She looks at the seat next to her, the place where Marc sat, and remembers she's going home alone. Home to a husband whose only question is, "What's for dinner?" Home to a daughter who—Nita's more and more sure—doesn't even like her. Without her son, she might be nobody's wife, nobody's mother. She might be a little girl again, waiting for her father to tell her to push over, he'll drive now.

At the next red light, Nita lets the car stall while she watches the colors change. Green, yellow, red. Green, yellow, red. Other cars speed around her, with honking horns and glaring eyes. She's not crying, she's not going to let herself cry. Not for all the things she doesn't have. Not for all that Louis won't give her. Not for how alone, how lost, how *left behind* she feels. Still, she wishes there was someone who'd hold her, who'd tell her it was all right. And in the wait for the next light, she catches herself muttering one word like a mojo or a spell she's about to cast. "Daddy," she calls out again and again, "Daddy."

5

SOME AFTERNOONS NOW THE AIR AROUND NITA tightens and she has to struggle for her breath. The spells hit her without notice; she could be polishing the glass teardrops on a chandelier or scrubbing an irritating spot on the floor molding when—Bam!—a shock runs through her head, her eyes sting, and her throat seizes up. In the background she might be playing Aaron Neville and all of a sudden his voice turns from silk to pins in her ears. Everything around presses against her: the hulking sections of the couch, the giant oval mirror on the wall, even the walls themselves inch in toward her. She wants to scream, but there's no one to hear. She wants to ask for help, but there's no one to ask.

The spells never last for long, but they drive a fear in her and she starts thinking of going back to church. She doesn't know where to go, though. She could catch a chill picturing the Catholic altars with their high arched domes and droning priests. But she doesn't know any other church in Lafayette and she's not about to jump on a folding chair and shout "Hallelujah!" with her sister.

Vina Lee hasn't stopped calling for help since Nita's last visit to Mermentau. Every week a new threat crawls under her door and she asks Nita for another check. They're gonna cut off her phone; they're gonna take away the freezer and the TV. They're gonna cut off the lights; she's gonna run out of those pills and—*le bon Dieu!*—what'll she do when they're gone?

At first Nita sends checks, small ones in printed cards and scented envelopes. Even if she can't bring herself to visit Mermentau again, she wants to help her sister and her mama. She wants to give them whatever she can. Of course, Louis doesn't like it. Soon as he sees the missing checks, his face turns red. He says nothing, but acts as if she was somehow robbing him, as if she was taking money that wasn't hers.

With his mouth open and nothing but hot breath coming out, he stands in front of her. Nita thinks he looks like a pit bull, like an angry dog about to snap its chain. Hair jumps out of his shirt collar and a purple vein throbs on the side of his face. All that beer he drinks after work has left him with a melon belly and red eyes. She can't believe she's married to him. She can't believe this man clenching his fists is her husband. The thought depresses her so much that she pushes her hands to her forehead and tries to ignore him.

Louis sees the worry in Nita's eyes, the fever in her cheeks when that damned sister of hers keeps calling and he can't stand what her family does to her. Always moaning, complaining about some new illness or debt. Is he running the frickin' First National

Bank of Acadiana? Is he supposed to stand by while his wife gets hounded for money?

Louis refuses, he just refuses to let them drive Nita crazy. He doesn't want to fight her, so he lets her keep writing the checks. But if he picks up the phone and finds Vina Lee or Gilda on the other end, he gives them a hot earful. And—to Louis' surprise— Nita doesn't stop him from yelling; she even seems grateful when one night he tells her sister not to call again or he'll slam the phone down so hard her fucking ears will bleed. After that, Nita doesn't say a word when he cracks open a third can of beer. And she doesn't roll her eyes when he retells the kids his favorite old joke: "What's the loneliest place in Louisiana?" he asks. And together they call out, "Bayou Self!"

For once, Louis feels as if he and Nita were fighting the same demon, crossing the same lake of fire together. His mother was right: it's that damn family that's been making Nita crazy, that's been coming between them. All along he's been looking for a reason why she's so wound up, so tense and nervous. Maybe she hasn't seen her family much since they married, but they plague her mind like locusts in a rice field. He should've known what the problem was; he should've tried to help her sooner.

So when one of Vina Lee's sons writes a hot check with Nita's name on it, he's glad for the excuse to have their phone number changed and unlisted. "That'll buy us some peace," he announces to Nita, hoping maybe she'll come to his side of the bed again, maybe she'll want to be held and touched, maybe she'll see that the only family she needs is under this roof.

But Nita doesn't go to his side of the bed, and she never forgives him for cutting off her family, for cursing out her sister. She also never forgives him for keeping her cooped up like some rare bird weekend after weekend. She asks him for a trip out of town, at least a ride to Holly Beach, but he says no. "I'm on call, now," he tells her, "twenty-four hours a day, seven days a week."

When she tells him again that she needs to get out of Lafayette, out of this house, he just hangs his head and shrugs his bulldog shoulders. "I thought you liked it here," he says. "I thought you could get everything you need."

Ha! she thinks, only if you have no ambition. Only if you have no dreams. Only if you're content to sit behind a desk and let everyone call you coonass all day long. Nita hates that word, hates the way that Cajuns let themselves be on the wrong end of every joke.

She doesn't know how Louis can like it here, how he can be satisfied with so little. Doesn't he ever get bored? she wonders. Doesn't he ever want to see something new?

He doesn't want to spend the money, she decides. Louis's stingy, it's true. He checks the odometer on her car nearly every day and cringes when he finds the rubber on her tires the least bit worn. He'd fill her gas tank with a thimble if he could, just to make sure he's getting every dime's worth. And Louis never buys her anything, either, never surprises her with a gold pendant or a pair of glittering earrings or a bottle of her favorite Shalimar perfume. She has to buy those things on her own, then have them gift-wrapped so she can surprise herself when she gets home. Louis never notices the new jewelry, though, or the new fragrance. Half the time, he forgets her birthday until she reminds him. Then he hangs his head and mutters, "So what d'ya want?"

Sure, if she asks for it, he buys the new microwave with the revolving tray or the bamboo steamer. But he never thinks of anything on his own. Not in the way that he thinks of Jo. He's always buying that girl some new treat: a bag of Mary Janes, a handful of Pixie Stix, a swirling plastic mood ring. He tries to hide the treats, but Nita finds them tucked under a pillow in Jo's room or hidden in a shoebox under the bed. She can't believe he would go behind her back like that, like a thief working in reverse. When has he ever thought of *her* in the middle of the day? Or Marc? In fact, what has he ever bought Marc? And what, what has Jo ever done to deserve a shoebox full of gum, candy, and plastic rings!

All through elementary and now into middle school, that girl's done nothing but bring worry and grief Nita's way. Something's wrong with her, Nita's sure of it. Not a day goes by without Jo falling into some new bag of trouble. Already she's been kicked out of school twice for smoking in the girls' bathroom. She's cursed out more teachers than she can count and run away from home so often that Nita's stopped chasing her. Jo always comes back soon enough, with a ripped skirt, scuffed-up knees, and a look that says, I hate you! I hate you! I hate you!

Oh yes, she can see the hate in Jo's eyes, burning like bits of coal. At first, Nita thought she was imagining that look. But she's grown certain, absolutely certain that her daughter resents her. Why else would she invent more and more outrageous ways to shame her? Breaking pencils with her teeth, stealing markers from the teacher's desk, and changing from the skirt Nita makes her wear to a pair of shorts anywhere she pleases. "Your daughter's dropped her skirt again," the teachers say, in high clipped voices. "She's dropped her skirt in the middle of the schoolyard." Their reports make Nita feel uneasy, even guilty, as if *she* was the one out exposing herself in front of the student body, as if she was the one caught cheating on another test or sticking gum in some boy's hair.

Lord knows Nita tries. She talks to her daughter on the corner of her bed. "Don't you wanna be like your brother?" she asks. "Don't you wanna make good grades?"

But Jo stays silent, glaring at her with those blue eyes turned to flame. Nita can't stop wondering what burns inside that girl (is it a devil? is her daughter possessed?). She also can't stop the voice that rises from within, the scream that breaks out of her mouth.

Again and again, Nita throws her arms in the air and warns that if Jo doesn't watch out, she's gonna make a mess of her life. She's gonna end up in the projects or in a shack like Vina Lee and Monetta Lou. "Do you want that?" she hears herself shout. "Do you wanna watch the plumbing back up and roaches climb the walls?" But Jo just keeps staring at her, with her arms folded tight against her chest, and Nita swears that every time she turns her back, her daughter sticks her tongue out. Ten years old and she sticks her tongue out at her own mother.

Nita hates to admit it, but Jo looks as odd as she acts. Her hair kinks up at the slightest hint of humidity (which in Louisiana is almost every day and is always less of a hint and more of a roar) and her face breaks out in weird little splotches that Nita tries to cover with powder and an ivory foundation. Then, too, Jo's eyes always look tired, as if she stayed up all night rubbing them just to guarantee she'd have circles in the morning. And no matter how many times Nita tells her to stop, that girl's always biting her lips. They stay cracked and bleeding, like an old nigger who's been out in the sun too long. "Stop it!" Nita finally shouts, squeezing her hands behind her head, trying to control her rage. "Stop it! Do you wanna look like somebody's poor cousin? Do you wanna look like bayou trash?"

"Shut up!" Jo shouts back. "I'll bite my lips if I want to! I'll bite my lips and you can't stop me!"

Then, when Jo's favorite answer—"Shut up!"—is replaced by a filthy new comeback, Nita really loses it. After the principal calls her in to discuss a report card with a forged signature, a report card full of black D's and red F's, she tears open a sack of rice, pours it on the floor, and plants Jo down on her knees. But that girl won't stay put and she won't admit to any wrongdoing. Even as Nita pulls her by the hair and presses her face to the mirror, Jo refuses to confess.

"Well, if you didn't make those stinking grades and sign that sorry card, who did?" Nita demands.

Jo glares back in silence and Nita can feel the air around them thicken. Her throat tightens and the black hole of her daughter's future throbs in her head. She won't let Jo do this. She won't let Jo shame her again. Nita raises her hand to the ceiling and screams, "Who signed that report card? Who made those grades? Who's the liar in this room? Answer me! Who?"

Jo's breath is almost visible. Nita can see her reaching inside for some new weapon and before she knows it, the words are out. Jo stands with her hands on her hips, looks right at her, and shouts, "Screw you!"

Nita can deal with a lot, but she can't deal with a daughter who curses, a dirty girl with a foul mouth. She chases Jo out the back door and into the yard. She tries scrubbing her from head to foot, rubbing her mouth out with soap, with lye, with a whole purple onion. But nothing keeps her from shouting those words again and again, "Screw you! Screw you!"

As Nita's hand grabs a spatula, she slips out from behind her eyes. She watches the flat metal come down hard and fast on her daughter's arms, back, and legs. She deserves it, Nita thinks, she deserves it for all the hell she puts me through, embarrassing me at school, at the mall, in the grocery store, every chance she gets. Hollering for this and that until her face turns blue and everyone around thinks she's got a witch for a mother.

Whole minutes pass before Nita slips back behind her eyes, before she realizes it's *her* hand holding the spatula, *her* scream charging the air around them. At first Nita's eyes well up as she sees a fresh swollen bruise on Jo's arm, a purple wound she'll have to cover. I did that, she cries to herself, I hit my own girl, my own blood. She moans and presses Jo's face to her breast and wishes her daughter didn't hate her, didn't wish her dead with every step.

But then the bruise begins to anger her. Like a purple eye, it stares at Nita, refusing to fade. And the bruises that follow only make it worse. What Jo constantly inflicts on *her*—the icy stares, the sassy comebacks, the nasty tantrums—none of that hurt breaks out on her own skin, none of it swells or bleeds. More and more, she's convinced Jo traps her into these beatings. After all, she never cries when Nita hits her. She never says a word until her father comes home. And no punishment ever sticks. As soon as Louis walks through the door, he calls Jo's name and she's off her knees and out of her room, running straight for her daddy's arms. "Daddy!" the scream rings out in Nita's ear, "Daddy! Daddy! Daddy!"

What's wrong with buying things for your daughter? Louis wants to know. What's wrong with bringing her treats? On his lunch break, he plugs a quarter into a gumball machine and pockets a bubble-wrapped toy or a hard yellow gum with a smiley-face for Jo. If he has to stop for gas, he slides over the change for a bag of candy, sometimes even a whole bar. Nita won't buy the kids sweets anymore. She says all that sugar will leave holes where their teeth ought to be and she's not about to raise a couple of kids with rotten coonass smiles.

Still, once a week, Jo cries in the middle of Delchamp's for a bag of M&Ms and Louis winces as Nita shakes her head no, then shakes Jo into a stunned silence. She never shakes Marc like that, never raises her voice or tells him to shut up. But then Marc always listens to his mother. He wouldn't touch a piece of chocolate if St. Peter himself handed it to him along with the keys to heaven. That boy knows only one voice in the house, one face. But Louis can't see the harm in a little sugar, so he thinks nothing of tucking a Milky Way under Jo's pillow.

Besides, he likes to watch the look in her eyes as he comes home and she tries to figure out what he's hidden. Her baby blue eyes grow wide, then narrow, and her mouth draws into a thin line, just like Nita's. In fact, Jo is slowly growing into Nita's face. The slope of her nose, the perfect pout of her mouth, the way her chin forms the bottom of a heart. Maybe her skin's not as dark, but even Nita's skin seems lighter now that she wears powder and carries an umbrella to avoid what she calls "the blasting rays of that awful Louisiana sun."

To Louis, Nita looks more and more glamorous, with her fancy scarves and monogrammed handbags and dark red lips. Her hair falls in clean lines, then bounces into a curl above her shoulders. Some sparkling bit of gold clings to the fabric above her breast or dangles from her earlobes. She's nearly thirty now, but she looks almost as young as when he married her. And she always smells like oranges or peaches or azalea flowers. With ease, she could walk out of the pages of a magazine. Or star on TV, like Jacklyn Smith, like one of Charlie's Angels. When she turns her head his way, he still sometimes loses his breath for a moment. She might be talking to him, complaining about something she needs, but all around the air buzzes and he can't get past the thought, *This is my wife.*

Of course, Louis sees the bruises. Of course, he sees what his wife does to Jo. And he's angry. Pissed off. Goddamn furious! Sometimes he can barely speak to Nita without stammering, without jamming his fingers into the palm of his hand. But—like steaming rain on a hot tin roof—his anger dissipates in the light of

Nita's face. Does he forgive her because she's beautiful? Does he ignore Jo's beatings in the hope that he'll be forgiven too, that Nita will be grateful for his silence? That may be. He's seen it before, seen how beauty works its own voodoo, how it chops up truth like a kaleidoscope. He also sees how Nita hides the bruises. She never hits their daughter in public, or in front of him. But he can see through the heavy stockings and the long sleeves. He knows the marks that lie underneath.

So, yes, he gives Jo the treats, and he tries to ignore the yellow and purple marks and the question that runs circles in his head. Instead he laughs as his daughter tells him a story about a girl who grows fantastic wings. Only the wings aren't for flying, they're for swimming, and she can't ever seem to make it to the water. She always runs into a raccoon or a possum and they trip her up and she can't ever find the bayou or the river or wherever it is she's headed. Anyway, it all ends very badly, but Jo hunches her shoulders when she reaches the end and puts her palms up in the air as if she was balancing a great weight. "Say two," she says, drawing two fingers before her eyes. Louis knows what she means, "*C'est tout*. That's all." It knocks him out that she tries to speak Cajun, that she makes up a story about a bayou girl. And he feels grateful that someone in this house needs him to listen.

One long, hot Sunday in November, Louis sits outside to watch his daughter spin circles on the front lawn. The forecast calls for a cool front in a day or two, but the air's still heavy and almost impossible to bear. Despite this, Louis watches as Jo makes her own breeze, spinning round and round with her arms stretched out. Every so often, she stops to perform a new stunt for him. She stands on her hands or uses a yardstick as a baton. She finds a handful of moss and arranges it on her head. "Look at me," she says, "look, Daddy, I'm an old lady!" She puts pinecones in her shirt to make a pair of breasts and uses a palmetto leaf as a crown. She does somersaults and splits and swears to Louis that when she makes it to high school, she's gonna be a cheerleader. He believes her, too. He believes his daughter could do just about anything.

As she begins to spin again, he hears a clap of thunder. One, two, three, he counts. Then lightning zigzags across the sky and Louis thinks, Good, let it rain. Let it be the kind of cool rain that chills the air and stops summer short.

Thunder claps again and this time he only counts to two before lightning flashes. The azalea and camellia bushes begin to curl their leaves. The tall sugar pine trees drop a few needles and even the old live oak across the street seems to sway a bit. There's a salty-sweet smell in the air, which makes Louis thinks of how the Gulf of Mexico is only a short drive from here. Every year, the gulf water seems to rise higher, even as the marshy bottom half of the state sinks. One day the balance will tip and Acadiana will wash away, turning oak trees into water logs and moss into seaweed. But Louis would never leave. He'd pull on hip boots and wade through the bog like any good Cajun.

In defiance of the forecast, the storm's about to break early. Louis doesn't mind. He likes the way that weather in Louisiana knows no law, the way it proves everyone wrong.

Jo will prove Nita wrong, too. Louis's sure of it. Marc may have the grades, but Jo's got the *envie,* the drive. She's gonna be the one to make it. He sees her now, picking up the yardstick, fighting the approaching storm like Joan of Arc fighting the British. Spinning in circles, flying against the wind like Amelia Earhart. If she falls, he promises himself, if she comes crashing down, he'll be there to catch her.

6

THE PHONE NEVER RINGS NOW. NITA STARES AT THE receiver in its cradle, wishing someone would call. But who? Louis' mother is the only one who has the new number, and Nita certainly doesn't want to pick up the phone to find that sharp voice on the other end. She almost wishes Louis would call, that he'd have some question to ask her in the middle of the day. But he never calls and he's never home before nightfall, either. When he finally walks through the door, he barely says hello. He marches straight to the fridge for a can of beer, then plops down in his La-Z-Boy to stare at the TV. Nita doesn't even bother to set the table anymore since no one eats at the same time. Jo stays outside until long past dark and only comes in when she hears her father drive up. Even Marc seems far away. He's a freshman at Carencro High, an honors freshman, and he's always staying late for some class project, joining some new club, or else sleeping over with the doctor's son. He never needs her help anymore; the problems in his books have grown too large, too complicated, and—as hard as Nita tries—she can't make sense of a logarithm or a symbolist poem. She didn't know it was possible to be married, to be married and have kids and still feel completely alone.

Louis's done this. He's suffocated her. He's kept her from seeing her family for so long that they probably wouldn't even recognize her voice. If she was married to another man, he'd take her on Sunday visits. They'd host crab boils and barbecues and invite everyone they know. They'd laugh and dance until their feet bled and tears came shooting out of their eyes. Louis doesn't make her laugh, that's for sure, and together they visit no one. No one except Louis' mother, who never fails to find some new way to wound Nita. Anna holds every dish Nita washes up to the light, searching for a dirty spot so she can cluck her tongue and say, "*Mais ga' ça!* Just look at that! Someone's flunked the squeaky clean test. Someone wants us to eat like a bunch of niggers!"

And Louis never defends Nita. Never. If Pop was around, he'd make Anna hold her tongue. Nita misses that man and she misses her own father so much that she decides to do it, to do the crazy thing she saw on one of those detective shows. She takes out her charge card, picks up the phone, and hires a private eye.

Within weeks, Nita gets a call back. "No phone number," the man says, "listed or un. Just an address." She scrawls out the street number, then stops short when he names the city. "Crowley," he says, and in a daze she hangs up the phone without saying goodbye.

She can't believe it, can't believe he's in the same town where she used to live. She could've passed him on the street or run into him at the Piggly-Wiggly. She could've sat in his kitchen every morning for *café au lait* and biscuits dipped in dark cane syrup. Nita looks at the clock and figures there's still time. She can make it to Crowley and back before the kids are out of school. She rushes through the house, grabbing everything she might need. Her purse, her umbrella, framed photos of Jo and Marc. Newspaper clippings of Marc winning the poster contest, the spelling bee, the writing award.

All along I-10, she pictures her father's house. She sees the row of Mason jars in his kitchen, filled with herbs and roots. She sees the squat green medicine tree growing next to his house, dropping its long black pods on the ground, like a dragon shedding its claws. She sees Hilton standing on the porch in cowboy boots and a ten-gallon hat, tall and handsome and excited to see her.

But when Nita parks the car, she sees no medicine tree. No tree at all. The lot is bare and pocked with sinking holes of land-fill dirt and shellstone. And the house isn't a whole house, but half a duplex in a row of identical crumbling brick apartments. Project houses. She spots a circle of nigger kids chasing an old hound through an endless canopy of sheets and clotheslines. For a moment, Nita's sure she has the wrong address. But the numbers match up, so this has to be it.

There's a man standing on the front porch. His hair hangs in a long ponytail and he sits in a cane rocker with one leg on the ground. The other leg is missing, chopped off at the knee. The man's shirt is yellow from sweat and he looks as if he was one of her father's old drinking buddies, one of the men he made her call uncle. *N'onc* Duck? she wonders, *N'onc* Ti-Boy? Then she sees a woman's face through the screen door. "Hil-*ton!*" the woman shouts, "*Mange-toi!* Come eat!"

No, Nita thinks, *no!* That can't be him. But when he stands up on the single crutch, she catches sight of his smile, the same smile that used to appear over her bed in the morning. The warm broad smile that would ask, "*Rêves-toi bien, ma 'ti' fille?* Dream well, my little girl?" That's him, that's her father sitting on that porch. That's him with one leg. (Who hurt him? she wants to know. Who hurt her daddy?) And that's him with another woman. He's married; she forgot he was married. She planned on finding him alone, talking to him alone.

As soon as the screen door bangs shut behind Hilton, two kids—two boys—come running out, shirtless and neither one of them older than Marc and Jo. He's got kids younger than my kids, she thinks, I've got brothers younger than my son. She watches as the boys race each other through an endless row of white sheets, chasing the nigger kids and snapping plastic pins in the air.

The whole picture depresses Nita. And the thought of her father living like this, like a nigger, stings her eyes. Soon her makeup is smeared, her hands are burning, and a clot of nerves pinches her neck like a claw. She can't get out of the car. She can't let Hilton see her. Not until she knows what to say. All her practiced lines are gone. How can she ask him for help? How can she complain to him about Jo, about Louis, about how bored and nearly mad she feels?

On the drive home, she keeps promising herself that she'll go back, that she'll find a way to get her father out of that place. Her hands grip the wheel as Crowley once again becomes a dot in her rearview mirror. I'm gonna do it, she thinks, I'm gonna find a way out.

But she never gets the chance, never finds a way. Once Nita's back in Lafayette, she's swallowed up again by the house, by the constant cooking and cleaning. As she scrubs the sinks, tubs, and floors, on top of the fridge, behind the hutch, under the stove, a hard silence catches in the air. The sound echoes through each room like the end of a scratchy record. She reaches deep inside cabinet drawers, sweeps ceiling corners and windowsills. She splashes bleach on everything: in the clothes, the dishes, on the tile floors and baseboards. She tries baking, moving pots and pans, setting noisy timers. The house fills with the smell of boiling sugar, sticky caramel, and toasted pecans. But she can't escape the buzzing in her ears, the feeling that he's already gone, that she's already lost her father.

When the call finally comes, when Louis phones to say that he's coming home early, Nita knows. She knows from the clicking in her ears what he's about to tell her. She knows Vina Lee called him at work with the news. She knows the funeral already happened, that she won't even get to bury her father. She knows all this, but her ears still burn when he says it. When Louis looks right at her and says, "He's dead. Your father's dead."

Any hope Nita had left, any hope at all slips out of her, leaks into the air like a seeping toxin. Hilton's dead, her daddy's dead. She feels the fact enter her like a sharp needle, its poison rushing to her head, to her arms and eyes and every last nerve in her body, filling her until she thinks she might explode.

Suddenly, her hands are all over Louis' face. Her hands rain down on his head and he's caught up in a fast, furious storm. Nita's slapping him and he doesn't know why. What has he done? He came home as soon as he heard. He wanted to be with her, to hold her, to feel her hot tears against his neck. And now she's slapping him. Goddamnit, his wife is slapping him.

At first, Louis tries to block the hits with his arm, but then his hand is in the air too. He thinks about it for a minute, thinks about slapping Nita into sense. Maybe he should, maybe it's what she needs.

But when she looks at him with that green fleck in her eye and screams, "Do it! Hit me! Hit me!" a sour feeling rises in the back of his mouth. He pulls his hand to his eyes and struggles for something to say. Nothing seems right, not "I'm sorry," not "I know how you feel," not anything. So Louis remains silent while Nita runs around the room, pulling on her hair and beating the sides of her face with her fists. "No!" she screams again and again. "No! No! No!" He wants to stop her, to lock up her hands, tie her down and whisper in her ear until she's calm. But he can't open his own mouth. He can't say anything anymore. He just stands still while his wife runs toward the dark of their bedroom.

Nita's screams eventually soften into loud sobs, but her crying lasts long into the night. Even after the kids go to sleep, he can hear her in their room, kicking and beating her fists against the bed. He's afraid to go near her. But he's more afraid when she refuses to eat, refuses to speak. For days after, she stays in bed, with the light off and her face under a pillow. When she finally gets up, he finds her on the floor with a pair of scissors, cutting herself out of all the pictures in their family album. Each of the pictures is cut in half or rounded off to make it look as if she was never there. Or else there's a hole, a shadow where she used to stand. Louis can no longer ignore the question circling in his head, buzzing like an angry mosquito: What's wrong? What's wrong with Nita? What's wrong with his wife?

From now on, anything she wants, anything she asks for, anything she simply notices, he buys her. He trades her Volaré in for a purple and gold special edition Plymouth Cougar, then the Cougar turns into an official Indy 500 Corvette pace car, and the Corvette turns into a candy-apple red Cadillac with white leather seats. A velvet-green pool table for the den leads to a Pacman game and an Atari joystick. The bigscreen TV becomes a wide-screen; the twin speakers, Surroundsound. A VCR, Jenn-Air Stove-top, and Jacuzzi tub follow one after the other. The yard's not big enough for the kind of swimming pool she wants, but he fits a trampoline, a hammock, and an automatic swinging bench. When Nita admires the neighbor's crêpe myrtle tree, Louis plants a dozen. When she mentions a stained glass window, he buys two. His charge card practically sizzles, but he won't stop. He'll do anything, buy anything to keep Nita at home, in the picture.

Everywhere, all the time now, he follows her and Nita can't stand it. In the kitchen, in the bathroom, out the back door. Like a sad dog, everytime she turns around he's at her feet. Louis says nothing; he just stares at her as if he expected *her* to speak, or to pat his head, when all she wants is to get away from him, to disappear into another life. She's tired of the boxes, tired of shopping. Even talk of a new mall fails to excite her. And her son—her own son—becomes a disappointment.

Nita first notices Marc's lisp when she sits in the gym at school to watch him play the son in *The Glass Menagerie.* At first she thinks she's imagining his tongue hissing like a snake. But when she over-hears someone else say, "They shoulda let him play Laura!" she feels the shame crawl under her skin. The shame drives her out the door and back into bed. She misses the second half of the play and never finds out what happens to that crazy girl on stage. But she doesn't want the lights to come up, to face her lisping son in front of all those strangers.

That night, she can't sleep as she worries over Marc's future. What'll become of a boy with a lisp? He certainly can't win class president. He can't date the Homecoming Queen or give the speech at graduation. She sees Marc in a dark corner at school, all the other kids laughing and pointing his way.

In the morning, Nita drives him straight to Our Lady of Lour-des' emergency room. "My son needs an operation," she whis-pers. "There's something wrong with his tongue." The nurse gives her the fish eye, but she calls a doctor and within an hour the ex-tra flesh under Marc's tongue is snipped and stitched. "Thank God!" Nita tells her son. "Thank God it was that simple."

But it's not that simple. After she deals with the lisp, she has to deal with the smell rising from under Marc's arms. She tells him to use deodorant, then to learn how to shave the tarantula crawl-ing above his lip. "I won't have you looking like trash," she says, "I won't have you talking like a sissy and looking like bayou trash!" This is Louis' fault, she decides. His own father won't teach him, won't show him how to be a man.

Louis tries, he really tries to spend time with Marc. When he builds an extension to the house, thinking Nita might want a mosquito-proof patio, he invites his son to help out. But anytime Louis calls for a tool, Marc stares at him with blank eyes. He doesn't know what a ratchet looks like or whether to turn a screwdriver left or right. He acts as if a power saw was a roaring crocodile and a hammer was specifically designed to pound holes in plaster and miss every nail in sight. And if Louis raises his voice a bit—just a bit—the boy cries.

Finally, when Marc confuses motor oil for turpentine, Louis throws his paintbrush down and shouts, "Goddamnit! You may have book smarts, but when it comes to common sense, you're as stupid as a duckbill on a catfish!" The boy cries long and hard after that; he cries like a little girl with his hands tucked under his arms and his chin to his chest. Louis's glad the men at work aren't around to see his son like this. They'd slap him on the back and ask, "So when do we get to meet *ton aut' fils?* Your other son? The little genius who takes after you?"

Louis keeps buying new cars, new kitchen gadgets, new games and toys, but nothing seems to make Nita happy. Nothing, that is, except for Marc's endless string of A's and overflowing trophy shelf. The summer before his junior year starts, Nita takes him to Brother's, the fanciest men's store on Johnston Street, and buys him a whole pile of Izod shirts, pants, belts, socks, and sweaters, all with that little green alligator stitched on. The clothes come in the queerest colors Louis's ever seen: purple ringed with yellow, green crossed with maroon. One shirt is striped pink and white. Louis shakes his head; does Nita want their son to look like a goddamn candy cane?

But he says nothing—not one word—through all this. Not when he finds that Jo is wearing exactly the same clothes she wore the year before. Not when her shirts stretch tight over her grow-ing breasts and her pants become culottes, with their hems made for some high water disaster. Not when he hears Nita tell their daughter that a flunkee doesn't deserve new clothes, that a girl who gets more warning notices than a nigger honky-tonk doesn't need a new wardrobe. Not even when Marc comes home with an F in Workshop and she finally slaps him.

That F keeps Marc off the honor roll, which sends Nita spin-ning. Louis almost wants to laugh—after all she's the one who in-sisted he take the class. She's the one always calling him "whiz kid" and "wonder boy," staring at him as if he were made of gold, as if oil might come pumping out of his head at any moment. Louis should feel sorry for his son; he knows that. But that boy could use a little humbling. His head's gotten too big, stuffed with all those ten-dollar words and Yankee books. Maybe it'll shake him up, Louis thinks, and maybe it'll take some heat off Jo for a while.

But the heat from the F only catches fire in Nita's mind. She's losing everything, everything now, even her son. And she only becomes more convinced something's wrong with him when he tacks up a poster of Barbra Streisand on his wall. Not Farrah Fawcett, not Cheryl Tiegs, not the Cover Girl model, but *Barbra Streisand!* What normal boy wants a poster of a woman who looks like that?

A few days after Marc gets the F, Nita opens his bedroom door to talk to him, to see if the grade can be changed. She can help him. She'll figure out how he can make a new lamp, a lamp that lights when you plug it in. She'll joke with Marc, tell him that she never wanted him to be a carpenter anyway. But as soon as she opens the door, a scream rips its way out of her mouth. Her son. Her son! Spinning naked in his room like a fairy in the woods while that Jewish woman sings, "He touched me." *He* touched me!

"What's going on?" Nita demands as Marc pulls the bedspread around his body. "What kind of filth is going on in this house? What are you doing naked in your room? What are you doing!"

Right away, he starts crying. "Please, Mama. Please, please, please," he says. But the S catches on his tongue and Nita hears that lisp again, that horrible lisp like air leaking from a tire. She walks over to the huge head of Barbra Streisand with her mouth stretched open before a microphone, that kinky hair and 3-D nose lit by an invisible spotlight. "Marc," she says, narrowing her eyes and daring him to lie, "who gave you this poster? Who gave you that record?"

"No one," he says, without moving his lips.

"No one!" she shouts. "No one! And I guess no one told you to dance around naked in your room? No one told you to hang that poster on your wall?"

"Francis," he finally says, and the name hisses in the air.

"Francis?" Nita shouts. "Francis? The doctor's son?"

She should've known. She should've known there was a reason he was sleeping over at that house so much. She should've known there was something odd going on. What kind of boy has her son been playing with? She can't let this happen. She can't let all her dreams for Marc, all her plans go up in a puff of pink smoke. Nita closes her eyes, searching for a word, a warning, something to say that will change all this.

But when she opens her eyes again, she sees it, she sees her husband's face staring at her. That furrowed brow, that jutting chin and red face. For the first time, she thinks Anna was right: Marc looks exactly like Louis. Exactly.

The thought rattles her so much that she paces the room with her hands behind her neck. Marc's sobs fill her ears and she thinks back to how Louis mothered—yes, mothered!—him as a baby. She kept trying to tell him he was gonna ruin that boy. But Marc didn't even have a chance with Louis as his father. Not a chance! What kind of man would let this happen to his son? What kind of man is he? He never tries to cross her side of the bed anymore. Even if Nita doesn't mind, even if she's actually relieved, what does it mean that her husband won't—or can't—come to her at night? She wonders again, Is he queer? Is Louis queer?

All at once, it seems to Nita, the room goes black. She can't see anything, not even the wall in front of her. She hears a voice, a scream rising higher and higher in her ears. Her throat is so tight she thinks she might choke. Then her hands catch fire. Something's happening, something's flying across the room, something's hitting the wall and smashing to bits. She can see it now, see the wreck in Marc's room: his certificates and awards, all the frames scattered on the floor. Bits of broken glass and gold-plated wood littering the carpet. The bed twisted off its brass frame, the pillows torn and sheets stripped clean. Every last drawer of the maplewood bureau pulled open, Izod shirts and sweaters in a tangled bundle on the floor. She can't look at her son's red face, can't look at this mess anymore, so she runs toward her own room to bury her head under a pillow. To lie down in a field of cotton, a field of cane, far away from this house, far away from Louis, from the shrill noise in the air, the voice that says, "I hate you! I hate you! I hate you!" Her own voice, still screaming at her son, still screaming in her head.

7

LOUIS FINALLY DECIDES TO DO IT. HE DECIDES TO PUT
the house up for sale. After Nita complains about all the run-down
houses in their neighborhood and about the busted northside of
town—which is filling with niggers as fast as a Louisiana ditch fills
with rain—he decides, Maybe she's right, maybe a move is what
we need. The kids can start over at a new school. She can dive
once again into the decorations, throw herself into a sea of wallpaper and carpet samples. He'll even let her pick the house this
time. He'll let her direct the way through every last section of
Lafayette. Together, they can search the tight streets and tall, arch-
ing oaks of downtown. They can hunt the huge kudzu-covered
lots and wide boulevards of the booming southside. He'll put her
right down in the middle, if she wants, right in the center of
everything.

Sure enough, Nita chooses a house less than two miles from the Acadiana Mall. Every day he passes a block-long billboard that boasts "Inch for Inch, The Largest Shopping Mall Between Houston and Atlanta!" With an antiqued brick floor, three-color fountains, and a food court decked out in wrought-iron and blazing neon, Louis can't imagine his wife ever asking to move or leave town again. What could she possibly need that she couldn't get in that place?

The house also looks like something only Nita could've dreamed up: two stories, two *full* stories made to look like some miniature plantation home. Fat white columns up front, a winding staircase in the middle, and ceiling-to-floor windows overlooking the water oaks and tallow trees of the small bayou out back. And the whole thing sits at the end of what the realtor calls a cul-de-sac, which makes Louis laugh. "That's a hell of a fancy name for a dead-end street," he tells Nita. But already he sees her face pressed against the window, planning the changes.

Before the changes are finished, though, before they've even lived six months in the new place, Louis watches as his wife disappears again. The arched eyebrows that sized up the house through the car window, the sideways smile and floating voice that talked patterns and colors with the real estate agent, the sparkling heels twirling in the hallway all fade as his wife sinks back into silence. Nita still calls him to supper or calls him at work with a shopping list. She still rolls out dough, pours out sugar, melts butter. The kitchen fills with ambrosia and red velvet cake, spicy crab bisque and steaming crawfish pie. But Nita never sits at the table; she barely sits at all. Instead, she runs her sponge in circles in the kitchen while everyone else eats. Or she mops and remops a spot on the floor when it already shines like a mirror. The kids try to talk to her, ask her a question, but she just stares ahead at the wall or down at the floor. As Louis watches her, he becomes more and more certain that as a husband, as a man, he's a failure. Even if he can buy the new house, the new car, the quadraphonic stereo, or 4-head VCR, he can't find one thing that'll make Nita happy, not one damn thing. What good is his rising salary, his bonuses and overtime, when he and his wife dance around each other like ghosts in a Cajun song? When their own kids avoid the house and act like strangers from another country?

Even a trip to New Orleans doesn't help. On the long drive there, Nita seems fine. She scoots forward in her seat until her face is practically pressed against the front window, and she keeps turning around to make sure Marc and Jo see everything. She points out the tall sugar pine and black oak trees, the twisting cypress clumps and water oaks rising out of the Atchafalaya River and every bayou along the way. She puts her hands up when they cross the Mississippi River bridge, as if they were riding a roller coaster. She coos at the silvery light that makes the moss look like tinsel and the ribbons of silt look like eels or long snakes skimming the water's surface. And she counts every road sign along the way, every clicking mile. Her voice rises in his ear as she calls out her favorite parish names like a roll call of saints: St. Charles, St. James, St. Martin; St. Landry, St. Mary, St. Bernard; St. Helena, St. Tammany, and St. John the Baptist. Her excitement charges the air around Louis and makes him feel that here is something he can do: he can put his hands on a steering wheel, his foot on an accelerator and drive his wife exactly where she wants to go.

But as soon as they reach the outskirts of the city, Nita's mood begins to sour. She sinks back into her seat as tall gray cemeteries rise up on both sides of the highway, and she holds her hands like a steeple to her face when Louis somehow drives straight into the

Desire housing project. For ten, maybe twenty minutes, they roll through the worst parts of New Orleans. Nita complains the whole time that instead of passing the mansions and wedding-cake houses in her Garden District brochure, she gets a scenic tour of busted windows, boarded-over doors, a tour of nappy-headed women and shoeless babies. She makes Marc and Jo crouch on the floorboard, then clutches her purse as if any minute a gigantic black hand might come through the window to grab all her makeup and both her kids. Louis doesn't trust niggers any more than Nita does, but he can't understand what's come over his wife. She sees danger everywhere now and hears noises when there's only silence. At one point she even turns to shout at Jo in the backseat: "Shut up!" she screams, "Shut up! Shut up! Shut up!" when he swears that girl said not a word, not one solitary word.

Then, when they finally make it to the French Quarter, Nita complains that there are niggers everywhere. On every street, in every restaurant, in every store, there are nothing but black faces, pickaninny curls, cornrows, and poofy afros. Louis always heard there were a lot of niggers in New Orleans, but he figured they'd stay in the projects, not spill out into downtown like this. He barely has time to see the wrought-iron balconies, the cobble-stone streets, to hear the tinkling jazz pouring out the windows before Nita announces in a huff that it's time to leave. He wants a Hurricane cocktail; he wants a Lucky Dog or one of those crazy muffaletta sandwiches with umpteen kinds of spicy baloney and olives. But he shrugs his shoulders, fingers his keys, does as he's told.

As soon as they're back in the car, they hear on the radio that this happens to be the weekend of the Bayou Classic, the all-nigger version of the Super Bowl. "I knew it!" Nita cries, before crawling into the backseat with Marc and Jo. "You picked the worst weekend. The worst!" Louis doesn't know whether to laugh or put his head through the dashboard.

More and more, he knows he's in trouble. The old house hasn't sold yet, so now he's paying two notes and a utility bill three times what he paid before. Without his mother's help, without the money she gives him from two small wells pumping on the family farm, he'd have already drowned in a swamp of bills and red ink (and if he didn't need that money, he'd have to rub it in Anna's side; he'd have to tell her that she's joined the oil boom sure as a coonass joins a *courir* to run in the woods and chase a greasy pig on Mardi Gras day).

Then, on top of all the bills for the house—for both houses—there's the constant drain of Marc's high school. That boy joins every club, every contest, and every damn time Louis has to pay: club dues, lab fees, art supplies; official T-shirts, field trips, and more books than a frickin' library. He should feel sorry for Marc, really. Nita pushes the boy twenty-four hours a day, scanning every test, every paper he brings home, checking every school project and poster for a smudge or spot. She even combs over his clothes with a lint brush and straightens his hair with a curling iron. It's no wonder he's started sleepwalking at night. Nita finds him naked in the bathtub at two in the morning, scrubbing his skin red or walking down the hall with a pair of polished shoes in his hand. The boy doesn't know what he's doing, but Nita screams and screams at him until he wakes up and runs back to his room.

Still, how is Louis supposed to feel sorry for Marc when his wife treats him like some kind of Cajun royalty? She buys that boy a car when he's only a junior. And not just any car, but a Fiat Spider convertible, an Italian car! Pop would roll over in his grave to know that his son's money paid for a foreign car, and Anna would lose her hat and both her gloves if she knew the price. But Nita doesn't ask for his opinion—as she reminds him—and she insists that if Marc is gonna make it, he needs to have the best, the *very* best. Make it where? Louis wants to ask, at some speedway in Rome? He remembers what his Pop always told him, "A real Cajun never leaves home, never."

After Nita buys the convertible, Louis sees once again that Jo's wearing nothing but old T-shirts and worn jeans. The jeans cover her legs, but the shirts are never long enough to hide the bursting black and blue marks that glow and fade on his daughter's skin. Louis thought the beatings might stop when Jo turned thirteen, then fourteen, then fifteen, but they're as regular now as winter rain. He wants to cover her from that rain, to put his hands over her bruises, to block the beatings with his own body. But Nita never hits Jo when he's in the house, so he never has the chance to save his daughter. No, he tells himself, he never has the chance.

While he's at work, Nita keeps Jo cooped up in the house, like a criminal or some kind of wild animal. If she forgets to do a chore, Jo tells him, she's grounded. If she comes home late, if she talks back, she's grounded. If she doesn't make her bed, if she fails a test, if she even looks at her mother wrong, she's grounded. Nita won't let her go to the roller rink or the mall, to dances, parties, or movies. Some days, she locks Jo's room from the outside and— more than once—she's threatened to put a padlock on the door. The minute a boy calls, Nita hangs up the phone as quickly as if she was just electrocuted, or as if Satan himself called. And she's always sending Jo back upstairs to put on a looser shirt, as if her breasts were some sort of explosive device, some bomb that might go off in a too-tight halter.

At the same time, Nita herself dresses less like the Oil Center ladies and more like a high school girl. She buys big neon bracelets for her arms and pins her hair up with barrettes. Her makeup is heavier, with dark eyeliner, and her skirts are shorter, rising above the knee like a miniskirt. Louis' eyes wander up and down those legs, those coffee-colored legs that have been kept from him for so long. He stares at that hair, those eyes, as she passes him through the blue-green glow of the TV. He dreams of letting his hand race up her thigh, caress her ankle, touch the back of her knee. He still wants his wife; he still craves her in all the ways you crave the very thing you can't have: excitedly, angrily, mournfully. But there's something about her new look that disturbs him, that makes him wonder if she's trying to outdo Jo somehow.

His daughter's not perfect, Louis knows that. In fact, he knows before Nita does that Jo smokes, that she sometimes drinks, and that she's been sneaking out of the house ever since they first moved to Lafayette. Late at night, he hears her window lift, her voice telling some other girl to shush. He hears her feet scraping the side of the house as she climbs down the lattice and he grins to himself. Maybe he should worry, maybe he should try to stop her before she falls into trouble. But something within Louis lightens when his daughter escapes. When Jo leaves the house without waking Nita, he almost feels as if he personally freed her, as if he opened the door to her locked bedroom.

Marc, he might as well be someone else's son, but Jo is his to keep, his to guard. She listens to his long stories about Boudreaux and Thibodeaux and laughs every time. She knows Hank Williams' "Jambalaya" by heart and can finish any joke Louis starts.

"How many Cajuns does it take to screw in a lightbulb?" he asks.

"Two," she answers, "one to hold the lightbulb, another to hold the case of beer!"

"Okay," he says, "so how does a coonass get out of a fix?"

"Like a crawfish," she says, "he backs out of it!"

And if he lets loose with a beer belch, she teases him, "Hell, Daddy, you make me *honte,* you make me ashamed to be your child!" He's glad to know *someone* in this house will grow up learning a little Cajun, someone will look after that legacy.

Of course, he's still angry that Nita beats Jo. But the anger sits at a distance from him now. He watches it in the same way he watches his wife: through a six-pack, a twelve-pack, a fog of beer and dim recollection. He remembers wanting to hit her for burning his daughter, wanting to twist her arm until it snapped, just as he remembers lying inside her that first time, feeling her thighs press against him. But both memories dwell so far back in his mind that they've become one. And he can no longer understand the difference between desire and anger, any more than he can reach or understand his wife.

Or at least that's what Louis tells himself to explain what happens next. He comes home a bit early one afternoon to find Nita sitting on a corner of their bed with her feet tucked under her legs and not a single light on. Even in the dark, he can tell she's not wearing any of her new clothes, just a plain cotton dress with some kind of flower stitched on. The ceiling fan turns overhead and the dress billows and the ends of her hair lift and fall in the breeze. To Louis, she looks almost like a squaw again, almost like the girl he married, and the thought comforts him in the way a hand would, a soft hand on the back of his neck. He lingers in the doorway and lets himself think, Maybe she's waiting for me. He even thinks, he foolishly thinks, Maybe now she'll let me touch her.

Then he sees it, the cardboard box in her lap. She doesn't have to say anything; he already knows what she's found: the overdue notices, the credit card receipts, the new mortgage, the rising tide of debt. Still, she waves the box in front of him as if it was the Lost

Ark, and she glares at him as if he long ago stole something from her and she just found it.

"How long?" Nita shouts, her arms flying everywhere and her eyes shutting tight. "How long until you run through everything we have? How long until we have nothing, nothing! How long until we wind up in the projects, eating old cheese seven days a week?"

"What the . . ." Louis starts, then stops before finishing in his head, What the hell is she talking about? The projects? Old cheese? She's never once had to do without something she wanted. Not once. Each time they've moved, he's gotten her a better house, a better car. Each time.

Louis knows he should answer her; he should say something in his defense. But he can't stop staring at his wife. With no makeup on and her hair past her shoulders again, she could be a teenaged girl. She could be the girl who wouldn't answer his calls, the dream girl he wanted and got.

Suddenly, Nita jumps off the bed and the box tumbles over, sending slips of paper into the air like ticker tape or tiny white flags floating to the ground. He can feel the heat of her eyes staring at him as if she didn't know the reason for each and every one of those receipts. For just a minute, he wants to bring her face close to his, to run his tongue along her lips. Then he wants to hit her, to slap her into sense, to smack her so hard she'd bleed.

But before he can do anything, Nita pounces on him. Her hair, her arms, her wild eyes flash in and out of his face while she tears at his shirt and brings her hands hard and fast against his face. His nose fills with the trace of Shalimar on her neck and the scent nearly explodes in his head. In a daze, he reaches his hand out to her breast. He pushes his mouth against hers, then with both hands he pushes her back down on the bed. One hand rushes up her dress to pin her legs down while the other pulls at his pants. He wants this, he wants to slide inside Nita, to feel her throb against him. He doesn't care that she's fighting him, that she doesn't want the same thing he wants. He's tired of waiting for the right moment, tired of watching her mood. So with one quick thrust, he does it. He finds that place he's missed, that warm place, and feels all the longing slip out of him like steam.

When he's done, he looks down at Nita to find her eyes wet and her lips cracked with teeth marks. There's a metallic odor in the air and blood on the sheets. Did he hurt her? he wonders. Will she stop talking to him again? She's shaking and he wants to say something that might calm her, that might keep her under him. But all he can think of, all that comes out of his mouth is one word: "Boo."

THAT WORD HANGS IN THE AIR FOR A MOMENT, COL-lecting static, becoming charged until it pops in Nita's ear. Boo? That's all he has to say after practically raping her? After nearly splitting her open, making her bleed? That's all he has to say after driving her and the kids to the poorhouse? After lying to her about their debt? And then he has the nerve, the actual nerve, to clamp his hand on her breast, as if he owned it, as if going broke was the height of romance. He lies on top her with that water-melon belly, that red face, all that hair sprouting on his back. Nita wants to laugh and scream at once, but she refuses to give Louis anything, not a sound, not a tear. Instead, she slaps him when he's through. She slaps him good and hard and marches straight out the room, down the stairs and into the garage where she stares at the Cadillac. Maybe I'll drive away, she thinks, maybe I'll just get in the car and go. But her hands sting when she puts them on the steering wheel and that light, that mad light bursts in her head: she can't leave the kids, she can't leave Marc and Jo.

Still, her legs are raw and her stomach burns and she wants nothing more than to get out of here, to get out of Louisiana, to find a place where her head won't throb and the air won't choke the living wind out of her.

As far as she's concerned, they might as well change the name of this state to Lowsy-Anna. All around, everywhere you look, there's hardly any land to stand on, just miles and miles of bridges and murky brown water. Even the cypress knees in the bayous depress her. Those old stumps look like thousands of tiny wooden tombstones just barely breaking the water's surface.

She's sick of this place, sick of Acadiana, sick of the word *Cajun*. To Nita, it seems there's not a storefront, bumper sticker, or billboard in sight that doesn't include that word, as if it was something to be proud of, some great attraction. People around here act as if Acadiana wasn't just a handful of parishes, but a whole nation by itself. They even fly a flag with a gold castle, a gold star, and three white fleurs-de-lis. Nita's never heard of a Cajun castle and she thinks it's stupid to fly a flag for a country that never existed. Lafayette's not a real city, not with its crazy cowpath streets and everyone shouting bits of a language that you can't even study in school. She doesn't understand why Louis would settle for this, why he wouldn't want more for himself, more for his son. Why he'd teach his daughter to love this place, but hate her mother.

A few nights later, Louis asks her what she wants to do, stay here or move back to the old place? She sits silent for a minute, then laughs in his face. As if she had a choice! As if there was some difference between a spotted apple and a spotted orange. Either way, it's rotten. Either way, it's nothing she wants.

And when he drags her back to the northside, Nita almost never leaves the house. Even after winter finally settles in, the humid air stays so thick that she can barely breathe. In Louisiana, it never drizzles; it always rains by the buckets. But this year the buckets become tubs, barrels, heavenly vats. And everytime it rains, the front ditch swells and the water in the backyard seems to rise higher and closer to the house. If she tries to go outside, her skin prickles, her hair kinks, and she gets dizzy just stepping out the door. Some days the sides of her neck burn and——Nita swears——although they took out the steel pin and repaired a disc, she can feel the phantom pain running up and down her back.

Not all her days are bad. From time to time, she comes across some new idea. She spends weeks découpaging every planter in the house, or designing massive flower arrangements on driftwood. She buys paints, brushes, and canvases and makes still-lifes with figs and split melons. She dreams of getting rich from one of her crafts, selling paintings or puppets. During those moments, Nita laughs with the kids, both Marc and Jo, and tells them she's gonna be the mama in the song, the one that buys the mockingbird *and* the diamond ring.

But when Louis refuses again to let her get a job, to let her take an art class or to sell her planters at the downtown street fair, that phantom pain shoots right into her head and——before she knows it——she's pulling on her own hair and screaming in a mirror. She's cutting up her favorite dress, ripping it to shreds. Cutting up silk flowers and shoving bits of green Styrofoam down the garbage disposal. Smashing every one of her paintings against the side of the house and burying her paints and drawings in the backyard. Then she's smacking one of her kids with the back of her hand, with a hard plastic brush, the tattered end of a belt. Sometimes whole minutes pass before she hears her kids crying or her own voice rising like a siren in the air. Sometimes hours.

All of this is Louis' fault, she decides. He's kept her locked in this house, this prison. If it wasn't for him, she'd be a chef in New York like her father. Or a singer in a jazz band. Or an artist. Instead, she's stuck here in Lafayette, stuck with a bucket and a wet sponge in her hand. She'd rip the sponge in half and drive her Cadillac straight into the bayou if not for Marc.

Nita tells herself that he still has a chance, that her son might make it out of here if she helps him push. So she takes him out of drama class and tells him to stop sleeping over with the doctor's son. "No more after-school rehearsals," she says, "no more all-night study sessions. I want you home after school. Home, here with me!"

Almost every day, she polishes Marc's ever-growing wall of trophies, ribbons, and medals, and she tries to ignore the fact that he's shrinking before her eyes, that he barely eats and that her stocky boy now has a waist smaller than her own. She turns away when he crosses his legs at the knee and flaps his hands like a bird's wing. She even tries to ignore his sleepwalking in the night. After all, he's still her golden boy, her only real hope.

Jo, on the other hand, is lucky to make it to school on time. As soon as they move back to the old house, to that miserable northside of town, that girl slips right back into trouble as quickly as a crawfish slips into its hole. If anything, trouble is easier for her to find now that their old neighborhood—even their old block—is swarming with nothing but white trash. No one lives on the northside of Lafayette anymore, no one. She tried telling Louis to sell the place sooner, but he didn't listen, he never listens.

Just a few weeks after they move back, another house goes up for sale and all the women who wouldn't bother to talk to Nita before call her with the news: a nigger family walked through the house, a nigger family, black as tar! Though they don't buy the place, three more "For Sale" signs go up on their street alone. Two of those houses fall to seed, with unmown lawns and missing shingles. And in another house a new family moves in, a family that Nita has her doubts about: coffee-colored skin, jet-black hair, and one of those names you just know belonged to a slave. Louis is foolish enough to believe the Washingtons are white, but she knows better. Their yard stays overgrown with bitterweed, their ditch is choked with water ferns, and more than once, she's seen a boy cross the porch wearing nothing but a pair of baggy blue jeans. And she's sure that's the very house Jo wanders to, the very place she heads when she runs out the door.

Nita tries everything, everything to keep that girl out of trouble. She reads *Redbook* and *Ladies' Home Journal,* wondering how other women talk to their daughters. She offers Jo makeup tips, diet tips, advice on how to do her hair. She offers ballet classes, art classes, piano lessons, all the things she wanted but couldn't have when she was a girl—and still can't have. Jo just turns up her nose and says, "I'd rather eat a live bullfrog than put on some damn tutu!"

That girl curses all the time now, just like Louis. Though she's only a freshman, she collects warning notices and bad grades like other girls collect add-a-bead necklaces. And Nita can't make her wear anything but the rattiest clothes. No matter how cold it is, she never puts on socks and she refuses to wear earrings or barrettes. Some days, she wears her jeans ripped at the knee or her T-shirt inside out, and when Nita tells her to change, she answers back, "It's a free country and I'll wear what I want!"

Nita's sure, absolutely sure, that her daughter's on a highway to hell, that she's smoking, drinking, and doing God-knows-what when she sneaks out the house. (Oh yes, Nita knows about her late-night escapes!) But Louis won't listen. In fact, he barely budges from his La-Z-Boy, where he sits with a six-pack and the TV on high. He might blind himself to what's going on in this house, but she's not gonna stand still and do nothing. She's already talked to Jo's teachers at school. Every last one of them thinks she's got problems, that she ought to be sent off to that reform school near Baton Rouge. But Louis refuses to send his daughter away, just as he refuses to believe she's anything but an angel.

One afternoon, while Jo's running around the neighborhood, Nita decides to prove Louis wrong. She searches his daughter's drawers and closet, tossing shirts, jeans, bras, and panties in the air. She runs her hand inside Jo's shoes, checks the back of the mirror and every picture on the wall. After almost half an hour, she finds nothing and nearly gives up. But then she sees the edge of an album poking out from under the bed, an album covered in black with glaring red letters, some devil-worshipping band called Black Sabbath! When Nita drops to her knees, she finds a whole pile of albums she's never seen before: grown men in makeup with hair past their shoulders, each one dripping in leather, metal, and chains. Some are painted to look like demons, and one howls at the moon like some kind of wolf. Ozzy Ozbourne, Judas Priest, AC/DC, Kiss, even their names rankle Nita. Then, to make matters worse, she finds an empty cigarette pack in a shoe box and a collection of tiny airline bottles of Southern Comfort, each one drained dry.

But does Louis listen? No! He actually defends Jo's music and says he believes that girl's lie about holding the bourbon and cigarettes for a friend. "Some friend," Nita scoffs, "here, hold my *empty* pack of Marlboros and my *empty* bottles of booze!"

Soon after, Jo steals, flips, and totals Louis' company car in a ditch off Moss Street. The cops find her with a half-empty bottle of bourbon and her head cracked against the passenger window. A picture of the smashed Buick and a caption with their name lands in *The Lafayette Daily Advertiser,* and what does Louis do? He brings flowers and candy to her hospital room and promises to buy her a car as soon as she's well!

Nita's just about ready to throw in the towel, the washcloth, *and* the white flag when the real proof, the evidence Louis can't ignore, finally arrives. A teacher at Carencro High finds a letter Jo was writing in class to Boogie Washington. In her own hand, she not only confesses her undying love for that nigger boy, she admits to sneaking out the house to get stoned on hash, "Mary J," and PCP! She talks about finding "uppers" in the nurse's cabinet at school and gives that boy advice on how to fake a signature on a permission slip so they can skip class together. Nita's known all along exactly where Jo's headed. That nigger boy's room. That nigger boy's bed.

That's it! Nita decides. That's absolutely it! And before Louis has a chance to stop her, she's on the road to Baton Rouge, with Jo on the seat next to her in a silence that nearly vibrates between them. What else is she gonna do with a girl who's been expelled? With a girl who's headed straight for the projects and welfare, for sin and failure?

The reform school, *Belle Place,* turns out to be less a school and more a live-in Christian clinic, or a convent without the nuns. There are no classes, no boys, and no visitation rights for eight weeks. Jo will be locked in her room and let out only for supervised visits to the bathroom, the dining hall, and the chapel. Perfect, Nita thinks, she'll be kept away from that nigger boy, away from her father.

In those eight weeks, Louis drinks so much and so fast that he usually falls asleep in the La-Z-Boy before the ten o'clock news. Nita doesn't wake him; she's glad to have the bed to herself, glad to be left alone with the church pamphlets she's collected. Baptist, Lutheran, Methodist, Seventh Day Adventist, Pentecostal, even Jehovah's Witness, she tries them all, looking for a place that might tell her what she wants to know. How to free herself. How to save her kids.

More and more, she sees the house as a battlefield and Louis the sleeping enemy, the monster who might wake at any moment. Maybe she'll leave him after all. Maybe when Jo's better, she'll take the kids and run. Maybe together, they'll find a way out.

Just before Christmas, on the day of the nineteenth, Jo's released for a visit. Nita drives back to *Belle Place* to pick her up. She drives over swamp water, over bayous and cypress knees, over the long bridge with its oily lines that mark the rise and fall of floods. She's been reading all about the filthy water and air in Louisiana, the cancer cloud that hangs over the bottom part of the state. All the refineries, the plants with their glowing lights, the hazy gray sky frighten her so much that she buys a new rosary and two doctor's masks in a pharmacy, one for her, one for Jo.

Of course, Jo refuses to wear hers, but Nita doesn't fight her. She's too busy trying to block out the buzzing sound in the car, the rising pressure in her head. That sound is so loud by the time she reaches the house that she stuffs cotton in her ears and crawls into bed. She prays for sleep to come quickly, for the sound to fade, for her daughter's salvation.

8

LOUIS AND NITA ON THAT LAST NIGHT. THE SOUND OF wind in the trees outside the house. Leaves scratching against the window. As Nita tells it, the night is too restless, too noisy for her to sleep. She stays up late, listening to the drone of Louis' TV, the murmur of voices and canned laughter. She hears the rattle of the automatic ice maker, the low buzz of the digital clock. Even the rustle of the sheets disturbs her when she turns to face the wall. At some point, she must fall asleep, though, because suddenly Louis's lying next to her. She can feel his eyes staring at her back, watching her breath. So she tries to keep steady, to pretend that she's not awake.

Soon, she can hear Louis snore, that loud grunt and low whistle through his teeth. With his round belly and hairy arms, he looks like a bear, or a gorilla who fell from the sky and landed right next to her. She can almost smell the beer rising out of him, leaving his pores like steam from a sleeping volcano. If she lit a match, he might explode. He might burn up like an old rag soaked in gasoline. Maybe lying in his place would be a new man. A strong man. Someone like her father. Someone who'd hold her in his arms, tell her that everything's all right.

But it's not all right, nothing is. She knows that the minute she sees the light in her bedroom, bursting through the crack under the door like a searchlight, like a warning sign coming straight from Jo's room. That girl is up to no good again, Nita's sure of it. She's ready to run down the hall and scream at her daughter for waking her. In fact, she's halfway out of bed before the doorbell rings. 12:28 on the clock exactly and the doorbell rings! Maybe it's the cops. Maybe they've already found Jo in a ditch or face-down in another ugly mess. The bell rings again, hard and sharp, and Louis finally wakes up to see what the trouble is.

From her end of the house, Nita can't hear much. She can only make out the distorted voices on the police radio. But in her head, she sees it all. She sees Jo smoking dope with that nigger boy. She sees them draining a bottle of bourbon, racing up and down the dark country roads like some kind of mixed-up Bonnie and Clyde. She sees everything: his hand on her leg, that laugh on her face. Then she sees the wrecked car in the road, both cars. There are two and that nigger boy's running out of one, running down the road with his hands in the air. He killed her baby, she's sure of it. That nigger boy killed her baby!

Nita starts circling the room while she waits for Louis. Round and round she turns until she thinks she might wear a hole in the carpet or right through the foundation. She turns and turns until she reaches the idea, the fact she's been chasing: that nigger didn't kill Jo. He may have driven the car and he may have wrecked it, all right, but he didn't kill her. Louis did!

Yes, Nita knows it. She's absolutely certain. Louis drove her daughter to her death, sure as if he was behind the wheel. He drove her so far away that Nita couldn't reach her, couldn't save her. She tried, she prayed and prayed, but she couldn't save her baby.

Right then, she thinks of Marc. She's gotta keep that boy away from his father. Keep him from turning into another Louis. She's gotta save him, she's gotta save her son. She wants to go to his room, to crawl into his bed, to whisper in his ear as she did when he was a baby. She'll tell him again that he's perfect, that he can be perfect. She'll press him to her side, hold him when he cries, and this won't ever change: no one, not Louis, not anyone, will take away her son, her little man, her future.

But the lights swirling in the house and the sharp burst from the police radio fill her head, and she can't go to Marc, can't move from her own room. Soon that buzzing sound returns, that mad sound, like an angry mosquito in her ear. Nita crawls back into bed and—to take her mind off that sound—she begins to think of some new way out, some new place to go.

Houston, Dallas, Vegas; California, Florida, New York. She hears the names of other places in her head like a new prayer. Yes, she's gotta get out of here. She's gotta get out of this nowhere town, this nowhere state. Yes, she can see it now. She'll talk Louis into leaving, all right. They'll jump in a car and chase the white lines in the road, chase them to a new city, a big city where the skyscrapers and all their lights burn like a promise, like a holy testament, like a page on fire.

9

LOUIS AND NITA ON THAT LAST NIGHT. THE SOUND OF wind in the trees outside the house. Leaves scratching against the window. As Louis tells it, the night is too quiet, too still for him to sleep. He stays up late, later than usual, watching dumb show after dumb show, delaying the moment he has to slip into bed with Nita. He dreads having to lie next to a woman he can't touch, having to watch her back rise and fall with her breath. Even more, he dreads facing the question she's bound to ask, the question he can't answer: "Where's Jo?"

Louis would never want to lie to his wife. But tonight he certainly wouldn't want to tell her the truth. She wouldn't understand why he let their daughter out of the house on her first night back. She wouldn't believe the light that shone out of Jo's eyes when he walked through the door. How she wrapped her arms around him and pressed her lips against his. How she laughed at his dinner of microwaved eggs and cayenne pepper, "nuclear coonass," she called it.

Jo was halfway out the door before he even said yes. But she would've left no matter what he said. She would've crawled out the window, busted through a lock if she had to. No, he couldn't have stopped her, so he let her go. *"Laissez les bons temps rouler,"* he whispered after her, "have fun." Later, he'll wish he'd said more.

Just past midnight, Louis braves the bedroom and lets out a sigh when he sees Nita asleep. Her hair falls back against the pillow as neatly as if someone brushed it into place. Her hands seem arranged, too, folded over her silk nightgown. He almost expects to find a poisoned apple on the bed—she looks that peaceful. For now, she's his own Snow White. He can stare at her all night if he wants to. He can lie right here and watch her eyelids flutter, her lips move with the soft force of her breath.

At some point, Louis must have fallen asleep, since all of a sudden he's dripping with sweat and staring at a light coming from down the hall. The light fills the bedroom so quickly that his eyes hurt. He figures that boy across the street is shining a floodlamp in Jo's room and he worries it'll wake Nita. As he makes his way down the hall, the light flares and he thinks someone's staring at him. There's a pair of eyes in the window, he's sure of it. But by the time he reaches Jo's empty bed, the light vanishes to a pinpoint, just as suddenly as if the window itself was a TV screen and someone turned it off with a switch.

The whole scene unnerves Louis and keeps him wide awake until the doorbell rings and he crawls back out of bed. Now he thinks maybe Jo's home early, maybe she left her keys, maybe she needs more money. He looks at the clock—12:28 exactly—and almost cheers when he makes it across the room and out the door a second time without waking Nita.

As Louis approaches the den, he sees a wall of light again, only this time the wall is lit by the swirling red lights of a police car. "Goddamnit," he says out loud, "goddamnit all to hell," sure that Jo's in trouble, sure that Nita will nail her to the cross for good. All of a sudden, his wife's gone half mad with Holy Roller churches. Louis can't understand it. He'd been in a Protestant church once, just outside Iota. There was nothing on the walls, nothing at all. At least the Catholic church gives you something to look at: statues, saints, paintings of the Assumption and Ascension.

Out on the porch, the sheriff's deputy stands nearly at attention. He talks softly, saying something about a dark country road, an oncoming car, a sudden U-turn, but Louis hears none of it. At least he hears nothing clearly until the deputy says what he's there to say, "Sir, we need you to come with us. We need you to identify the body."

That's when Louis knows it, that's when he knows who was staring at him through the window. His baby's dead, Jo's dead.

He'll have to wake Nita. He'll have to find a way to tell her about the waiting cop car, the wreck on Gloria Switch Road. But before he does, he stops at Marc's door and turns the knob. The boy is awake and staring at the lights on the wall. He barely seems to notice anyone else is there. Louis sits on the bed, and as he does, he realizes he's never sat on his son's bed before. When he puts his hand on Marc's shoulder, he feels the boy shudder as if he was afraid of his father's touch. The thought catches fire in Louis' head and he decides to do exactly what Jo would do: he ignores Nita's rule and slides his arms around Marc.

Already, he knows his wife will want to move and he won't argue. She'll want to leave Lafayette, leave Louisiana, and he'll take her wherever she wants to go. In fact, Louis will still do everything else Nita demands. But at least this much will change: no one, not even Nita, will keep him from holding his son.

Louis presses his lips against Marc's cheek. Soon the boy is crying and he's crying too. Right there, against his son's stubbly face, he's crying. He's crying and Jo's face is burning in his mind like a saint's, burning like the eyes in the window, like the light in the room.

ACKNOWLEDGMENTS

FAITH AND PATIENCE:
Georges Borchardt and Cindy Spiegel

GUIDANCE AND INSPIRATION:
Michael Cunningham, Richard
Howard, Fenton Johnson, Richard
Locke, T. R. Mooney, Mary
McCay, Melanie McKay, Michael
Scammell, Christine Wiltz, and
especially, Lis Harris

TEA AND SYMPATHY:
Ramón Alvarado, Caleb Daniloff,
Christopher DeKuiper, Kyan
Douglas, Scott Fontenot, Stephen
Kijak, Eric Polito, Noël Ponthieux,
David Ross, Lesley Tolar, and
especially, Karen Schwartz